WINTER'S

DESTINY

A Novel by

NANCY ALLAN

WINTER'S DESTINY

Acknowledgments

To my devoted husband for his tireless edits, valued opinions, ongoing encouragement, unfailing enthusiasm, and his enduring love, I am deeply grateful. To my daughters and sons, each of whom read and gave valued input, I am so appreciative. I thank God every day for each of you. To my friend, Mike, my heartfelt thanks for your editing assistance and sound advice.

CHAPTER 1

OREGON COAST
November 10, 2011

Amy threw open the truck door and stepped into the ferocity of the night. The wind assaulted her, peeling her suit jacket off one shoulder. A powerful gust slammed into the side of the house and rounded the corner, howling. Like an invisible hand, it rocked the Jeep, knocked Amy into the door, and whipped an envelope from her grasp, sending it flying across the lawn and into the brush on the state land bordering her property.

"No!" Amy dashed after it until she was deep into the tangled foliage where it had been snagged by a branch. She reached out, straining, finally catching hold of it.

A shrill cry rose above the wind.

Amy froze, her arm in the air. The eerie tone came again, swirling around her in the gale like a voice calling her name. Dropping her arm, Amy stood bolt upright, her heart pounding in her chest, her ears perked. It was too dark now to see through the swaying brush. In the distance, the ocean roared as breakers collided with the rocky bluffs of Cape Peril. All around her was the angry rustle of leaves and branches, the moan of the wind, and…something else.

It was a foreign sound, only a foot or two behind her. Something brushed her arm. Amy let out a shriek and bolted for the Jeep, glad she had left the door open as the interior light acted as a small, flickering beacon. As she ran, roots and thick stalks grabbed her feet. The heel of her right shoe caught, bringing her to a stumbling stop. A bolt of white light streaked across the sky, illuminating the brush and then disappeared, immersing her in darkness. Pivoting on one foot, she bent down and groped around for the shoe. The deep rumble of thunder shook the ground. She abandoned the shoe and ran for the truck.

Suddenly, the interior light went out and the blackness of the night engulfed her. Amy kept going, stumbling in the direction of the truck, thistles, and twigs tearing into the sole of her shoeless foot, scratching her legs, biting into her hands, and lashing her face. She felt none of it.

A moment later she broke through the brush, onto the lawn. She stopped, breathless. The Jeep was on the drive just as she had left it, but the driver's door was now *closed*; the interior light off.

Walking on shaky legs, she nervously retrieved her purse and laptop from the passenger seat and limped toward the front door of the house. The two-story log home she had taken such care to design was drenched in darkness. Shakily, Amy pulled the house key from the side pocket of her purse, unlocked the door, and stepped inside, double locking the door behind her. She hit all the switches on the wall panel and light spilled into the entrance hall and up the open staircase. They hadn't lost the power. Yet.

She stood perfectly still and listened to the sounds around her. The house groaned with each onslaught of wind. Noise emanated from everywhere at once. She let the laptop, purse, and envelope slide onto the mat and took deep breaths, trying to slow her heart rate. A sound—upstairs. Amy's eyes darted to the upper floor. With sweaty hands she pulled herself up the banister to the bedrooms. She flipped on the light in each room as she passed by.

A creaking sound. She stopped, ears straining, nerves taut. She peered around the doorframe and into the master bedroom. Light from the hall spilled across the pair of double beds. Everything appeared as she had left it that morning. She pushed the bedroom door back against the wall and stepped into the room. A movement caught her eye. She swung to her right.

The sitting room was shadowed. There! In the corner. The old rocker moved slowly back and forth, as though recently vacated. Amy's eyes darted around the room then back to the rocker. Behind it, in the far corner of the sitting room, the drapes billowed. Wind funneled through a narrow opening in the window and across the back of the old chair, sending its wooden rails noisily back and forth over the hardwood floor.

Amy rushed into the sitting room, grabbed hold of the flying curtains, and yanked the window closed. She stood there a moment, heart pounding, unable to recall opening the window.

She had to get hold of herself. *What's the matter with me?* Yet, there was a strange feeling in the room.

Amy went back into the hallway and listened. The roar of wind and waves emanated through the skylights above. Amy was yanked from her thoughts by another sound. She stiffened, listening intently. Uncertain as to its origin, she moved quietly out to the upper balcony and peered down into the great room, her eyes scanning the shadows and the corners of the room.

Wind was gusting outside. The house moaned with each onslaught. Amy ran her hands through her hair.

Never had she felt so on edge…and so alone in her own home. She headed for the kitchen. "I need coffee."

Later, after two cups of strong coffee, she retrieved the laptop and the crumpled envelope, and walked into her study. She dropped the envelope onto an unopened stack of mail and stared at it.

No! Not now. Deal with it later.

Stepping across to her drafting table, she switched on the gooseneck lamp, and angled its wide beam onto a set of blueprints. Slipping a hip up onto the drafting chair, her right hand automatically reached for the pencil, her eyes scanning the floor plan

Outside, the wind howled. Its sheer force bent the old elm sideways, the giant boughs embracing the corner of the house. Behind her, the branches scratched the windowpane, like angry fingernails. Amy stiffened. Shivers ran down her spine. She turned and looked through the glass, but all she could see was a dim reflection of herself. She felt strangely vulnerable sitting with her back to the dark glass and made a mental note to install a blind.

The huge structural beams supporting the vaulted ceiling above her creaked as another powerful gust battered the roof and shrieked through the vent. Then an onslaught of torrential rain pelted the windowpanes with such fury that it sounded as though the glass would break.

The lights dimmed for a few seconds, then returned to normal. Amy put her pencil down and thought about the flashlight Dan had left charging, in case of a power failure. Seconds later, the lights went out completely. Alarmed, she waited in darkness, willing them to come back on. Finally, they did.

Amy was about to breathe a sight of relief when something struck the window behind her. She whirled around. Her eyes widened and all the color drained from her face. What she saw turned her stone cold.

Her heart...and time...stopped. She gaped at the image in the window.

Staring back at her was a woman in her early thirties, rain streaming down her pale face. Terror-stricken gray eyes locked onto Amy's.

The face was *identical to her own!*

The details of the woman's face registered somewhere in Amy's brain: broad forehead, brows and lashes so fair they were barely visible, same small, straight nose, dimple on the right cheek. Every feature was... *exactly like her own!*

There was a movement off to one side. A pale hand slid down the glass leaving streaks of crimson.

Blood. The woman was *bleeding!* A split second later the power went out and the room went black.

Amy fought to retain her senses. She reeled on the chair, her brain shutting down. She felt as if she were perched on the rim of a dark abyss. *Get a grip!*

Her heart raced in her chest. She looked back at the window. More movement. It was too dark to see clearly. A single thought. The woman outside needed her help.

Amy bolted from the chair, running down the dark hallway toward the outlet where she hoped to find the flashlight. Stopping about halfway, she ran her hand along the lower wall, expecting to feel it protruding from the receptacle. Nothing. She moved ahead a few feet, her hand flailing along the wall. There! She yanked the flashlight from the outlet and raced to the front door. Diving into unlaced sneakers, she snapped back the locks and swung the door open. Wind slammed it backward into the wall.

She raced down the porch steps, sheets of rain pelting her skin like buckshot, drenching her before she reached the sidewalk. The roaring gale shrieked around her and the wind tore her breath away. The darkness was alive with motion. Suddenly, afraid to go further, she stopped—terrified of what or *who* she'd see.

Don't think. Just move. She's hurt.

Forcing herself forward, Amy stepped around the pampas grass, inching toward the flower garden beneath the study window. The wind swayed the heavy boughs of the elm tree, creating dark movement across the front of the house.

Amy wiped her eyes trying to see through the driving rain. She raised the flashlight and directed its powerful beam into the garden. No one was there. She moved the light left, then right. Still no one. Swinging the light around, she searched the deep shadows under the elm, and then cast the beam across the Jeep and over the lawn. Nothing.

As suddenly as the rain had started, it stopped. Wiping the rainwater from her eyes, she stepped into the garden for a closer look. Blood had pooled in the window ledge. As she stared at it, the office lights blinked back on, spilling light into the garden. She jumped back in surprise, stumbling onto the walkway. A large puddle of blood had collected in a dip of the concrete near her feet. She followed the receding red trail down the concrete driveway to the road, where it ended.

CHAPTER 2

When the call came from dispatch, Sheriff Dallas Wayburne was standing in the center of a three-car pileup at the only three-way intersection in town. Sanville's ambulance backed from the scene, lights flashing. He couldn't understand why so little happened in this peaceful little town until a storm swept through; then all hell broke loose.

In the last two hours there had been five vehicle accidents, a kitchen fire, a burglary, one missing senior—found inebriated in the neighbor's wine cellar, and now a strange incident involving the disappearance of an injured woman on Lighthouse Road. All his deputies were engaged, so Dallas turned his Yukon onto the narrow, winding road to Cape Peril.

Twenty minutes later, he pulled up behind a man and woman arguing on their driveway. Getting out, he immediately recognizing the town's flamboyant doctor. Coat flapping in the wind, the doctor approached Dallas, hand outstretched, shouting to be heard over the gale, "Evening, Sheriff. Dan Johnson."

A vice-like grip close around Dallas's knuckles. Nothing ticked Dallas off more than a game-player, so he squeezed back twice as hard. Johnson extracted his hand, stretching the ligaments, and motioned to the woman shivering behind him. "My wife, Amy," he said flatly.

10

As she stepped forward, Dallas barely recognized the woman he'd pulled over earlier that day. She was now rain-soaked, hair plastered to her head, face covered in fresh scratches, and she shook like a California quake. "Evening, Mrs. Johnson. Looks like you've had some trouble."

Amy nodded, but before she could reply Dan turned on Dallas. "Forget about the call, Sheriff. Nothing happened. Amy panicked, that's all."

Dallas looked at Amy Johnson. Long strands of fair hair dripped down her open coat, her face was ghostly, her lips colorless. Yet, in spite of everything, she was an exceptionally attractive woman. She was also well known, not only for her unusual architectural designs, but for the work she did pro bono. He'd noticed her often over the past few years. What man hadn't? She'd stop traffic, if they had any. Now her soft gray eyes locked onto his. "I saw a woman—"

Johnson cut her off. "There wasn't anyone, Amy, or they'd still be here."

"You saw the blood—"

Dallas interrupted them. "Who called it in?"

"I did," Amy replied, "I saw the woman a few seconds before the power went out—"

"I told you, Amy, it was too dark to see anything."

The sheriff turned impatiently to Johnson. "Look, Dr. Johnson, we got a call concerning the disappearance of an injured woman from your property. If that's the case, we're losing valuable time. Were you here when the incident occurred?"

"No, but I got here right after. And as far as I'm concerned there was no *incident*."

"Would you excuse us, Doctor? I need to speak with Mrs. Johnson."

Unspoken words passed between the couple before Dan Johnson reluctantly left his wife's side and made his way back to the house. Amy looked up at the sheriff.

11

"Thanks." She told her story, shakily, but succinctly, leading Dallas toward the office window as she spoke. "She stood here."

Dallas put his hand on her arm to stop her and prevent her from disturbing the evidence. The touch, as simple as it was, set off an alarm for him. Instantly, he knew he would come to know this woman better. Amy stopped and looked up at him, her eyes searching his. She glanced down at his hand, still encircling her arm. Reluctantly, Dallas released her. "We need to preserve whatever evidence is there," he explained.

He shone his flashlight across the window ledge. Blood had pooled with rainwater. He examined the blood receding from a dip in the sidewalk. A crimson thread was still visible all the way to the front road. There it ended. He pulled out his camera and snapped a few photos, and then he examined the fresh scratches on Amy's face and hands. They wouldn't have produced the amount of blood he'd seen. "You hurt anywhere else?"

Amy shook her head.

"How'd you get these?" His thumb swiped her cheek gently.

Reluctantly, Amy related her dash through the brush when she'd first arrived home. "Guess I was a little spooked. Never felt like that before, especially on my own property."

Dallas considered her story, his natural curiosity peaked. "Must have been a mighty important letter."

Amy winced and looked back at her study. *Could be.*

"No sign of a vehicle driving away?"

She sounded exhausted. "No."

"You certain about the woman's description?"

"I know it sounds a little crazy, but her face was identical to mine. She had the same gray eyes, hair color, face shape, everything. Not only was it disconcerting to turn around and see a face looking at me through the

12

window, but it was a shock to look into a face a mirror image of my own."

The remark made him look at her afresh. He was seldom affected by a woman's looks, but Amy Johnson, even dripping wet, was breathtakingly beautiful. She was also well respected and intelligent. He knew enough about her not to doubt her credibility, although her story sure stretched it. "You wearing those sneakers when you came out to look for the woman?"

Amy looked down and nodded, shivering.

"Okay. There's enough blood here for concern. I'm going to call in the crime scene unit and our K-9 team. We'll need fingerprints and blood samples from you and the doc. Meanwhile, why don't you go on inside and warm up, Mrs. Johnson," he said, walking her to the porch. "And leave your sneakers outside. We'll need those."

Amy retreated into the house. Later, she saw a black van pull up the drive. A man in dark coveralls jumped out, walked around to the back of the truck, and opened the rear door. A German Shepherd leapt out, responding instantly to the handler, its tail wagging eagerly.

Amy turned away and went back into the living room where she paced in front of the stone fireplace, oblivious to the fire's warmth. Even though she had showered, her hair was almost dry, and she had changed into jeans and a sweatshirt, she still shivered, unable to get warm. Listlessly, she walked over to the living room windows, flipped on the yard lighting, and pressed her forehead against the cold glass. She peered into the black void over the bay, her thoughts on the woman she'd seen.

Who was she? How could she look like me? How's that possible? What is going on? Mentally Amy ticked off

13

family members. Not one of them resembled her. They were scattered across the continent, were of various ages, but she couldn't think of anyone who was close to her age, size, or appearance. Then who?

The moon slipped out from behind the clouds spilling a wide beam of white light across the bay. Huge breakers crested toward the beach. Near the house, trees and shrubs danced in the wind.

A powerful beam of light swept over Cape Peril. A helicopter hovered, its searchlights sweeping the cape, the lighthouse, down the steep cliffs, and out over the sea.

Amy pulled back from the window and examined Dan's reflection in the glass. He was perched on a stool in front of the bar, pouring another shot of whiskey into his glass. He downed it in a single gulp. "I should be at the hospital, not wasting my time here. I'm supposed to be on call." He slipped off the stool and walked over to the window, nodding in the directions of the helicopter hovering over the cape. "This whole thing's a big farce. Can't imagine what they're doing out there, besides wasting taxpayer's money. And to top it off, those idiots wanted *my* fingerprints and blood samples. Jerks."

With her back to him, Amy replied, "I wish you'd cooperate with them, Dan. They need to be able to identify the prints they're lifting from the window, from ours. They must wonder why you made such a fuss about it and why you kept insisting *nothing happened* when the opposite is so blatantly obvious."

"Oh come on, Amy, I was trying to prevent bad publicity." He returned to the bar for a refill.

Amy glanced over her shoulder at him. "Always worried about bad publicity."

Dan slammed the whiskey glass down on the granite countertop. "I do. You go around saying this woman looks like you and the people in this town will label you crazy. I don't want them thinking I'm married to a

14

lunatic. For all I know, you saw your own damned reflection."

Amy was stunned. She whirled around and stared at her husband. "Surely, you don't believe that."

Dan shrugged and lifting his whiskey glass, downed the last ounce.

Amy could feel anger creeping through her like hot lava and this surprised her. Complacent by nature, she seldom got angry and was ill-equipped to handle it. "You care about what people might think, but you don't give a damn about what happened here, tonight. Instead, you did your best to discredit me—to make me appear witless!"

He swiveled around on the stool and looked directly at her. "Sometimes you get carried away over things, make a big deal out of nothing. You know how you can be."

Dan poured another shot. "Not only that, I didn't want the police out here snooping around, like they're doing right now. And I don't want this hitting the press, which is exactly what's going to happen." Angrily, he downed the shot.

Amy said sarcastically, "The publicity thing again."

Dan rubbed his eyes in frustration. After a beat he said, "Okay, let's say you did see a woman. Maybe she was hurt." He saw Amy's look. "Okay, maybe she was bleeding. And just *maybe* she kind of looked like you. It was dark. How could you have seen her face?"

"I told you. I turned around and she was right there...outside the window, not five feet away. And that was before the power went out."

"Doesn't make sense. None at all. Were you drinking or what?"

"Drinking?" Amy stepped over to the bar and lifted the whiskey bottle. "No, Dan, I wasn't drinking. That's your diversion, not mine."

"All right. Don't get all riled up. It was just a question."

Amy stared at her husband. At thirty-eight he was still good looking—although he worked at it—the gym four times a week to keep his body toned, the stylist twice a month for a trim and a dye job, manicures, tanning beds, and who knew what else. Nevertheless, nothing could alter that charming boyish face that women loved. As an OB/GYN, his practice was overflowing with doting women. Amy pictured them, one after the other, on his examining table, Dan's hands sliding over their naked skin, probing intimate areas of their bodies. *How long had it been since those hands touched me? How long since Dan and I have made love? How long since he had spoken to me with any respect? Or, since we've had a normal, intelligent conversation?*

His voice brought her back.

"What?" She realized that she was staring at him and turned away.

Dan repeated himself. "I said, 'Why are you looking at me like that?'"

Amy shook her head. "Never mind. I'm going to make a fresh pot of coffee. Want anything?"

"Yeah. Make me an Espresso. In fact, make it a double. And see if there's any of that deli meat left in the fridge. I'll have that too. Never had time for supper, thanks to this fiasco."

Amy made a plate for Dan while the espresso machine dripped dark black coffee into a demitasse. She took the plate and espresso over to him. "Want anything else?"

"Yeah. Tell everybody to go home. You've created a hell of a mess here, Amy."

She turned away. "I'll go see how they're making out." Amy left Dan and walked into her study. She was conflicted. On one hand, it bothered Amy immensely that Dan was angry with her for causing so much trouble. She didn't like upsetting him that way. On the other hand, she was worried about the woman she'd seen. The whole thing had left Amy with an ominous feeling she couldn't shake.

From the window, she watched the scene outside. Two patrol cars were on the drive, lights flashing. Crime scene tape traveled from the garden below the window all the way to the road. The sheriff was talking to his team as they were wrapping up. The dog handler got in his truck and pulled away. Turning, the sheriff spotted Amy in the window and motioned her outside. Amy threw on her coat and padded out onto the porch in socks, closing the door firmly behind her. She didn't want Dan involved.

Dallas bounded up the stairs two at a time, landing outside the front door as she stepped onto the landing. Amy looked up at him. Sanville's sheriff was well over six feet, lean, big shoulders, weathered face, and pale blue eyes that, at this moment, seemed to be looking right into her. She took a step back and caught her breath. The sudden rush of emotion stunned her. Dan had been the only man she'd ever loved, and even though *the love* had slowly drained from their marriage, she had never considered another man. Amy felt herself flush. Dallas was speaking to her. She took a deep breath, tried to compose herself, and met his gaze.

"We're finished for tonight, Mrs. Johnson."

"You didn't find her."

"No ma'am. But Max picked up the trail."

"Max?"

"The tracker dog. We use him in situations like this. It was Max that found that fellow who went missing from Mabel Beach last month.

Amy nodded, remembering.

The sheriff continued. "Blood is a powerful human scent for a tracker dog, even with the rain we had. His handler let Max sniff a sample and then dispatched him from the road, back down the drive to your garden, and then across the lawn and into the brush, where you described the incident earlier tonight. The rain made it difficult, but Max was able to pick up the scent here and there, all the way to the lighthouse and a clearing in the trees where a car had been parked."

Surprised, Amy said, "You mean, she was right there, in the brush?"

"That's right."

Amy tried to make sense of this. "So, you're saying she came by car and parked it over at the lighthouse. Then, she walked all the way here through the brush?" Amy's thoughts flashed back to the eerie sound she had heard in the brush *like a voice calling her name*. She shuddered.

"Appears that way," Dallas repeated. "She left some pretty good fingerprints on your window as well as a clear set of footprints in the garden. Problem is," he hesitated, "there's a second set of footprints there. That pair belong to a much larger, very heavy individual. The rain must have stopped around that time because those large mucky boot marks are visible on your drive, along side the trail of blood." Dallas pointed out the markings as he spoke. "Interestingly, the small set of footprints enter the garden, but they don't leave, suggesting the victim was carried to a waiting vehicle."

Amy grew more distressed. "But I would have seen that."

"It must have taken place before you arrived outside. How long did it take you to get from the study to the garden, keeping in mind that you said you didn't react immediately?"

She thought back. How much time had she lost before her dash down the hall? She'd been in shock. Time had passed, but how much? "Maybe five minutes. Maybe more. I'm not sure." She rubbed her forehead, and then looked over her shoulder toward the garden.

"I'm confused, Sheriff. You say someone carried the woman to a vehicle. If that's the case, did she come with someone, or did someone come after her?"

The sheriff removed his hat and ran a hand through his thick, dark hair. He twisted the cap back into place. "There was a second vehicle."

"How do you know?"

Dallas considered a moment before answering. "We know a car was parked over by the lighthouse. We're assuming the person in question parked there, out of the line of sight of your house. Meanwhile, we found tire tracks near the lighthouse that go right over the edge."

Amy's eyes widened. Are you saying…?"

"The car was pushed off the cliff."

CHAPTER 3

Sleep was impossible. Amy tossed and turned; her dreams were a disturbing collage of the evening's events. The woman's face appeared repeatedly, awaking Amy each time. Was she seeing that woman or herself? About 2 a.m. she sat bolt upright, bathed in sweat. In the twilight, Dan's sleeping outline was visible in the next bed. She missed the comforting warmth of his body next to hers, especially tonight. After Jamie was born, he'd replaced their king bed with two doubles, complaining that Amy's getting up for the baby disturbed his sleep. When Jamie began sleeping through the night, she tried to convince Dan to go back to their king bed, but he refused.

Amy slipped out of bed, tiptoed to the closet for her robe and slippers, and without using lights, went out into the hall. She stopped outside Jamie's room. The nightlight by his bed cast soft light across his pillow where *Mush,* his favorite bear, was sitting. How had he forgotten *Mush?* He never went to Nita's without it. Amy made a mental note to drop it off for him in the morning. She padded down the stairs to the study.

Nagging thoughts of deadlines and unfinished blueprints prompted her to turn on the Mac. She selected a drawing file in the hope of re-focusing her thoughts onto something productive. The floor plan

20

flew open on the big screen, she made a few modifications, but her concentration waned. She closed the file and left the study.

Amy roamed from room to room listlessly, questions stalking her like ghosts. *Who was that woman? Where did she come from? Why did she come here? Why does she look like me? How's that even possible?* Amy stopped at the door to the library that was tucked off the living room. Old photo albums lined the lower bookshelves. She hadn't looked at them in years, and didn't want to now; but maybe, just maybe, they held a clue.

Walking into the room, she dropped cross-legged onto the braided rug, and gazed reluctantly at the albums, dreading their contents, afraid to see the painful memories that they harbored. It was some time before she gathered enough courage to pull out a pink book filled with her pictures and images of her childhood. *Our Daughter* was embossed on the cover. Reluctantly, Amy lifted the hard cover.

Her mother's handwriting leapt from the first page. Amy's birth was recorded as 12:12 a.m. June 2nd, thirty-two years earlier in Beaverdale, a small town southwest of Portland.

A tiny footprint, a miniature handprint, and a clipping of platinum hair, like Jamie's, attested to her fragile beginning. Further along, old photos of a scrunched little face stared back at her. "Pixie," she said involuntarily, recalling her old nickname.

Photo after photo recorded her growth and development. The infant blossomed into a toddler with a head of flaxen curls and a mischievous smile, also like Jamie's. Amy thumbed through the pages and swallowed hard when a 5x7 photo of her parents jumped from the page. She wanted to snap the book closed to protect herself from the memories. *No!*

Inhaling deeply, she willed herself to continue. Quickly, she turned the page. This time it was a photo

21

of her dad that stopped her. He'd been gangly and fun loving in his youth, but over the years he'd changed. *He had matured into a wonderful, confident, caring man.* A deep, dark sadness welled up in her. *If only... No! Don't think about it.*

Her finger slid across to an enlargement of her mom--young and vibrant--cradling Amy lovingly in her arms. Photos depicted the years passing happily. Finally, Amy came to the last and final family photo. Her father, his hand on her shoulder, beamed proudly. Her mom had both arms around her. Suddenly, Amy was in the room with them. She could feel the warmth of her father's strong hand, mother's excitement, and their protective love. Her mother's hearty laughter rang in Amy's ears. "Oh, Mom." Amy pressed the book close to her chest and squeezed her eyes shut. "Dad, Mom," she whispered, "I miss you so much." The album slipped from her hands...and she wept.

Memories overwhelmed her, memories she had carefully locked out for years. Her father's excitement at her accomplishments, her mom's warm embrace, and days filled with wonder and joy. She had loved her parents with all her young being. Then, suddenly, they were gone. Obliterated. A horrific accident. Bodies so mangled that closed coffins were necessary. She'd never had the chance to see her parents one last time and say her *goodbye*. Amy could never get past that. A single word, but so important.

A year of her teenage life disappeared. She fell into an abyss of darkness, grief, and crippling heartache. It was like being hit by a truck at full speed. Her soul had been crushed.

Amy recalled the premonition that haunted her for days before their accident. Afterward, she'd wished she could have deciphered the strange, ominous feeling. Had she been able to do that, she may have found a way to save their lives. Finally, Amy wiped her tears and pulled the album back into her lap. Her mother's photo stared up at her. Her beauty held an astral quality. Had it foretold her fate?

Amy was hit by the realization, that at age thirty-two, Amy now looked almost *exactly* like her mom at the time of the photo. Amy pushed herself off the carpet and walked to the fireplace mantle where there was a recent photo of herself. She pulled it out of the frame and returned quickly to the library where she placed it beside her mom's. She stared in astonishment. *We're almost identical!*

And now—there's three of us...

Amy thumbed through the baby book again, reading the captions her mother had written. Then, one by one Amy searched each family album for a clue to the existence of the woman she had seen at the window. There wasn't a sign of another child who resembled Amy.

Hours later, Dan's disgruntled voice awoke her. "What the hell are you doing down here?"

Her eyes flew open. Light streamed in the windows, rays dancing across her face. She squeezed her eyes closed, and sat up, trying to understand what she was doing on the rug in the library. When she remembered, a heaviness re-settled over her.

She trailed Dan into the kitchen. He reached for the cereal box; she grabbed the coffeepot. "You look like shit," he told her, pulling a bowl from the cupboard.

"Thanks. Want toast with your cereal?" Amy stumbled around the kitchen waiting for the coffee to brew.

"No, I don't want toast." He pulled the milk from the fridge and read the date. "It's expiring this week. You need to go shopping, Amy. You know I hate stale milk," he grumbled, pouring it over his cereal. "You're not keeping up with things, Amy."

She sat down across from Dan, eyeing him. Nothing was good enough anymore. She didn't buy the right groceries, she allowed dust to settle on the furniture, she let Jamie spread his toys across the carpet, and on and on. The complaint list grew longer every week.

He interrupted her thoughts. "I've been thinking about last night. You're obviously stressed out. I think this would be a good time for you to take that vacation your firm owes you. Go away for a while. Nita can look after Jamie." He looked over at her purposely, waiting for a response. When none came, he continued, "You've been working too hard. You need a break. Go somewhere for a couple of weeks. I'll let Nita know."

Groggily, Amy got up and poured the rich steaming coffee into her mug and held the pot in his direction. He held out his cup and she poured. "No, Dan, I'm not going anywhere. And I'm not leaving Jamie. What I am going to do is find out who that woman is, and what's going on."

"No! Amy, don't do that. Leave it alone. You hear me? Things are getting out of hand. I don't want you making a bigger deal out of this than you all ready have." He ate in silence then dropped his spoon. "Damn it, I wish you hadn't called the sheriff." He picked up the spoon and tapped the tabletop with it. "Complicates things."

Surprised, Amy said, "Really? Most people don't think of the sheriff as a complication unless they're on the wrong side of the law." She cocked her head and looked at him intently, once again feeling anger rise within her. *Does he ever care about anyone but himself?* "You know, for a doctor, you've got shockingly little compassion for people."

Dan dropped the spoon and stared at her. "What did you say?"

Amy turned away. *Where did that come from?* The truth was, she was weary of Dan's self-centered, uncaring attitude. She turned back, her eyes steady on his, "You never care about anyone, except yourself, Dan. It's tiring."

He blinked, unable to believe what he was hearing. "What's happening to you, Amy? In all the years we've been married, you've *never* talked to me like this," he thought a minute and then added, "It's not like you at all. Of course, we both know you don't handle stress well."

She took another sip of coffee, savored the flavor, and inhaled the aroma, praying for revitalization. Mug in hand, Amy turned toward the hall and headed for the stairs.

Dan stood up. "Where're you going?"

She threw the answer over her shoulder. "Shower. See you tonight, or tomorrow, or whenever you decide to come home."

Dumbfounded, Dan stared after her.

CHAPTER 4

As Amy drove toward town, she turned up the morning news. Local reports were first, including mention of a woman reported missing near Cape Peril. *There's the publicity Dan's worried about.*

She pulled up to her Grandfather's ranch style bungalow within the golf course community, where he once enjoyed a daily round of golf with Grams and his friends. Amy parked behind what she had nicknamed, his *eight-wheel ride*. The van was in the carport, the electric scooter mounted across the extended steel bumper. No room in the garage. It housed a lifetime of keepsakes and memories. What didn't fit in there had been stuffed into the crawlspace.

At the front door a weathered sign hung above the mailbox, boldly stating, *The Haddens*. Only one Hadden lived here now.

Amy glanced at her watch and pounded on the door. It wasn't quite eight a.m., but he'd be up; he'd been an early riser all his life. The door opened and Amy leaned across the wheelchair to give her grandfather a warm hug. He smelled of soap. His craggy face was lined with crevices and ridges; his reading glasses perched halfway down his nose, and the hazel eyes peering over them, danced with delight. "Checking to see if I'm still alive, are ya?" he bellowed.

"I know you're still alive, Gramps," she replied. "No point visiting a corpse." Gripping the handles of the wheelchair, she swung it into the living room, kicking the front door closed behind her. "How're you doing?" she asked him.

"Better, now you're here," he hollered.

Amy motioned for him to lower his voice. He refused to wear a hearing aide. "Sorry," he yelled.

"Get you anything?" Amy looked at his bony frame and frowned.

"Nope. Had breakfast hours ago. Day's half over."

"I can hear you," Amy said loudly.

"Keep forgettin'. Hardly talk to anybody anymore," he grumbled pointedly.

Amy curled into a corner of the old leather couch that had been in her grandparents' living room since she could remember. "Something happened at our house last night," Amy told him. When she saw that she had his undivided attention, she related what had occurred, pausing occasionally for his reaction. Seeing none, she continued.

Even though Gramps Hadden was in his seventies, his mind was sharp. The two of them had always been close. She knew him as well as he knew her. He was the quiet type—a thinker, not a talker. Until sixteen years ago, he had been an astute businessman, opening his own carpet store just after her birth. Under his management the business had thrived, multiplying into a national chain within a decade. Then tragedy struck. His only daughter and son-in-law were killed. He sold the stores, gave the funds over to an investment firm, and became withdrawn and absent-minded. After the accident, he began spending time away from home, alone, at his cabin. Amy's laughing, fun-loving grandfather disappeared, although he'd been, and still was, one heck of a card player.

He taught her to play when she was two. She learned that he never revealed his hand, at cards, or in life. In later years, they'd play long into the night, Amy vowing to beat him. It finally happened when she was twelve.

Now the old man's stoic expression aggravated her. She watched for a sign, a twinge, any reaction at all that would indicate that he knew *something* about the woman Amy had seen. But of course, being the poker player that he was, he revealed nothing. Amy concluded by repeating Sheriff Wayburne's summation. "...the car was pushed over the cliff."

He sat perfectly still. They eyed each other. Silence hung heavily between them. Amy watched for an indication he knew *something*. Finally, she saw it in his eyes. A flicker. Was it fear? Knowledge? *What?*

He cleared his throat. "Amy, I think it best if you to take Jamie and go away for a while."

Amy stood up. "That's the second time I've heard that today." She began pacing across the worn living room carpet, never taking her eyes off her grandfather. "Why do you want me to go away?"

"Safer," he said quietly, looking down. "For you and Jamie."

Amy caught the fear in his voice. "Safer? What do you mean?"

He looked up at her, grimacing. "They could come back."

"They?"

He shook his head.

"Gramps," she stopped where she was. "*Who is they?*"

He covered his eyes with his hands and shook his head.

Amy whirled on him, "Gramps, tell me what you're not telling me!"

He sat stubbornly silent. Then he whispered, "How about a coffee?"

Amy glared at him. "Coffee! I want to hear something that makes sense. There was a woman at our house last night that looks just like me. Do you know who she is?"

"What does it matter? Doubtful you'll see her again."

"Are you saying you know who she is?" Amy sat down in front of him, watching him, waiting out his silence.

He twisted uncomfortably in the stainless steel chair. "I'm not sure who you saw, Amy," his voice was barely a whisper, "but I know you have to be extremely careful now. You and Jamie." Their eyes locked. Neither moved. Finally, the old man reached for her hands. "Amy", he paused, struggling to find the right words. "I can't tell you much, but what I can say is this. Horrible things have happened to our family in the past. *Accidents.* Your parents' death, my fall at the cabin...other things..." he struggled, agonizing over how to explain.

Amy squeezed his hand. "Gramps, those were *accident*s. Accidents happen to people now and then. What do they have to do with *this?*"

He rubbed the back of her hands with his thumbs and when he looked up, Amy saw the pain in his eyes. "Please, Amy, take Jamie and go somewhere safe."

She stared at him, and then pulled her hands from his grasp. "I'm not going anywhere. Jamie's in school and I've got a big project to finish. I need to find out who this woman is." She searched his weathered face knowing he was holding back. "I need answers, Gramps. I came here for your help."

The old man leaned back in the chair and rubbed his leg with gnarled knuckles. He always did that when she asked him for something he wouldn't, or couldn't, give.

Recognizing the motion, she sighed and pushed herself off the sofa. He could be so damned stubborn. There was something he wasn't telling her. "Damn!" Her arm flew out, sending a golf trophy crashing to the floor. "How can you just sit there after what's happened and not help me? You're holding back. Whatever it is, I need to know. Gramps, please!"

His determined expression hurt. She didn't understand it, but she knew it was pointless to pursue it right now. Reluctantly, she gave in. "All right, I'll make coffee," she said, picking up the bronze trophy and placing it back on the shelf.

Handing Gramps his mug a few minutes later, Amy sank back into the couch. They sipped in silence, each deep in thought.

Gramps spoke first, "What's Dan say about all this?"

"He's worried about bad publicity."

"Asshole."

Amy added, "And he wants me to go away for a while."

Gramps's eyebrows shot up, "First things he's said in years that makes sense," he scratched his chin and added under his breath, "the egotistical prick."

"Don't get started on Dan. You two never did like one another, but this isn't the time to get into that."

"Well, I've got my reasons," he said peering over his glasses.

Amy never did know what those were and Gramps never did tell her. She had always assumed in was simply a mutual dislike between the two men.

Gramps continued, "I keep telling you to stand up to him. He pushes you around. Talks down to you. Treats you like live-in help. You deserve better than that, Girl."

Amy stood abruptly. She didn't want to hear anymore. "Enough of this," she said. "Want to come with me?"

"Where to?"

"We'll go see Grams." She saw his face fall. Grams was the love of his life. They'd been together forty-five years when Alzheimer's—at least that's what they thought it was—took hold of her. Amy knew it pained Gramps to see her like that.

"What would I want to see her for?"

Amy tipped her head sideways and frowned.

He leaned forward in the wheelchair. "Now don't you go giving me that look of yours. You know darned well the woman's lost her marbles. She doesn't know who I am anymore. Last time I was there she thought I was the janitor. Told me to stop gaping at her and start sweeping."

"Maybe it was a hint."

"Now don't go getting surly. She's best left alone."

"That's the last things she needs, Gramps, and you know it. If there's even a chance for Grams, we need to do all we can for her."

"You go ahead. I figure if I hang around that place, I could end up in the next bed. Not good for a person's health, getting too close to those places. Besides," he cleared his throat noisily. His voice broke and he looked down, "I'd rather remember her the way she was."

Amy bent down and wrapped her arms around his frail frame, hugging him. "Want anything before I go?"

He looked up. "How 'bout a round of poker."

Amy laughed in spite of herself and stopped at the front door, looking back at him fondly. "Soon, Gramps. Take care."

CHAPTER 5

Amy swung the Jeep Cherokee onto the US101 for the ten-mile drive down the Oregon coast highway to the *Summerset Meadows*, the special care facility that had been her grandmother's home for the past few years. The neurologist couldn't be sure Cynthia Hadden had Alzheimer's, as test results hadn't proved it conclusively, but she had many of the symptoms. At the very least, he said it was dementia.

As Amy drove, she reflected upon her grandfather's reaction. She was sure it had been *fear* she'd seen in his eyes. *But why?* She considered the traumas he had suffered over the years. He'd lost his only daughter in a tragic car accident. Her death had almost broken him. He was close to his son-in-law, making it a double tragedy. Shortly after, Gramps had the fall at the cabin that had broken his right leg and crushed the left. Then, a few years ago, he'd lost Grams to Alzheimer's. *Now, he's probably afraid he'll lose Jamie and me, and we're all he's got left. Still, there was more than fear in his eyes and in his voice. There had been something else, a flicker of recognition. Gramps knew something. And if he knows, then Grams knows. Or did.*

Still pondering this, Amy parked in the vast parking area in front of the sprawling facility. She hurried up the long walk, up the front steps, and through the busy lobby where she signed in before climbing the stairs to her grandmother's floor. The private room was airy and bright with a large ocean view window that provided a distant vista of the rugged coastline. The older woman, her tiny frame clothed in sweats, sat in a chair staring blankly through the thick glass, a blanket draped across her lap, her eyes fixed on the horizon.

Amy assessed her from the doorway, searching as always, for some sign of improvement. Cynthia Hadden's sparkle and intelligence were gone. The essence that made her the special person she once was, had been stolen by the destructive process of the disease. Yet, her beauty remained, diminished only minimally by Mother Nature. Studying her profile, Amy could see that even though her grandmother was in her seventies, she was still attractive. She had passed those unusual features on to her daughter, and to Amy.

And perhaps... to someone else.

"Grams," Amy called to her. The white head turned slowly; two gray eyes searched the room and found Amy, but they showed no sign of recognition. Amy pulled up an armchair and sat down opposite her grandmother. "Came by to talk, Grams."

The old woman dropped her chin and eyed her suspiciously. Amy waited for her grandmother to adjust to Amy's presence, and then choosing her words with care, she began talking about her mother. Gently, Amy placed a photo of her mom on her grandmother's lap blanket. The older woman stared at it blankly at first, and then with shaky fingers, she plucked it off the blanket and turned it to the light. A smile eased the tension from her face. "Sharalynn," she whispered.

Another strange aspect of the disease was her Grandmother's inability to remember who Amy was, but with a struggle, the older woman could often recall the years prior to Amy's birth. Amy wasn't sure where the line was drawn, or whether it was simply a foggy zone where memory fragments drifted in and out.

"Sharalynn's wedding day," Amy reminded her.

Grandma Hadden's eyes seemed to look inward. "Small wedding...our garden." She rubbed the photo with the tip of her index finger.

Amy encouraged her. "Yes. You lived in Beaverdale then."

"Beaverdale...by the bridge."

Amy grew hopeful. If her grandmother could remember her daughter's wedding, maybe she could remember her daughter giving birth, just six months later. "That's right! We had to cross the bridge to get to your house." Amy pulled a baby photo of herself from her purse and slipped it into the elder woman's other hand. "Sharalynn had a baby girl."

Her grandmother inspected the second photo, her face brightening once more. "My pretty--" she twisted in her chair. "Can't remember..."

Amy swallowed the lump in her throat. It was so hard to hear those words. Her grandmother had been there for her, always. When Amy's parents were killed, Grams had pulled Amy into her arms and taken her home to live with her and Gramps. She had encouraged Amy to go on to university, telling her: "You've been drawing and designing buildings since you were a little girl. This is your chance to go to university and learn to do it for real. Lord knows, you've got the brains." When Amy graduated with a degree in Architecture, her grandmother was there with an armload of roses. "Now, my dear, you can change the world, literally!"

Leaning forward, Amy placed her hand on her grandmother's knee and said gently, "The baby's name is Amy."

"Amy! Yes...Amy." The old woman looked up at Amy in amazement. "How'd you know?" Her eyes glazed with sudden memories. "My Amy. Smart...quick like—like..." she stumbled, unable to find the word she wanted.

"Lightning. That's what you used to say, Grams, *'quick like lightning.'*" Amy realized that the moment had come. She pulled a second baby photo of herself from her purse and hesitated. She was taking a huge chance by positioning two of the same photos side by side with the hope of triggering a memory. At best, Amy might learn something. At worst, her grandmother would simply not understand why Amy had placed two identical photos on the lap blanket. Convincing herself she had nothing to lose, Amy positioned the second photo beside the first one. Now, the two baby photos of Amy were side by side. She didn't expect what happened next.

The older woman stared at the identical photographs. Her eyes darted back and forth between them. Suddenly her head flew up and she looked up at Amy in alarm, her eyes wide. "The same!"

Amy nodded, "Yes, Grams, they're exactly the same."

Cynthia Hadden's gray eyes darted around the room and her fingers began to tremble. She dropped the photo of Sharalynn. Her hands flew to her face. She rocked back and forth in her chair. "No," she wailed, "No, no, no!" Amy reached over to comfort her, but the woman's cries grew frantic. When the nurse came running in, Amy fled, tears streaming down her cheeks.

CHAPTER 6

As Amy left the US101 at Sanville, she noticed dark storm clouds building over the Pacific and a fresh breeze whipping up whitecaps close to shore. She pulled into an area of estate properties, slowing in front of a sprawling two-story set well back from the road. Amy turned down a long, drive and parked behind her sister-in-law's Camry.

The front door burst open and Nita stepped onto the porch, her ample arms motioning for Amy to move her car.

Amy grabbed Jamie's favorite stuffie from the passenger seat and stepped out, the wind whipping her long hair across her face. "I'll only stay a few minutes," She told Nita, waggling the toy. "Just wanted to drop *Mush* off. Jamie must've missed him last night. He hates going to sleep without him."

Suddenly, a small flaxen-haired boy burst past Nita, "Mommy! Mommy!" He raced down the steps, running toward Amy, the wind pushing him around like a toy. He squealed with delight.

Amy knelt and drew him into her arms and his tiny body connected with hers, giving off a penetrating warmth that made her heart swell. She kissed his soft, rubbery cheek and inhaled his sweet scent, then pulled back and looked at him. "Brought Mush."

He smiled, his little hands seizing the teddy bear. "Can we go home now, Mommy?"

She looked up at Nita, wishing she had the nerve to tell her son, "Yes." Amy wanted nothing more than to pick him up, put him in the Jeep, and leave. Instead, she said, "Mommy will be back for you tomorrow night, Sweetheart." She ran her hand through his unruly, platinum curls. "Big hug now." Two twiggy arms scuttled around her neck and a damp kiss was planted on her cheek.

Jamie pulled back and examined the wet mark with two huge gray eyes that sparkled with mischief. "Bye Mommy, be good," he told her through a smile. Always a smile.

Reluctantly, Amy let him go, watching as he climbed the stairs into his Aunt Nita's outstretched arms. He squirmed and looked back at his mom, waving.

As Amy stood, she was overwhelmed by the sudden irresistible compulsion to snatch Jamie from her sister-in-law. She and Nita had never been close. Her sister-in-law was cool and aloof and her words held a biting edge that often oozed with sarcasm. Rather than run verbal warfare with the woman, Amy kept conversation, and time spent with Nita, to a minimum. Looking hard at her sister-in-law, Amy tried to discern her sudden anxiety. She shivered and said, "Feels like it's going to rain. You can smell the ozone in the air."

Nita's short, black hair whipped her face. "Weatherman says we're in for another storm. Not the whopper we had last night though. I guess it's that time of year again." She ran her eyes down Amy's tall, slim body, her mouth forming a snarl. "I'd invite you inside, but you probably want to enjoy your time without Jamie."

Amy winced, and trying to ignore the mockery, pointed to the second story window. "Better close your upstairs window. See you tomorrow night." Her voice trailed off as she turned and dashed to the Jeep. Yanking open the door, she dove inside. Before backing from the drive, she glanced at the porch. Empty. Nita had taken Jamie inside. Amy stared at the closed door, swallowing down an intense sense of loss that she couldn't understand. She put the Jeep in reverse. Home, Amy thought,.

The wind was gusting by the time she reached Lighthouse Road. Since the Cape Peril Lighthouse was no longer manned, the narrow, winding coast road had fallen into disrepair and washouts were frequent during winter storms. The Jeep Cherokee rounded a sharp curve in the road. She was at *The Wash*, where the road met the sea. When the waves were up during high tide, the combination of seawater and rain often flooded the road.

A smoky shaft of afternoon light sliced through the cloud and into the rolling sea. With the force of the entire Pacific behind them, the waves crashed heavily onto the bluff, sending spray high into the air, and across the windshield. Amy turned the wipers on high and negotiated the Jeep through the potholes as she continued along the narrow road toward Cape Peril.

She loved the ocean and the coast. For a reason she could never explain, she found herself drawn magnetically to the sea. It gave her a compelling sense of wellbeing. Her grandfather's voice echoed in her mind. *"The ocean always makes things right, Girl.*

CHAPTER 7

No one was at the Johnson residence when Sheriff Dallas Wayburne arrived, so he walked the property, the beach below, and the state land all the way to the Cape Peril Lighthouse, searching for missed clues and insights into the case.

Amy pulled onto her drive, parked the Jeep beside the Yukon marked, SHERIFF, and walked around the house, looking for him. Stopping at the staircase to the beach, she leaned over the wooden rail, to see if he was down there.

Dallas walked up behind her. Knowing the roar of the waves would impair her hearing, he yelled, "Hello!"

Amy whirled around, her hand flying to her chest. "Sheriff! You scared me."

"Been told that more than once," he said, motioning to the house. "Can we talk inside, where it's quieter?"

He followed her to the wrap-around veranda, bypassing the wheelchair ramp, and through the French doors to the breakfast room. He commented on the ramp. "Did you put that in for a family member?"

"My grandfather," she told him, closing the double doors.

Dallas walked into the living room. The house was a larger, much more sophisticated version of the mountain cabin he and his father had built years ago: cedar walls and ceilings, massive beams supporting high vaults soaring over thirty feet from the floor, huge stone fireplace that rose to the rafters, and tall wood-framed windows that spanned the back of the house. He looked out across the bay to the open Pacific and whistled softly. "Wow. Some view."

Amy answered from the kitchen: "That's why we bought the property. Coffee? Tea?"

Normally he would decline, but for reasons he couldn't quite understand, he accepted, and strolled over to the small breakfast table.

Amy glanced at him over her shoulder. "You haven't found her yet." It was a statement thrown to him, as she reached for the coffee beans.

"No, not yet," he replied, removing his hat and dropping it onto the glass table. He sat down on one of the three chairs.

"Did you find out who she is?"

"Not for certain."

"Did you ID her fingerprints?"

"Not yet."

"Not much progress." Amy chastised him. "When do you think you'll know something?"

Dallas leaned back in his chair, a smile tugging at his lips. "I could be wrong, Mrs. Johnson, but I believe that I'm the one who's supposed to be asking the questions."

Amy gave him a quick glance, and hid a smile, "Yes, of course."

He added, "An investigation takes time."

"You're right. I'm anxious, that's all. And, as Dan has reminded me, I've never been good at handling stress."

Dallas watched her move lithely around the kitchen, her movements as quick as her thoughts, nothing wasted. She was dressed casually in jeans and a warm sweater. Her striking profile enhanced by long, honey hair swept into the same high ponytail his ten-year-old daughter frequently wore. In spite of Amy Johnson's youthful look, her presence was overwhelming. That was the part he was having trouble with. He'd best have his coffee and leave. *Maybe I've been without a woman too damned long.*

Dallas considered her husband. Doc Johnson was a well-known OB/GYN on the coast. Problem was, like many people in Sanville, Dallas had seen the doc with other women more than once. It was difficult to understand why any man married to a woman like Amy would risk his relationship with infidelities. Either the doc was oblivious to his wife's beauty, or he was insatiable. Unless...there was something amiss with Amy Johnson. "We did learn something," he said.

Amy pulled two mugs from the cupboard and turned around. "Oh, good."

Dallas let the remark slide, eyeing her calmly before continuing. "We salvaged the car that went over the cliff. One of the print sets inside the car match the set we lifted from your study window, but like I said, no ID yet."

Amy froze. Her skin-- flushed from the cool breeze outside—paled. Her eyes grew wide. "Tell me she wasn't inside the car when it went over."

"Nope. I'm almost certain she was put into a second vehicle and driven away."

"Was anyone inside the car when it went over?"

"No, ma'am."

"Was it her car?"

"It was a late model Taurus, rented yesterday morning from the Budget office at the Portland airport. Woman by the name of *Alesha Eickher* rented it. Recognize the name?"

Amy shook her head. "No, but there's something about the name *Eickher*..."

Dallas continued, "She has a Paraguayan driver's license. Arrived in Portland yesterday morning on a flight from Miami. We're checking arrival documentation with immigration in Miami."

Amy poured coffee into two mugs, placed them on the table, and slipped back into the kitchen for cream and sugar. "What about the hospitals and clinics. She was hurt."

"Checked. Dead end."

"So she's vanished?"

Dallas added cream and four teaspoons of sugar to his coffee. "Doubtful."

Amy raised her brows as he added two more spoons of sugar. "Doubtful?"

When she sat down, Dallas looked at her closely. Her beauty, in spite of facial scratches, was astonishing. He hadn't been in the company of a woman, other than for friendship, since his wife had left. "Why," he wondered, "is this woman having such an affect on me?" He turned his attention to questioning her and listened carefully as she related Friday's events again. On the window ledge in front of him, were three framed photos of a small, platinum-haired boy with soft gray eyes. When she was finished, he asked, "How old's your boy?"

Amy smiled at the sudden shift. "Jamie's five. Very bright for his age, according to the teachers. They say he's way ahead of the other kids."

Dallas nodded. He heard pride in her voice and wondered if he sounded the same when he talked about his daughter, Maya. He kept the questions coming. "How many kids did your mom have?"

"Just me. There was a problem during my delivery. She couldn't have any more children."

"How old was she when she married?"

"Eighteen."

"How long before you came along?"

Amy reached across the table for the sugar and added a spoonful to her coffee. "Six months." She looked at him, expecting a reaction, but he let it go.

Dallas pulled a notebook and pen from his pocket and made notes. "Your mom have any children before she and your father were married?"

Amy frowned. "Not that I know of."

He sipped the coffee thoughtfully. "How many children did your grandmother have?"

"My mother was an only child."

"You sure?"

Amy dropped her chin in her hand and looked at him. "Sheriff, if you're trying to understand how this mystery woman could be about the same age as me *and* look like me, good luck. I live in what's left of this family and even I can't figure that out."

Dallas sat back in his chair. "Don't worry, we'll sort it out. We always do."

Amy eyed him curiously, and then shifted the conversation in a different direction. "You have a southern accent."

"Texas. Moved here when I was fifteen. Never could shake the accent though. Gives me away every time." He laughed. "You know what they say, you can take the boy out of Texas but you can't take Texas out of the boy."

Amy smiled. "I thought it was the farm they couldn't take out of the boy."

"That too. Or in my case maybe it was the ranch." Dallas realized he was actually enjoying himself. Her smile was radiant. It made her eyes sparkle. He stood abruptly. *Time to go.* "Well, thanks for the coffee, Mrs. Johnson."

Amy followed him to the front door. He stepped outside and picked up the bag he had left on the mat when he had arrived and pulled out a heeled leather shoe. "Here's the shoe you lost in the brush last night.

Thought you might want it back, although it's a little damp."

Amy took the shoe, her fingers brushing his. The slight touch was electric. Their eyes met. Dallas thought. "I've got to get out of here."

CHAPTER 8

Loneliness and something more, emptiness, swept over Amy as she watched the sheriff drive away. During the short time he'd been in the house, she had felt safe. More than that, she'd enjoyed his company. His easy manner exuded confidence and strength. He was distinguished-looking and yet she could picture him on a horse, racing across the Texas landscape, as he must have done for years.

Now, alone, she felt tense. The feeling of uneasiness returned. It's the coffee, she thought; I have to stop drinking so much. She thought about Dallas's questions, the woman she's seen at her window, Gramps telling her to leave with Jamie, and Grams incredible reaction to the two photos of Amy.

She felt such trepidation—a sense of foreboding that nagged at her inside. The ominous feeling hung over her and just wouldn't go away.

Amy wandered into her home study. It was her workspace, saving the long drive to Portland, where her firm had its offices. It allowed her to make only one or two trips a week to the city to meet with clients, liaison with the design team, and pick up change orders and contracts. The rest of the week she worked from her home office.

She knew she was fortunate in many ways: she had a great career as an architect, doing what had inspired her

45

since childhood; she had a wonderful little boy who was the center of her very existence; her husband was a successful doctor with his own practice; and she lived in the most beautiful place on earth with a wall-to-wall view of the sea.

Her eyes rested on the crumpled envelope she had retrieved from the brush. She had brought it back with her from the Portland office yesterday, where it had suddenly appeared on her desk just before quitting time. She knew instinctively that it held something unpleasant. Not wanting to be late picking up Jamie from after-school-care, she had grabbed it and left Portland without opening it. Then, she'd almost lost it when the wind tore it out of her hand.

Now, Amy picked it up and examined the handwriting on the front. Her name had been penned with care, but there was no return. She dreaded the thought of what was inside, but she'd put it off long enough. Reaching for the letter opener, she slit the fold and pulled out a single sheet of paper. There was no salutation.

I'm sorry to have to write you, but I don't have the courage to say this to you directly. I admire the work you do and it was in this regard that we were introduced a few years ago, at your Portland office. Since then, I have attended your husband's clinic and referred a couple of my friends to his practice.

During one of my visits, he made advances toward me. This experience was degrading. Out of respect for you, I didn't make a formal complaint, although I may still do so.

My closest friend has informed me that something similar happened to her. Unfortunately, your husband and my friend have developed a relationship that extends beyond the examining room. I understand she's pregnant and I am fearful of the outcome. Not only am I concerned

*for my friend's wellbeing (in spite of her foolishness), but I
also feel that you should know of your husband's
impropriety.*

The words blurred. Amy's hand dropped to the
desktop and the letter fluttered onto the stack of bills.
Minutes ticked by. *All those late nights—the clinic, the gym,
the hospital, the conferences. She should have guessed. When did
it start?*

Her thoughts flashed back seven years, to the day
Dan asked her to marry him. She could see him as he
had looked at that moment: a handsome, self-assured
man of thirty standing with his back to the sunset, bare
feet planted in the sand, and a ring sparkling in his right
hand. Dan Johnson had promised her a romantic life
on the coast, where his young practice was already
flourishing. They were married as soon as Amy
received her degree. *We were in love then,* she told herself.
We were!

Almost two years later, when they learned she was
pregnant, Dan had been ecstatic. After Jamie was born,
Dan's attention shifted to their new baby. At first, he
was a doting father. Then, things changed in their
marriage. They didn't resume their lovemaking with any
frequency. Dan started to pull away from her. One
particular evening, six months after Jamie's birth, she
and Dan had been getting ready for bed. She had
walked up behind him and put her arms around him,
resting her cheek against his back. She felt him stiffen at
her touch. She had been shocked by that and asked
him, "Don't I appeal to you anymore, Dan?"

He had been stepping out of his trousers. The
question stopped him. "Of course. Why ask such a
stupid question?"

She slid around and looked at him. "Because, we
hardly ever make love anymore."

Dan turned away from her and busied himself laying out his clothes for morning. "Long days at the clinic and the hospital, that's all."

"That never bothered you before."

He became agitated. "Come on, Amy, what's the big deal?"

She had watched him, noticing that he wouldn't or *couldn't* look at her. Disappointed, she had turned around and stared at the double bed that Dan had bought her. She remembered thinking, *how many men allocate a separate bed for their wife?*

Dan had continued to drift away from her...and now she knew with certainty where he had gone. Perhaps, that was the beginning of his infidelity, but the truth was, she *had not wanted to know about it!* She believed his excuses so that she wouldn't need to face the facts. Facing the facts would mean dealing with the burden of being married to an unfaithful husband. It would mean calling Dan on his infidelities. Decisions about their future would have needed to be made, and she wasn't up to that. She wasn't up to any of it. Would she have left him? Will she leave him now? Was there any hope for their marriage and their future?

Amy put her hands over her face. She hated confrontation. She avoided it at all cost and always had. She had never stood up for herself over even the smallest issues with Dan. He'd won almost all disagreements simply because Amy couldn't bring herself to fight for what she wanted.

She had been stupid, so stupid! Confused, hurt, and humiliated, she closed her eyes. She ached so much inside that she felt ill.

Zombie-like she walked barefoot onto the veranda and stared at the ocean with unseeing eyes. She had to get away from the house. His presence was everywhere and it was strangling her. She found herself at the beach stairs, and gripping the rail, oblivious to the cold wind, she descended the uneven staircase.

The ocean always makes things right.

Amy ran, her bare feet flying over the hard, damp sand, her thoughts penetrating the seven years she had shared with Dan. It had been so good in the beginning. He had been the perfect doting husband: kind, considerate, and loving. Where had that gone? What caused the change? Was it her? Had she changed? Had she unknowingly pushed him away? Had she failed to meet his needs? Had she put Jamie before Dan once too often?

Gramps hadn't always disliked Dan. That developed after Jamie was born. Did Gramps know about Dan's transgressions? Is that where Gramps's dislike stemmed from? How many others know?

Time passed. Eventually, exhaustion slowed her. Finding herself near the cape for the second time, she turned wearily back toward home. *Home?*

The offshore fogbank had absorbed the sunset, sending a stiff cold wind into the early twilight. She had not stopped to put on a jacket and her bare feet were numb with cold. The heavy waves curled higher onto the beach, their icy wash stinging her ankles. Amy looked at the rising breakers with sudden awareness. One loomed higher than the rest, draining the bay in front of it. She'd been careless. Oregon's infamous Sneaker Wave was a rogue wave that moves faster than others, absorbing them, growing higher, steeper, thicker, and more powerful, until it unleashes its fury onto the coast, and occasionally sweeps people out to sea. It can surge a hundred feet beyond the water's edge, then retreat, sucking back anything or anyone in its path.

Amy dug her feet into the sand and raced up the beach, the roar of the sea pounding in her ears. Out of the corner of her eye, she saw a massive wall of green water curling behind her. Adrenaline pumped through her arteries and she spurted forward. She leapt over a log, and bolted for the rock embankment, striking it at full speed, desperately wedging her body into a crevice. The wave, a huge green claw, impaled itself on the embankment, sending tons of water into the air. The force of it flung her backward into the crevice, smashed her head and shoulder against the rock, pinning her, and drenching her with cold seawater. Pain ripped across the back of her eyes. She gulped salt water and choked, wishing desperately that the crevice was deeper.

The suction would come next. She knew she had to hold tight or be carried out to sea. Digging her feet into the rocky ledge, she stuffed her body into the wedge and wrapped her fingers around an extruding stone. The giant wave receded, its powerful suction tearing at her, ripping her fingers off the rock, and lifting her out of the crevice. She clawed at the rock, but the suction was too strong.

Amy was submerged now, unable to breathe, being swept backward over the sand. She clawed at it, hoping to stop the backward momentum, but the sand traveled with her. She tumbled in the receding surge. Her lungs were bursting. Something struck her foot. It was the log she had jumped over a few minutes earlier. She wrapped her arms and legs around it and held on tight. For a moment it held firm. The water receded past her and she surfaced, gasping for air. Then the log shifted, and they began to slide together down the beach. They were being sucked out to sea!

Amy could see deep water approaching fast. Only a few seconds left. The log hit something hard and came to a jarring stop, throwing her forward. She dug her feet into the sand and for a second she obtained a foothold, then the sand washed out from beneath her. She propelled herself forward again and dove for a boulder that protruded from the wash. Grabbing it, she held on while water and sand swirled past her. When she looked up, the surge was gone.

Amy tried to stand. Her legs were barely able to hold her, her body drained. She gasped and choked and coughed water from her lungs; then staggered up the beach, wet clothes clinging to her body. Shaking with cold and exhaustion, she collapsed at the bottom of the staircase and vomited seawater into the sand. With watery eyes she looked out at the angry sea.

Sneaker Waves.
Life is full of them.

CHAPTER 9

Amy was in a deep, troubled sleep when a sound awoke her. She was lying on her side, back to the bedroom door, but she dared not roll over until she could figure out what had awakened her. She scanned the window side of the room: the curtains were still, the rocking chair empty. Dan's bed was unoccupied. He hadn't come home.

Nothing moved.

Then she heard it again. Closer this time. Behind her, near the door. A footstep? Her heart began to pound, her ears alert for the next sound, her body tense.

Was it Dan? He always went straight to the bathroom, closed the door, and switched on the light. Not only that, he always made a lot of noise. So it wasn't him.

Amy had no weapon and vowed to get one for the bedside table. Every muscle in her body was poised for action.

Suddenly, two gloved hands grasped her head and pushed her face into the pillow.

Amy kicked out, her body flying off the bed.

"Don't move!" Male voice--garbled. Strong hands.

The intruder slammed her down hard onto the mattress, shoving her face back into the pillow. Her heart went into overtime. She couldn't stand closed spaces, let alone being smothered. It was her only phobia and it was debilitating. Now, it mixed with the fear for her life.

His hand squeezed the back of her head where she'd been bruised and cut by the rogue wave. "Lie still and you won't get hurt!" He wheezed in her ear. "Stop! That's better. Now listen carefully. You made a big mistake calling the Sheriff. Back him off before it's too late. You hear! Back him off fast or your boy will pay for your stupidity."

Fear pierced right through Amy's chest. *No. Not Jamie!* She tried to nod, to tell him she understood, not to hurt Jamie, but his grip was viselike.

"Understand?" The pressure on the back of her head let up slightly.

"Yes!" Amy choked.

"Good," said the muffled voice, "I'm going to let go. Don't raise your head. Don't move! Got that?"

"Yes!" Amy's muffled reply sounded more like, "Us!"

He released her and said nothing more. Amy remained stone still under the pillow, sweat pouring off her. There was no air! She bit her lip trying to control her panic. Twisting her head away from the pillow an inch at a time, she finally freed herself and inhaled deeply.

At last, she could see across the room. It was dark, but she knew he was gone. The room was heavy with his presence. Sitting up, she grabbed the phone and with shaky fingers, she speed dialed Nita. After three rings her sister-in-law's groggy voice answered. "'Lo?"

"It's Amy," she whispered hoarsely. "I know it's late, but could you please check on Jamie."

"What? It's three in the morning!"

"Nita, someone broke into our house. He threatened to hurt Jamie. Please Nita, make sure he's okay."

"Broke in your house? When? Now?"

"Yes! Nita, please!"

"Be right back."

Amy paced the floor beside her bed. For all she knew *he*—whoever *he* was-- could still be inside the house. *Hurry up!*

Nita came back on. "Jamie's sound asleep. Everything's fine. You want me to call 911?"

"No! They'll hurt Jamie if we do that. You understand me, Nita? *Don't call anyone.*"

"I don't understand—"

"Wake up Brandon—"

"He's awake."

"Check your doors and windows. Make sure they're locked. Let the dog out. If anyone comes onto the property he'll bark. And Nita?"

"What?"

"Bring Jamie into the room with you. Don't let him out of your sight. I'll call you in the morning."

"Amy—"

"Bye. And thanks, Nita." Amy set the handset onto the charger and tiptoed to her closet where she had tucked away the baseball bat she had bought for Jamie's birthday. She gripped the handle and walked softly into the hall. Cautiously, she worked her way through the house, arms and shoulders tensed, ready to swing. She checked windows and doors, and turned on lights. On the main floor she felt a cool breeze coming from the laundry room. Tightening her grip on the bat, she crept to the laundry room door, readied the bat, and looked inside. No one. The window was wide open, and below it, leaves and dirt littered the floor. *He came in through here!* Amy shuddered, yanked the wooden window closed, and turned the lock.

The break-in jarred her. She felt violated even though he had not hurt her. She was angry that *he* broke into her home, but most of all, she was terrified for Jamie. She paced the entrance hall, the family room, the library, and ended up in the kitchen, where she put on a pot of coffee. She paced while she waited for it to brew.

He had grabbed her head and pushed her into the pillow, but in the split second before his glove touched her, she had inhaled. There had been a distinctive and familiar odor on the glove, but she couldn't place it. She poured coffee into a tall mug, knowing she would never go back to sleep.

Something terrible was happening, but she wasn't sure what it was. She had seen the injured woman and called the sheriff's office. Now, Jamie was in danger. How could she get the Sheriff to *back off*? She needed help, but if she couldn't get it from the police, then where? Dragging anyone else into this would be crazy. She was trapped. *Gramps is right. I should take Jamie and get out of here.*

Amy had her back to the living room. Something inside the house had changed. She could feel it. Looking up, Amy saw an image on the microwave glass. A man was behind her. Amy gasped and whipped around, coffee flying from her cup.

"Dan!" she screamed. Her cup crashed to the floor.

He stood perfectly still, his eyes on her, his face inflamed with angry red bumps.

Amy leaned on the counter, her heart hammering in her chest. Why had Dan made this sudden, silent appearance behind her when he usually makes enough noise for three people? "What are you doing! Why did you sneak up on me like that? What's the matter with you? And why are you standing there, gaping at me? Jesus!" Angrily, she reached under the sink for a cloth, and then knelt to wipe up the spilled coffee.

Dan didn't move, nor did he speak. Instead, he watched her mutely, a crazy, disjointed look on his face. Infuriated, Amy's cloth flew in all directions at once, slapping against chair legs and cupboards. She stood up, tossing the mug into the sink. "What the matter with you!" she yelled. "It's like the twilight zone around here—a lookalike that somebody wants dead, a car pushed over a cliff, a warm fuzzy letter telling me about your affair, a Sneaker Wave out of nowhere—" Her voice rose to a breaking crescendo. "and then some thug breaks in here and threatens to hurt Jamie…"

"Rogue wave? Thug? You're talking crazy."

"Crazy! You have no idea what's been going on, but threatening to hurt Jamie is the last straw." She knew she was screaming, but couldn't stop herself.

"Who would hurt Jamie? You're losing it, Amy."

Amy stood and let fly with the towel. It struck him on the cheek and fell to the floor. She suddenly felt better and used her sleeve to wipe the tears from her face. She had never done anything like that. Maybe Dan was right—she was losing it. Too much going wrong too fast. *Get a grip!*

They stared at each other for what felt like an eternity. Finally Dan broke the silence. "I'm leaving."

"You just got here."

"No Amy. I'm leaving permanently."

Amy gaped at him. "What! Because I threw a towel at you?"

"No. Because it's time, that's all."

"Time! You mean you set an alarm seven years ago, and it just went off?"

"Don't be ridiculous."

"You've spent the last—how many years—screwing around. Now, you're tired of playing husband and you're bailing, is that it?"

"You don't understand."

"Really? You've got a libido from hell that croaks the minute you come near me, and *I don't understand*?"

Dan backed away from her. "We'll talk when you calm down."

"I don't intend to calm down, Dan. You've screwed your patients, compromised your practice, and now you're destroying our family."

He stared at her, the red welts standing out on his face.

"Is it that woman you got pregnant? Are you leaving me for her?"

Dan's mouth fell open. "How did you hear about that?"

"You couldn't stand me after Jamie was born. What makes you think you'll feel any different about *her*?"

"You don't know what you're talking about. Her problem's been taken care of, so forget it."

Amy was appalled. "Just like that? Forget it?" Her voice sounded strange. "Are you kidding? You screwed that woman while you were married to me. And she had to get in line! How do you think I feel being dumped for a laundry list of women—"

"Stop!" Dan yelled back. "Those women meant nothing."

Amy dropped her voice. It was an angry hush. "Just an opportunity to practice lots of safe sex, huh?"

Dan was momentarily speechless. "What's up with you? Where's all this coming from?"

Amy ran her hands through her hair angrily. "The unfaithful husband runs off. Is that what this is?" she asked flatly.

He started for the stairs. "It's not like that. You don't understand."

"I'm supposed to *understand?*"

"It's complicated." He put one foot on the bottom step and stopped to look at her. "This has nothing to do with any of–of *that*. It's something else altogether."

Amy stared at him, dumbfounded. "Really? You mean there's more that I don't know about?"

Dan continued up the stairs. "Lots more."

"Dammit!" Amy threw up her hands in frustration.

While he packed, Amy stood at the far end of the living room; her eyes fixed on their wedding photo, her thoughts once again on re-run. Finally, she switched off the living room lights so she could see across the bay and walked out onto the veranda. The moon glistened on the dark ocean surface. The night was silent except for waves washing softly over the sand. Everything beyond her porch looked normal. How could that be?

In the past thirty hours her entire life had turned upside down. Nothing made sense anymore. She tried to sort her thoughts from her feelings, but couldn't separate them. Her brain had mutated into a mass of swirling confusion and chaos. Amy closed her eyes. She was scared, not only because of everything that had happened, but because she was completely alone with no one to turn to. She felt her life tumbling away. Tears ran down her cheeks. With Dan gone, she would be left to run the house alone, raise Jamie alone, make decisions alone, and worst of all, live as an adult—alone. She was terrified of what lay ahead.

She had arrived at a turning point in her life.

Stepping back inside, Amy locked the sliding door behind her. She saw Dan drag four heavy bags outside. He left without another word, slamming the door closed behind him. She double locked it and stood dumbfounded in the entry. Her emotions churned, but she could no longer make sense out of what she was feeling or thinking. Even the house felt different—still and uncertain.

Amy forced her emotions on hold, a survival trick she'd learned after her parents died. She couldn't deal with Dan's departure right now, nor could she bear to be alone. She was worried about Jamie and needed to think. For now, Jamie was safe with Nita and Brandon. Whoever had threatened her wouldn't know where Jamie was. The danger would come when she picked him up from Nita's, twelve hours from now. Quickly, she showered and dressed, leaving the house before dawn.

CHAPTER 10

By the time the sun rose above the treetops, Amy had reached the small community of Beaverdale, where she was born. It was her hope that she would find some answers in her birthplace. Her plan was twofold. First, talk to her grandparents' neighbors to see if anyone remembered her mother and father. They had lived with her grandparents when Amy was born. It was a long shot, but she might learn something that would help. Second, Amy wanted to visit the records department at St. Mary's hospital, where she was born.

Exiting the I-5, she passed through Beaverdale and continued on to the countryside. The day promised blue sky and a cool fall sun. Fall leaves swirled around the jeep as it bounced over the rutted bridge deck near her grandparent's old house. Amy drove down the hill, and came to a stop in front of the white, impeccably landscaped sixties house that they owned decades earlier. An aging paperbark maple stood like a sentry next to the drive. Childhood memories rushed back.

The blue-green river that ambled behind the house triggered a different memory. It was the day Amy had gone fishing with the small fishing pole her dad had made for her. She'd waded out to a boulder, midstream, climbed up on it, and cast the line like her father had taught her. Suddenly, the line pulled taut and the pole flew out of her small hand. She jumped to catch the

60

rod, but her foot slipped off the rock and she found herself in deep water on the far side of the boulder. Amy could still see herself dropping through the slow moving water, onto the rocky riverbed. The current dragged her helplessly along it. She looked up and wondered how to get back up to the surface. Her small body screamed for air, but she knew there was none. She scrambled up a submerged rock, but the surface was still too far away. Terrified and needing to breathe, she pushed against the rock, launching herself upward. Kicking hard, she clawed the water until she finally broke the surface. Two strong hands pulled her out. Her dad had reached her just in time. Amy recalled the huge lecture he had given her, not for falling into the river, but for fishing without a worm.

The childhood memory made her think of Jamie. Nita should be up by now. Picking up her iPhone, Amy punched in the number. The call was answered right away. "Nita, it's me."

"Amy, is everything okay?"

"I'm okay. How's Jamie?"

"Brandon took him over to the ballpark to play with the kids. Jamie's having a great time, as always."

Amy sighed with relief. "So listen, I'll pick him up around six, if that works for you."

There was a pause, then, "Sure."

"See you later." Amy slipped the phone into her pocket and climbed out of the truck. Glancing around the cul-de-sac, she saw that it was likely a tight knit neighborhood when her grandparents lived there. She hoped some of the residents from that era were still around and would remember her parents.

Amy headed for the house right next door. When no one answered her knock, Amy tried the next house up the road. An elderly woman poked her head out the door. Amy introduced herself and told the woman why she was there. "My grandparents, the Haddens, lived in

61

that house over thirty years ago," Amy turned and pointed to the old basement home by the river. "Did you know them?"

A wrinkled hand flew out to greet her. "Nice to see you, Amy. I'm Dorothy. I sure do remember your grandparents. I think I remember your mom too. Not that my memory is the best these days. But if I recall, she was expecting." The woman smiled, "I guess that was you!"

The smile was infectious. "I guess it was," Amy agreed.

Dorothy continued, "After your mom and dad moved away, I remember seeing you as a little girl, when you and your parents came back to visit. Imagine that." The old woman patted Amy's arm. "Your grandmother, Cynthia Hadden and I, were good friends you know. Even kept in touch after they moved to the coast. But I must say, I haven't heard from her in quite a while."

Amy nodded. "Dorothy, is there anyone else still living in the neighborhood who was here back then?"

The old woman patted her pin curls and looked up and down the street, her eyes settling on the house Amy had just tried, next to her grandparents'. "Emily Boxer's been here even longer than we have. Try her."

"She's not home right now, but I would like to call her, later. Do you by chance have her number?"

The older woman disappeared for a few minutes and then reappeared with the phone number written on a small piece of paper. Amy thanked her and started down the steps.

"Give Cynthia my best," Dorothy called after her.

Amy turned around. "My grandmother's not doing very well. They think she has Alzheimer's."

Dorothy's face fell. "Oh. Such a shame. She was so bright. Must be terrible for your grandfather. Or does he have it too?"

"Not yet. But he's afraid it might be contagious."

Waving, Amy continued up the street. At the next house along, a woman in her thirties with short, spiked hair stepped onto the porch. "Hi! Back again, huh? How'd you make out?"

Amy was taken aback. "Excuse me?"

"You know, tracking down the Haddens?"

Amy gaped.

"Did you find them?" The woman coaxed a package of cigarettes from her robe pocket and knocked one into her hand.

"Uh, no." Amy was stunned. Then it hit her. Her *lookalike* was here!

The spiked-haired woman lit the cigarette and inhaled deeply, eyeing Amy skeptically. "Did you try the directories like I said?"

Amy shifted. "You must have been talking to my—" What could Amy say? Could she suggest that it was a *sister?* "My sister," Amy mumbled.

The woman choked. "Sister? You're kidding me, right?"

Amy was beginning to wonder. Not knowing what to say next, she just stared at the woman.

"Well, your sister's a dead ringer for you, that's for sure." The woman glanced at Amy's jeans and jacket. "Even dresses kind of like you."

"When was she here?" Amy asked, recovering.

"Friday morning."

"Friday morning," Amy repeated thoughtfully. "Did she drive a white Taurus by any chance?"

"Yup. Something like that anyway."

"So, she came here and asked you about the Haddens?" Amy's curiosity grew.

"Yup. She was pretty jumpy, I mean, you know—nervous. Kept looking up and down the street."

"Were you able to help her?"

The woman put the cigarette to her lips, sucked in the smoke, then plucked a piece of tobacco from her tongue and flipped it Amy's way. "Yeah. We got to talking. She said it was lunchtime where she came from. Now where was that? Can't recall. Hey, you oughta know, being her sister and all."

Amy shrugged. "Can you remember anything else?"

The woman puckered her lips and blew a couple of smoke rings. "Yeah. She said she had an urgent message for the Haddens. That's why I kind of got into the whole thing with her. She didn't say what the message was, but she was uptight enough to give me the idea it was pretty serious-like."

"Is there anything else you can tell me?"

"Nah, that's about it. I gave her a few suggestions on how to find the Haddens and she took off."

Amy held out her business card. "Look, I appreciate your help. My home phone and cell are on the bottom of the card. If you remember anything else, please call me."

The sum total of Amy's inquires revealed that her *lookalike* had been inquiring here Friday morning. Amy found that information astounding. Her *lookalike* must have learned that the Haddens and Amy now live in Sanville, but how had the woman found Amy's home address?

She returned to the Jeep, her head spinning. It was a strange feeling to be told that you're following the same path as a woman who looks *exactly like you*. Amy started the truck. She needed food. She'd barely eaten anything since Friday night and she was famished.

The town center mall had fast burgers so she ordered a high cholesterol lunch. She wasn't in the mood for her usual healthy fare. When she had swallowed the last fry, she turned the Jeep north toward St. Mary's hospital, and parked in the crowded lot.

Inside, she asked for the Records Department, and after much pleading, was lead down a corridor to the Records Supervisor's office: A stick thin, all business—no nonsense woman peered up at her over thick bifocals. Protruding eyes inspected Amy up and down before a frown settled across her ruddy forehead. "Well?"

Amy read the nameplate and offered her hand in introduction. "Good afternoon, Mrs. Goodrich. My name's Amy Johnson. I'm trying to locate my birth records."

The records supervisor ignored her hand. "We don't give medical records out to the public, Ms. Johnson."

Amy wasn't put off. "I was born in this hospital thirty-two years ago, Mrs. Goodrich. I'm interested in knowing the name of my physician."

The record's supervisor told her, "There are no records prior to 1981." She picked up her pen and went back to her work.

"Where would I find them?"

The supervisor didn't look up. "You won't."

Amy's foot tapped impatiently. "And why is that?"

The woman's head jerked up and she slid her glasses down her nose. Her voice was cold. "We had a fire here in 1980, Ms. Johnson. The lower two floors of the hospital were gutted. All the records were destroyed."

CHAPTER 11

Amy swung the Jeep onto Nita's empty driveway, jumped out, and ran to the door. She pushed the doorbell and waited impatiently. She could barely wait to pick up Jamie. She missed him terribly. The dog barked from inside the house, but no one answered. It was six o'clock; where were they?

Disappointed, Amy decided to wait in the truck. She tried Brandon's cell, then Nita's, but they were both directed to voicemail, so she left a message on each. While she waited, Amy thought about Mrs. Boxer, the neighbor who lived beside her grandparents and who wasn't home that morning. Amy pulled out the slip of paper with the number Dorothy had written down for her and decided to try it. A quivery voice answered.

Amy responded, "Hello, Mrs. Boxer, this is Amy Johnson. I'm Cynthia and Art Hadden's granddaughter. They used to live next door to you."

There was a long pause. "Oh yes, I remember Cynthia and Art. And you're their granddaughter?"

"Yes, that's right."

"You were just a little tyke back when you'd come visit them. How are you, My Dear?"

Relieved that she remembered, Amy replied, "I'm fine, but something has happened, and I was hoping you might be able to help. First, tell me, did you live next door to my grandparents back in the eighties?"

"Oh yes, my husband and I have lived here over fifty years."

Amy grew hopeful. "Do you happen to remember my parents? They lived with my grandparents when I was born."

"Sure do. Now, what were their names? Oh, I remember, Sharalynn and Dave. They moved in with your grandparents when Sharalynn was pregnant. I'll never forget that—she was as big as a dirigible. Looked like she was going to burst."

Amy found this surprising considering her small birth size. "Really?"

"Yes, and I do recall that a specialist was involved."

"I don't suppose you remember his name," Amy said.

"No, sorry," Mrs. Boxer relied, "that was a long time ago."

Amy tried again. "Do you happen to remember who my mother's doctor was?"

"No, but I do recall that he was concerned about one of the twins."

Twins!

"Hello? Amy? Are you there?"

"Twins?" Amy asked. It made sense. It was the *only thing* that made sense. *Why am I shocked to actually hear it?* "I wasn't aware that my mom had twins," Amy finally said. "But if she had twins, what happened to the other one?"

There was a silence. "You don't know, my Dear?"

"I don't."

"I wonder why no one told you," Mrs. Boxer said.

"Told me what?" Amy tried to be patient.

This time the silence lasted too long. Finally, Mrs. Boxer whispered, "One died."

CHAPTER 12

Amy sat stunned. The more she thought about it, the more she realized that somewhere deep inside her, she'd always felt as though someone was missing from her life, someone very special. Now, Amy knew who that was. From inception there had been two of them. They were twins. And sadly, her twin had died at birth.

Or had she?

Why had no one ever mentioned the twin to Amy? Why had no one ever spoken about this? Why the deep silence?

Amy glanced at her watch. It was almost seven o'clock and still no sign of Nita, Brandon, or Jamie. Where were they? Amy decided to call Gramps and let him know that she and Jamie were planning to stay the night with him. She wouldn't mention what she had just learned about her twin until she got there. Then, she would insist on Gramps giving her a *full explanation* about what happened. She wasn't going to let him off the hook again.

He answered the fourth ring. "Hadden." The old man sounded grouchy.

"Hi, Gramps, how's everything?" Amy said loudly.

"I've been worried about you and Jamie. I was hoping you were going to call and say you were both in France, or Australia, or someplace."

Amy sighed. "What I was calling for, Gramps, was to tell you that I'm at Nita's picking up Jamie. We're going to come and stay the night." There was no way Amy was going to take Jamie home after the break-in and the warning she'd received.

"Sure," he answered. "Always love having you both, but you won't be any safer here than at home, if that's what you're thinking."

Amy changed the subject. "We'll talk more about that when I get there." *Lots more.* "Meanwhile, I've got a question for you, Gramps."

"Who said I've got an answer?"

Amy ignored the remark. "Who was our family doctor when I was born?"

"Why?" he asked suspiciously.

"I need some medical background."

"What for?"

"It's important," Amy insisted.

"He's dead."

Amy almost dropped her cell phone. "Dead?"

"Yup. Burned up in the hospital fire not long after you were born."

CHAPTER 13

Yard lighting cast shadows from Nita's two-story home, onto the driveway. The house was dark, except for the porch light. Amy grew increasingly impatient as Brandon's cell continued to go to voice mail, so she backed from the drive and headed for the park, thinking she may find them there. No luck. She tried a few more places; then returned to the house. This time the dog greeted her as she stepped out of the Jeep. Amy gave him a fast pat and ran up the walk to the door. Nita opened it with a surprised expression. "You're not here for Jamie, I hope?"

Alarm bells sounded. "Of course."

"Dan picked him up hours ago, Amy. Didn't he tell you? You weren't feeling well, so he—" she saw Amy's look, "well you did sound kind of—" she cleared her throat, "—out of sorts. Anyway, he picked up Jamie, like I said."

The color drained from Amy's face. Dan had moved his personal things out in the night, *what reason would he have to pick up Jamie? Especially when he never picked up Jamie.* Worried, Amy asked, "Where's Dan now? Did he take Jamie home?"

"No idea. What's wrong? Amy, wait!"

Amy dashed to the truck and rammed it into reverse. She had no idea what Dan was up to, but she knew it had to do with his sudden decision to leave her, and it

70

looked like he might be planning to take Jamie with him. *There's no way I'm going to let that happen!*

She skidded onto Lighthouse Road, almost colliding head-on with a big delivery truck. She swerved hard right, skimmed the front end, and then struggled for control of the Jeep as it fishtailed, slamming its rear end along the side of the truck. The exterior mirror grazed the van box and exploded into the air. Amy threw the Jeep onto the soft shoulder and came to a sliding stop. Taking no time to recover, she angled the truck back onto the rutted pavement and glanced in the rearview mirror. The big truck was gone. She was surprised, and a little angry, that the driver didn't bother to stop.

Amy pressed harder on the accelerator and a few minutes later she skidded onto her own driveway, sliding to a diagonal stop. Dan's Mercedes wasn't there, but lights were on inside the house, and the front door stood slightly ajar.

Amy ran inside. Glancing in her study, she saw it was exactly as she had left it. She rushed to the family room and stopped with a sharp intake of breath. Everything was gone including Jamie's small computer center. She checked the library next. Dan had no interest in the old furniture she had brought from her grandparent's home. The room was untouched. The living-dining area was vacant; the furniture, paintings, and rugs were gone. Only the wedding pictures had been left behind. Numb, Amy looked in the kitchen. Everything was the same as she'd left it. Nothing removed. The small kitchen table and the three chairs were still by the window.

Amy ran upstairs. The guestroom was untouched. It was Jamie's room that stopped her dead. In a trance, Amy stepped inside, her hands running over the bare walls. Everything—every piece of furniture, every toy, every item of clothing—was gone. His room was completely bare. "No!" she cried, "Dan, you bastard!"

She was momentarily stunned. Why had he done this? Looking around the empty room, she wondered what her little boy would make of what was happening. Jamie had been born in this house. Moving was not one of his life experiences. He would wonder why Daddy took their belongings out of their home, and where Mommy was. And in the end, Jamie wouldn't understand this anymore than she did.

She glanced into the master bedroom. One bed, her dresser, and the rocker were the only furniture left behind.

Amy knew one thing. She had to find her son and bring him home. To do that, she had to find her husband. Dan was close to his sister, and Nita was protective of him. Would he go there? Nita would take Jamie in a heartbeat and that would certainly make things easy for Dan. Amy reached in her pocket for the cell and speed dialed Dan's cell. Voicemail. She tried Nita. Voicemail again. She tried Brandon. Same thing.

Something was really wrong. She recalled the delivery truck she had passed on Lighthouse Road. *A moving van!*

CHAPTER 14

Amy tore down the stairs and out the open front door running headlong into Dallas. He grabbed her arms and brought her to a dead stop. "Hey, where's the fire?"

The concern was visible on his kindly face but a voice echoed in her mind: *You made a big mistake calling the sheriff.* Remembering the threat to Jamie, she pulled back, twisted free of his grip, ran for the Jeep, jumped in, and jammed the key into the ignition. The engine fired.

Before she could back out, the driver's door flew open. A strong hand grabbed her wrist. "Now hold on just a minute."

"Let go! There's no time." Amy tried to twist from his grip.

"Mrs. Johnson, step out of the vehicle; you're in no condition to drive right now." He looked at her haunted expression and swollen eyes.

Amy pretended to relent. The second he released her wrist she rammed the transmission into first and with the driver's door still wide open, she floored it. The truck leapt forward and swerved around Dallas. A hundred feet up, Amy swung the wheel around, sending grass and dirt flying before the Jeep hit the driveway and peeled onto the road.

Dallas dove out of the way and ran to his Yukon. He caught up to her in no time, but pulled back when he saw her Jeep sliding from one side of the narrow, pot-holed road to the other. It was all but out of control. At the speed she was going, Amy would either end up over the edge or send someone else over, should they be so unlucky as to be coming from the other direction. Dallas radioed ahead and gave his deputies instructions: "We're going to need the spikes. Lay them down before the turnoff. And get a move on!" He shouted. "She'll be there in less than twenty minutes. Let's hope nobody's headed her way."

When he reached a straight stretch on the road, he accelerated, almost catching up with her truck before it hit the spikes. The tires blew, spinning the Jeep crazily. It grazed a pole and bounced to a stop. The deputies were ready and approached cautiously, hands on the butts of their guns.

Dallas pulled his Yukon onto the wide, grassy siding, waved them back, and jogged over to the Jeep. Blood trickled from the cut on her forehead and her eyes were closed. Dallas opened the door and the motion brought her around; her eyes fluttered open. Dazed, she fell back into the seat.

"Mrs. Johnson. Can you hear me?"

She turned her head, recognition flashing across her face. Then without warning, she jumped out of the seat, her fists pounding his chest and arms. "Don't do this! I have to find my son. I have to find Jamie!" Her shoe flew out and Dallas groaned as it impacted his bad knee.

"Want some help, Sheriff?" his deputy called.

With one quick move, Dallas grabbed her arms and swung her around, backing her into the Jeep. "Kick me again and you'll be visiting the inside of our facilities," he said through gritted teeth, pushing her firmly against the truck. "Now, do I need the cuffs, or are you going to calm down?"

They were eye to eye. He saw hers refocus and the anger diminish. Her body relaxed slightly. He grabbed her wrist. "Come on."

Limping, he took her to his Yukon and motioned her to the passenger seat. "Sit." He hooked an arm over the open door and looked down at her. "I'll call an ambulance."

"I don't need an ambulance. I need to find my son."

He looked at her thoughtfully for a moment. "Wait here. And I mean *wait*. Don't even flex a muscle; I'm in no mood for trouble." He hobbled around to the back door, opened it, and keeping an eye on her, reached into his first aid kit. When he returned, she was on the cell phone. "I've got to go, Sheriff. I don't know what's happening to my son. I can't sit here, doing nothing."

Dallas put an index finger under her chin and tipped her head up so he could apply the alcohol swab to the cut on her forehead. She jerked away. "Stay still. It's only alcohol. You're harder to work on than a trapped rabbit." When he was finished he stood back and examined his handiwork. She looked a mess.

"What are you going to do with my Jeep?"

"It'll be flat-decked to the impoundment lot. You can have it back in the morning, but it'll need new tires."

Amy checked the time impatiently. "Are you arresting me, Sheriff?"

"You're in the front seat. It's when you're in the back, that you've got a problem."

"If that's the case, please call me a cab. I'm not going to find my son sitting here."

Dallas ignored her. "What happened at the house?"

Amy hesitated. "All I can tell you is that they're threatening to hurt Jamie because I called 911 Friday night. God knows what they'll do if they find out I'm talking to you right now, especially after I was warned."

"Warned? You mean, threatened?"

Amy turned away from him. "Don't ask questions, Sheriff. I can't tell you anything. They made that pretty clear. Call the cab, please."

He gripped her arm and swung her around in the seat to face him. He bent over so that his face was close to hers. His voice was hushed, angry, and almost inaudible, but Amy heard every word clearly. "Listen to me, Mrs. Johnson. You're in over your head. These men will kill you *and* your son. They didn't think twice about pushing that car off the cliff and according to print results, you're dealing with a couple of killers. The only hope you have is to level with me—and fast—before they make their next move." His pale blue eyes blazed with an intensity that was frightening. "Do I make myself clear?"

Amy considered her options. The moving van was long gone. Neither Dan, Nita, nor Brandon was taking calls. If any chance existed of finding Jamie now, she would need the sheriff's help. There was no other choice. She closed her eyes and nodded.

Dallas spoke briefly with his deputies, then maneuvered his Yukon around the spikes, and headed into town. He glanced at her. "Okay. Start talking."

Amy told him what had happened since they had spoken twenty-four hours earlier. She finished by saying; "Things are getting progressively worse by the hour."

Dallas parked his Yukon in the secure parking area behind his office and led Amy inside. He motioned her to a chair opposite his desk. "I'll be about fifteen minutes. There's coffee around the corner," he said pointing out the door.

While he made calls, Amy found the small lunchroom and poured something black and caustic looking into a paper cup. With that in hand, she paced back and forth in front of the microwave, wired with worry for Jamie. She would never forgive herself if anything happened to him. Why hadn't she gone to Nita's and picked him up first thing this morning? If she had, he'd be with her now. She berated herself for about ten minutes then tossed the coffee down the sink and returned to Dallas's office.

When the last call ended, he looked up at her. "Okay, here's what we've got so far. First, the moving van you saw on Lighthouse Road belongs to Coast Moving. Your furniture is at the company's storage facility. You can do what you like with that information. You might want to approach them regarding the damage their moving truck did to your Jeep. The driver collected his pay and then quit. Next, I paged your husband. His service says he's out of town for an indefinite period. The message is the same at his clinic, and the hospital confirms this. No one seems to know where he is. I tried your sister-in-law's home and cell as well as her husband, Brandon's cell. They each have a similar message on their phones." He paused and looked across at Amy. "What's the matter?"

Amy's mouth had dropped. "I called each of them not long ago. I didn't hear anything like that." Her concern for Jamie grew.

"Like you said. Things change every hour." He rested his elbows on the arms of his worn chair and rubbed his chin in thought. "We're in a bit of a bind. Dan is Jamie's father, so legally I can't stop him for having his son in the car. What I can do is bring him in for questioning related to the investigation that we have underway. Your husband's tags as well as those of Nita and Brandon Williams have gone out statewide. If they're driving, they'll be spotted, sooner or later. We're checking the Portland airport and we've notified Child Protection Services. If Nita or Brandon are found with Jamie, the boy will be apprehended." Dallas stood. "A patrol car will keep an eye on your sister-in-laws place. By the way, what does Brandon do for a living?"

77

"He's a rep for Heavy Lift Equipment, meaning he's out of town a lot."

Dallas grabbed his jacket off the wall hook behind his desk. He took her arm, "Come on. After everything that's happened it'd be ludicrous for you to go back home, and you've got no way of getting there. I sent one of my deputies to your house to lock up and check around. Do you have somewhere to stay, here in town?"

"I don't want to impose on my friends, nor do I want to drag them into this, so I called my grandfather earlier and arranged for Jamie and I to stay with him. It would've been too risky to take Jamie home after the break in and the threat on his life."

"You're not worried about dragging your grandfather into this?"

Amy combed her hair with her fingers. "I have a feeling Gramps was involved long before I was. There's something he isn't telling me. The thing is, if that's the case, I'm sure there's a good reason for him to hold back."

Dallas opened the door to the parking lot and held it while she walked out. "His house is on my way home, so I'll give you a lift."

Amy cocked her head. "You know where my grandfather and my sister-in-law live. You have all their contact numbers. You've got their license plates and vehicle registrations. Did you do background checks too?"

Dallas guided her toward a newer pickup truck. He opened the passenger door. "Part of the job."

"Anything interesting?"

"Maybe."

Amy jumped in the truck. When Dallas got in, she asked, "How about me? Did you check me out too?"

Dallas appeared amused. "Maybe."

"Hm."

Dallas's cell rang. He listened quietly. "Okay. Check on it every hour or so." He glanced over at Amy. "There's no one home at your sister-in-law's, but we'll drive by every hour or so."

"I wonder where Dan would take Jamie," Amy said as much to herself as to Dallas.

He replied, "Could be wrong, but I'd say that he and his sister, Nita are taking Jamie to a place where you can't find him, but I don't think they're too far away. Just a hunch." Ten minutes later Dallas pulled up to the Hadden's house. "Porch light's on. Looks like he's expecting you."

Amy nodded. "He is." Amy twisted her hair around her index finger. "How's the investigation going, Sheriff?"

"We've made some progress. As I said earlier, we got IDs on the prints found inside the Taurus. Fortunately, the car hit the rocks down below the lighthouse so it didn't get submerged and the prints were pretty good. One set ID'd to a meat cutter who's wanted on a string of crimes in the south. Murder charges are pending against him. The second set of prints belong to an accomplice who is wanted for conspiracy to commit murder. These guys have a long history of brutality and violence. I haven't been able to make the connection between them and the woman you saw Friday night, but you can bet it's not good. You need to understand that these men are about as dangerous and as deadly as they come."

Amy shuddered. "Do you think it was one of them who broke into my house last night?"

Dallas rubbed the steering wheel thoughtfully. "Possible."

"And the third set of prints?"

"They match the ones we took from your study window." Dallas shifted sideways in his seat. "And they turned out to be almost identical to yours."

Amy stared at Dallas, speechless. They sat in silence for a few minutes before Dallas said, "By the way, we also got some lab results back."

"And?"

"The blood samples taken from outside your study window were O Negative. Pretty rare blood type. Do you know your yours, Mrs. Johnson?"

Amy became very still. "O Negative."

CHAPTER 15

Gramps Hadden looked across the table at Amy. She had purple shadows under her eyes. However, it wasn't her appearance that worried him the most. It was her silence.

He pushed his donut around on the plate and asked, "When do you plan on telling me where Jamie is?" He took a bite of the donut and chewed thoughtfully. "And Lord knows, you look a sight with all those cuts and scratches," he hollered.

Amy reached across the table and rubbed his arm. "I can hear you, Gramps."

The motion was lethargic. Her eyes had lost their sparkle; her face was taut with worry. "Tell me what's going on, Amy. Where's Jamie. You said you were bringing him with you."

Amy tried to swallow the lump in her throat. Eventually she said, "Dan took him. Picked Jamie up before I got to Nita's. Then Dan moved most everything out of the house, including all Jamie's things." Amy dropped her head into her hands. When she looked back at her grandfather, her eyes glistened with unshed tears. "It was a huge shock. No warning." Amy whispered angrily, "The bastard!"

The old man slammed his fist down on the table so hard, it sent his plate dancing. "That son of a bitch! I'll be damned if he's going to get away with this. Call Wayburne."

"There's not much the sheriff can do. After all, Jamie is Dan's son too." Amy pushed her uneaten donut away. "My life's hell, Gramps. It's hard to think straight. I can't sleep. I'm constantly groping for answers." Amy wiped her eyes with her fingers. "Friday night I saw a woman who looks exactly like me. I don't know if she's still alive. I don't know who's after her. I don't know who broke into our house. I don't know why Dan picked right now to leave me. I don't know why he took Jamie. *I don't know a friggin' thing anymore!*"

Amy jumped up, sending her chair flying. "What I do know is, Mom had twins and not a single one of you bothered to tell me! And why the hell not? How could you, every single one of you, keep that from me all these years!" Amy righted the chair and leaned over the back of it. "It's time you told me the truth about the past, Gramps. Your silence has to end now. I don't know what's happening or what's going to go wrong next. What I do know is, it's going to come out of nowhere, and it's going to be painful." She twisted around to look at him. "I can't sit still and do nothing. Jamie's life is at stake!" She faced her grandfather. "For godsake! Tell me what I need to know so that I can make the right decisions and do the right things. This is far too dangerous for me to be stumbling around in the dark any longer!"

Hadden studied her. His hands opened and closed into fists and when he spoke his voice was strangely subdued. "You're right, Girl. It's time you knew. Your grandmother and I were trying to protect you. We never wanted you to know what we found out. We figured the less you knew the better off you'd be. Grams and I hoped this thing would die its own death, but it seems like it's going to haunt us for the rest of our lives."

He pushed his wheelchair back from the table. "The woman you saw Friday night probably looks like you. Can't say for sure." He closed his eyes. When he looked up, they were bloodshot.

Amy stood frozen. "Go on."

He reached for his cane and stood unsteadily before limping over to a wall photo of Sharalynn. He stared at it and then said: "There's no way to break this to you gently, Amy, so I'm just going to come right out and tell you. Your mother gave birth to twin girls—you and another. We were told the first-born died. None of us ever saw her, not even Sharalynn." Gramps shook his head, "Poor Sharalynn. She was so devastated over losing that twin, she couldn't even talk about it."

He was quiet for a long time. Finally, he continued, "Then, one day out of the blue, when you were sixteen, Sharalynn got a phone call from a girl whose voice sounded just like yours. Sharalynn thought you were fooling with her, but it was the urgency in the girl's voice that made Sharalynn stop and listen. The girl cried and told Sharalynn that her name was Alesha and that she was Sharalynn's daughter, the firstborn twin who was supposed to have died. The girl knew the name of the doctors, the hospital, the time of birth. Everything. She wanted to meet her real parents. It took Sharalynn a while to accept what the girl was saying, but the clincher came back to the girl's voice. So, it was arranged that your parents would meet her in Portland after your dad got home from work." His voice broke, "but as you know, they never made it to Portland."

Amy's voice was hoarse. "The accident."

Hadden lifted the photograph of Sharalynn off the wall and stared at it. Then, he whispered, "It was no accident."

"Excuse me?"

"It was no accident, Amy. Your mom and dad were murdered."

Amy paled and collapsed onto the chair.

Gramps continued, "An eighteen wheeler crossed the center line and hit their car head-on. The driver fled the scene. At the time, they figured the guy was drunk. The police investigated the accident, but they never did find him."

Amy sat stunned. She could still see her parents before they left on that last night: Mom in her blue dress and Dad with his crazy, nervous grin. Mom had such exciting news. She was going to tell Amy all about it when they got back home. For years Amy wondered what it was her mom was going to tell her. Now, at last, she knew. Amy has a sister. A twin. And her name is Alesha.

The old man hung the photo back on the wall and limped back over to Amy and gave her a hug and stroked her hair. His voice cracked. "Never wanted to tell you that, Girl. The whole thing is so damned heartbreaking..." He sidestepped to the wheelchair and sat down heavily. Amy reached over and touched his leg. "There's more, isn't there, Gramps? It didn't end there, did it?"

"Nope, it didn't end there. That's how we found out the truth about the accident."

"Tell me what happened at the cabin," Amy said.

His voice was husky. "I went to the cabin a lot after the accident, as you know. Wanted to be alone. I'd go up there and work from sunrise to sunset trying to rid the demons I was living with. A couple of weeks after the funeral a black sedan pulls up. Two big guys get out. They tell me to keep my mouth shut about the phone call Sharalynn got from the girl." The old man rubbed his legs.

Amy touched his hand. "What did they do to you, Gramps?"

The old man shook his head. "What's done is done."

"Tell me, Gramps. No more holding back."

He exhaled slowly. "One guy punched me. Almost knocked me cold. The other guy got in the sedan and drove the front wheel over my legs. Crushed my left leg and broke my right. The doc fixed up both legs best he could, but even with the prosthetic, I can't be on my left leg long."

Amy swallowed hard. The room tilted and she grabbed the arm of the wheelchair. Something hot burned in Amy's stomach. "Jeez." She reached for his hand. "Gramps, I'm so sorry." They sat like that a while, Amy gripping the old man's hand, each deep in their own emotions. Finally Amy asked, "And Grams? What did they do to her?"

Hadden cleared his throat. "Told your grandmother they'd kill *you* if she so much as uttered a word."

Amy could feel darkness closing around her. *Too much too fast.* She gripped the arm of the wheelchair. *Get control! If you don't, you'll lose Jamie. Think of Jamie!* Amy took deep breaths in and out, until the darkness faded.

She walked out of the room. His words burned in her mind: *Your parents were murdered.* They threatened Gramps and crippled him for life. They threatened her grandmother into a sickening vow of silence. And now they were threatening to hurt Jamie.

Jamie. She had to find him fast, before they did. But how? She needed to know everything. The wheels of the wheelchair rolled up behind her. Without turning around she said, "What about the fire at the hospital, the one that killed our doctor?"

Hadden nodded. "Real convenient. Got rid of Doc Lamont and the birth records too."

"Was Dr. Lamont involved? Did he know about the other twin?"

Hadden shook his head. "Doc Lamont was a good man. If he knew, he would've blown the whistle on them. Maybe he was going to do that. Maybe that's why they roasted him. Or, maybe he was a loose end. They're killers, Amy. That's why I'm so worried. That's why it's so important for you and little Jamie to go away someplace safe for a while, before they turn on you."

Amy massaged her head. A giant headache pounded inside her skull. "Have you told me *everything*? Is there anything else? Anything you've left out?"

Gramps shook his head. "That's it, Girl. That's enough for anybody."

Amy pushed her hair behind her ears and paced the floor. She stopped and looked over at her grandfather. "Who are they?"

Hadden swung the wheelchair around and peered up at his granddaughter. "I don't know who they are, but something tells me we're about to find out."

CHAPTER 16

A cool dawn mist hovered over the ground, enshrouding the trees and shrubs, and rendering the world colorless, which matched Amy's mood perfectly. She had gone about a mile and was still running hard, sweat trickling down her back, and her sneakers tapping hard against the sidewalk. She pushed on in an effort to purge the cold that had crept into her soul. Morning fog blanketed the ground and encircled the trees.

She sprinted into the park, and fighting fatigue, Amy turned onto the jogging trail. She passed no one. It was too early. Even the birds weren't up yet. The park was eerily silent and forlorn. Just like her. It wasn't until she neared the other side that she slowed to a walk. Spotting an empty park bench, she dropped down onto it and wiped her face with her sleeve.

Gramps hadn't told her everything, there was more, but he had said enough to fire a spear of terror deep into her heart. Had the killer threatened her with Jamie's life the same way he'd threatened her grandmother with Amy's, years ago?

Amy wasn't about to let anything happen to her son. He was the very essence of her being—the miracle she had waited for since becoming a woman. He had a whole life ahead of him, and damn it, he was going to live it. She could see his small face--his big, round gray eyes sparkling up at her mischievously, and the magical smile that compelled people to stop and smile back. He was dear and sweet and innocent. A moan escaped her lips and she buried her face in her hands.

Eventually, she got up and walked through the mist to the park entrance. She pulled her cell from her pocket and woke up Sanville's only taxi operator. When he arrived, she directed him to the impoundment lot. Yesterday, she'd arranged for mobile service from the tire shop. The Jeep now had four new tires. The driver's mirror was shattered and the rear corner was dinged, but the truck was drivable, for now. Amy paid the impoundment and towing fee and drove home. She needed to get clothes and a few personal items. While she was there, she'd use her online access to the University of Oregon's Knight Library, and the big monitor on her computer to scroll quickly through the archives. All the way home her eyes darted between the road and the rear view mirror for any sign of being followed.

At the house, to avoid emotional distractions, she walked inside, locked the door behind her, and went right into her study. She knew it was risky being at the house alone, so she planned to be quick. Sitting down in front of the Mac, Amy clicked on the library icon. A second later, she was logged in. A search for the newspaper articles covering her parents' accident brought up black and white photos of the scene, including a number of shots of the Dodge. It was barely recognizable, mostly twisted metal and debris. The photo tore her breath away. She fought nausea. The eighteen-wheeler that struck her parents' car head-on had sustained only minor front-end damage. The Dodge was underneath the truck. She had never seen photos of the accident scene and found them devastating. The media reported that her parents had died instantly. The driver had fled the scene. There were no follow-up articles.

Next, she searched for items on the St. Mary's hospital fire and found a front-page photo and article. There had been a single death. Dr. Joseph Lamont's body had been found in the basement of the building. The grainy black and white newspaper photo depicted the middle-aged doctor as a balding, heavy-set man, with a kindly face. She located his obituary and noted that his wife had survived him. That was thirty-two years ago. Would she still be alive?

Amy checked the online Beaverdale directory, found six listings for *Lamont,* and picked up the phone. The first three tries got her nowhere, but the fourth gave her a man who was quite helpful. "You must be looking for my mom," he told her, "She's living over in Edgemont now."

An hour away. "I'd like to drop by and see her."

"She doesn't like visitors and she doesn't go out. She developed agoraphobia many years ago. You know—fear of being outside, in crowds, of wide-open spaces, and so on. For my mom, it's a fear of being outside of her apartment. It's so bad now, she's housebound. I keep telling her she should try going out, but she refuses, even for groceries. Gets them delivered."

"Can I call her?"

"She doesn't take calls and watches the call display. She only answers calls when she recognizes the number. You're welcome to drop by, but I doubt she'll open the door." He gave Amy the address and directions.

Amy thanked him, grabbed her laptop, packed some clothing and personal items into a small suitcase, and headed to Edgemont.

Did Mrs. Lamont know anything about her husband's death or the hospital fire? Was there a police investigation? Was there was a related reason for the agoraphobia?

An hour later, Amy tapped at the apartment door. When no one responded she called through the door, "Hello? Mrs. Lamont? Are you home? Mrs. Lamont?"

A husky voice barked a response from the other side of the door. "Go away!"

"Mrs. Lamont, my name's Amy Johnson, I just want to talk to you for a couple of minutes. I won't stay long, I promise."

A terrified wail came through the door. *"Johnstone? Did you say, Johnstone?"* The voice shrieked through the door and Amy stepped back in surprise. "Get away from here! Leave me alone or I'll call the police!"

Amy stared at the door. *Johnstone.* It had been said distinctly with a *T.* Why did that name distress the woman? What did the name, *Johnstone* mean to *her?* Disturbed by the woman's unexpected reaction, Amy returned to the Jeep, pulled out her laptop, and using wifi, logged onto the library site once more. She went back through archives of *The Beaverdale News*, unsure what she was looking for. Then she saw it. A newspaper photo of a woman reclining in a hospital bed holding a newborn baby in her arms. A doctor in his late thirties with thinning dark hair, heavy brows, and protruding jaw stood in the background, a stethoscope draped over his white coat. The quality of the photograph was poor and it was apparent the photographer had caught the physician by surprise. The caption identified him as *Dr. Johnstone*—spelled with a "t". The article reported that the woman had been expecting twins, but one infant had died at birth. This was exactly what had happened to her mother. Coincidence?

On a strong hunch, Amy ran through listings of obstetricians licensed in the state of Oregon during the late 70's and early 80's. Dr. George D. Johnstone had maintained his license to practice in Oregon until 1980, and then his name disappeared from the registry.

Changing her search to include all states, the OB/GYN re-surfaced in Houston in 1981, where he remained listed on their registry until 1995.

Had he retired? Died? Moved? It was time to call some Houston hospitals.

After two fruitless hours on the phone, and realizing it was getting dark, Amy followed a stream of westbound traffic out of town and exited onto the dark two-lane highway toward the coast. Soon the traffic disappeared. She picked up her cell and punched in the number for the Sheriff's office for the sixth time that day, hoping for word on Jamie. She asked to speak to her friend, Debbie.

"Hi, Deb. It's Amy. Is there any news?"

"No, Amy, sorry, nothing yet. I know the sheriff's doing everything he can. Between you and me, Dan needs a kick in the ass."

"I need to find him first. Then, we'll form a line."

"Don't worry, Amy, I'll call the minute we hear anything."

Amy dropped the phone on the seat. Fear of what could happen to Jamie swam at the back of her mind constantly. Trying to steer her thoughts from her son, Amy reflected upon her day's findings. She finally had a name: Dr. George Johnstone. He had a case almost identical to her mom's, where one twin died. *Could he be the OB/GYN who delivered me?* Gramps's neighbor, Mrs. Boxer had mentioned a specialist had been called in for her mom. Amy needed to find out if Dr. Johnstone was her mother's obstetrician. The dates fit the time period.

As Amy turned onto Highway 101, she reached for the cell and punched 2 for her grandfather. She wanted to let him know she would stay with him another night. The call went to voicemail. She frowned and tried again a few minutes later, with the same result. *Strange, he never goes out after dark.*

CHAPTER 17

Amy ran into fog on the way back, so it took longer than usual to get to Sanville. A row of cars crawled along single file, each following the taillights of the car ahead, with the hope of staying on the road. At last, she turned off the highway, headed north toward First Avenue, and turned onto her grandfather's street. A patrolman stopped her and motioned her to turn around. Behind him, the road had been cordoned off. Half a block up a fire truck and other emergency vehicles blocked the street, their lights flashing. The air was thick with black smoke.

Worried, Amy reversed the Jeep, threw it against the curb, and leapt out, running toward the fire. She dodged vehicles and neighbors, dread filling her chest like wet concrete. A second later she saw the house. *Gramps!*

Huge jets of water sprayed the burning bungalow. Tongues of flame reached for the shingle roof. A hot wind blew in her face, choking her with acrid smoke, and the stink of charred wood and melting synthetics.

She pushed anxiously through the bystanders, searching for Gramps. The van was still in the carport. She moved faster through the crowd, her brain screaming, *Gramps! Be out here, please.*

Suddenly an explosion blew out the living room window sending shards of glass raining onto the lawn.

Amy froze, her eyes fixed on the blackened building. *He can't be in there, he just can't!* She pushed along the front of the crowd seeing his face everywhere and yet, nowhere.

She recognized a neighbor and yelled to be heard over the din. "Have you seen Art Hadden?" The old man gave her a fearful look and shook his head. With sick realization, Amy turned around once more and stared at the house. *No!*

She ducked the yellow tape and spurted for the front door. A deputy caught her before she was halfway across the lawn. "Hey! You can't go in there!"

"My grandfather—" She screamed. "He's inside!" He put his hands on her shoulders and forced her back behind the tape. "Please," she begged, "Help my grandfather. Please!" Amy looked at the people around her. It was clear that no one was going to go into the burning house, not even the firemen.

She shoved through the crowd and dashed into the neighbor's yard, around to the far side of his house, and into the backyard. No one noticed. Once behind the house, she used the foliage for cover and scrambled toward her grandfather's bungalow. There were no flames coming from the rear of the house. Hoses shot jets of water from the front street. The overspray soaked her.

There was a small ground-level window that accessed the crawlspace under the house. Amy considered her options. Gramps always kept the back door locked, and she could never break it down. The only other way inside the house was through the crawlspace window on the side of the building. She had to be fast if she wanted to get through it without being seen. Or worse, stopped.

In a crouching run, she dove for it, her right shoulder breaking the glass. A fireman saw her and yelled. For a split second their eyes met, then Amy

93

shoved her body through the narrow opening and ducked inside

The crawlspace was shallow, damp, dark, and smoky. There was about three feet of clearance beneath the floor joists. She glanced around. Her grandparents used the space to store mementos, boxes of Christmas decorations, and bins. Amy bent over and scuttled toward the two-step ladder that led up to the access door and the main floor. By the time she got there her lungs were starved for air. Peeling off her wet jacket, she wrapped it around her head and face, inhaling though the damp fibers.

Still crouched over, she stood on the short ladder and pushed hard on the access door. It swung upward, and Amy found herself in the smoky kitchen. She coughed and pulled her jacket tighter around her head and over her mouth and nose. Her eyes watered. Smoke hung all around her. How would she find him when she could barely see? "Gramps!" she screamed, but the racket inside the burning house swallowed her voice.

Pushing herself off the floor, Amy ran toward the dining room, but leapt back when she had only gone as far as the doorway. *Too hot.* Flames danced up the walls.

Her lungs were burning now. Blinded by smoke and tears she ducked down, finding it cooler near the floor, the air less putrid. "Gramps!" She was running out of time! Scrambling crab-style back across the kitchen floor, she headed for the hall. Once there, she re-positioned the wet jacket over her head and face and crawled forward on her hands and knees. *Too hot. Hurry! No time! Gramps, where are you?* The bedroom was about three feet away, but it felt like a mile. She propelled herself into the room, landing beside the bed. She ran her hand over the hot surface—no Gramps. She yanked the blanket off the bed and threw it around

94

her, for protection. Her eyes watered profusely now, blinding her. Coughing, barely able to inhale, she crawled around the bed. No Gramps and no wheelchair.

That left the living room. Oh dear God. That room was all but totally consumed by fire. She returned to the hallway and belly-crawled forward. Everything was hot. There was no oxygen in the air! Her lungs were on fire and she couldn't stop coughing. The heat intensified with every inch. She was crawling into an inferno.

Her head struck something hard—the bureau outside the living room. She was almost there. She pulled herself up and turned toward the living room, but she could see nothing. The heat was cooking her. She tried to call out to him, "Gramps!" But ended up choking instead. An overhead beam pulled away, dangling precariously, sending sparks flying around her. Smoke, heat, and fire were everywhere, but no Gramps.

She could no longer feel anything. Her body went numb. The searing heat disappeared; she felt cold. Then her feet left the floor.

CHAPTER 18

Dallas climbed the worn staircase to his apartment over the dreaded dentist's office. Juggling grocery bags and dry cleaning, he unlocked the door, stepped inside, hit the lights, and looked around. He needed a cleaning service.

Putting food away was no problem. It either went into the near-empty pantry or the near-empty refrigerator. That job finished, he popped the top off a Lone Star beer, took a long swig, and walking over to the scanner, flipped it on. A second later, he caught Hadden's address and the word *fire*. He dropped the beer in the sink, grabbed his coat and hat, and ran back out the door.

The patrolman was looking the wrong way when Dallas arrived at First Street, so he whipped around him and broke through the tape, maneuvering his pickup down the crowded street. He came to a fast stop behind the fire truck. Ahead, the road was clogged with emergency vehicles, onlookers, firemen, police, an ambulance, and hoses snaking through the street. He barely recognized Hadden's house. "Hellndamnation!"

The core of the blaze centered on the front right corner of the bungalow, where flames reached over the rooftop, throwing searing heat back to the road.

Sam Eden, Sanville's fire chief, was barking orders when Dallas interrupted him. "Anybody inside?" Dallas yelled.

The chief gave him a sidelong glance. "It don't look good for old Hadden. By the time we got here the fire was too far gone for my guys to get in and out of there safely. Worse thing is, his granddaughter went in for him."

"What?" Dallas tensed, "Amy's *inside?*"

"Been in there a couple of minutes now."

"Anybody go in after her?"

The Chief shook his head. "We tried, but it's too risky. The roof is going to cave any minute. Hey, wait! Wayburne, you can't do that. Come back here!"

Dallas grabbed a yellow jacket, helmet, and respirator from the fire truck and yelled for the paramedics to meet him in the back lane. Throwing on the protective clothing and respirator, he ran through the neighbor's property, into Hadden's backyard. Two firemen tried to grab him, but his years on the football field paid off. He dodged them and raced up the wheelchair ramp to the back door. Locked! Two powerful kicks and the old wood splintered. He pushed it open. As he slid across the kitchen floor, something broke free in the front of the house, near the living room, and crashed to the floor sending sparks flying down the hallway.

Then he saw her.

Dodging toppled furniture, he dashed down the hall, reaching Amy just as she collapsed. He flipped her over his left shoulder and wound his way back toward the kitchen.

Suddenly, the house swayed on its foundation. The ceiling over his head buckled sending drywall and wood splinters raining down upon them. He moved as fast as he could, re-entering the kitchen at the same second the far side of the room disintegrated. The roof was collapsing.

Move! Move! Move! Ten feet to the back door. He ran for it, plunging outside, as the roof caved behind him. He didn't stop running until his shoes hit the lane. There, gasping for breath, he dropped onto his knees. Paramedics lifted Amy onto a stretcher, put an oxygen mask over her mouth, and hoisted the stretcher into the back of the truck.

"Get a move on." Dallas told them. They pulled out and Dallas limped back through the neighbor's yard, onto the street. Fire Chief Sam Eden was furious. "You crazy bastard! All the years I've known you, this has got to be the gull-darnedest, stupidest thing you've ever done. Lucky you didn't get fried in there."

Dallas slapped the fire chief's back. "Had to get that woman out of there, Sam. Your job's to put out fires. My job's to do everything else."

The Chief grunted. "You barely made it out of there, Dallas. Only thing that saved your ass was your old football days. You always broke the speed records, but this one tops 'em all."

Dallas stripped off his gear and dropped it into the fire chief's hands. "Call me on my cell if you find Hadden."

Dallas waited impatiently in the Emergency waiting room. As usual, the place was in turmoil—white coats and uniforms going every direction, would-be patients waiting for treatment, and a young girl sobbing. How people actually got medical treatment in these conditions was beyond him.

"Sheriff?"

Dallas turned to see Sandra Wilson, the head nurse waving him over, pen and clipboard in hand. "You can go in now, Sheriff. Amy will be fine—minor burns, cuts to her upper arm and shoulder, a few scrapes, and surprisingly, her lungs aren't too bad. She's pretty upset about her grandfather though. She says she's got to go back to the house. We've sedated her to calm her down and to help with the pain." Sandra stuck the pen behind her ear. "We've been trying to locate Dr. Johnson, but it seems he's out of town and didn't leave an emergency number."

Dallas grunted. "If you find him, let me know." The nurse caught his tone of voice and raised an eyebrow.

Dallas followed her to a curtained cubicle. She parted the curtain so he could step through and closed it behind him. He stood beside the stretcher. Amy was still, her eyes closed; an intravenous solution dripped into a vein in her hand, an oxygen mask covered her mouth and nose. Her arms and hands were lathered with a jelly-like substance. A reddish-purple lump grew from her forehead and one eye was swollen and purple. She must have heard him because her eyes opened immediately.

Dallas shook his head. "You look terrible."

Amy pulled the oxygen mask away and tried to speak. "My grandfather?" Her voice was raw.

"We don't know yet, and we probably won't for a while."

She closed her eyes. When she reopened them, she asked, "Pull back one curtain, please. I don't like being closed in."

Surprised, Dallas reached around and opened the curtain. He looked back to find her staring at him. He shifted uncomfortably.

Amy tried again to speak. "The paramedics told me you went into the burning house and got me out just as the roof caved in." She swallowed. "Can't believe you did that."

Dallas raised his brows meaningfully. "You going in there was a little crazy, you know that, right?"

She cringed. "Somebody had to."

That Dallas understood.

Her eyes never left his face. "But you didn't *have to*."

He stepped away from the stretcher. "Get some rest. I'll let you know the minute I hear anything."

"Sheriff?"

He turned around to see her trying to get up. "Don't get up—"

"I can't stay here. Please, I have to get back there."

He pushed her gently back onto the stretcher. "Come on now, you keep that up and they'll hog-tie you to the damned thing. You know how they get in here when you don't do what you're told."

"I can't stay here. Please."

"You're in no shape to be released. Now, lie back. I'll stop by tomorrow and see how you're doing." He dropped his cap back on his head and seeing her settle back down, he slid the oxygen mask back in place and headed off.

He had driven most of the way back to Sanville when his cell phone rang. "Wayburne."

"Sheriff, it's Sandra in Emergency. Sorry to call on your cell, I know you're off duty, but it's about Amy Johnson."

Worried, he asked, "What is it?"

"She's gone. We've checked most everywhere. A couple of people in the waiting room saw a woman who looked like Amy, slip out the front door."

Dallas cursed and yanked on the wheel, made a U-turn, and headed back toward the hospital.

Sandra continued, "The thing is, we're not sure how she can stand up, let alone walk, considering the amount of sedation and pain meds she's been given. After you left, we increased the dosage."

"I'm on my way."

Dallas was three blocks from the hospital when he spotted Amy walking unsteadily down the shoulder of the road. He pulled up beside her and lowered his window. "What do you think you're doing? You have any idea how far it is back to Sanville?"

"Can make it. Better 'n the hospital." Her words were slurred.

Dallas jumped out, grabbed her arm, and steered her around to the passenger door.

He helped her inside and headed to the US 101. "Where do you want to go? It's not safe to be at your house. In fact, that'd be crazy. Do you have any friends you can stay with?"

Amy shook her head. "No." Dallas was thoughtful. "I have a cabin up in the mountains, about an hour from here. You're welcome to use it. You'd be safe there."

"That's—nice, but I have to go back—to my grandfather's. I have to know."

"There's nothing you can do for your grandfather."

Amy sighed. "Should get my Jeep."

"It'll be fine where it is. You're in no shape to drive anyway."

"Do I have any other—options?"

"Guess not. Dallas turned south onto the US 101. They drove in silence and Amy dozed. A while later, Dallas turned inland, drove twenty-five minutes, then engaged the four-wheel drive, and worked the pickup up a steep incline to a level clearing. Dallas helped Amy out of the truck and guided her across the clearing. She shivered in the cold night air, so he took off his jacket and wrapped it around her, before climbing an uneven path toward a dark structure nestled in the trees. Her feet kept slipping on the rocky path. "Oh, help, sorry, oops. Where are we? Dallas?"

"I'm here."

"Where?"

"Right here. Give me your hand."

"Whoops!"

He reached down to help her up. "Hang on to my arm."

"Okay. Where're we?"

"Almost there."

"Where's there?"

"My cabin. Remember?"

"No," she said. "Don't see anything."

"You will." Dallas unlocked the front door and they went inside; the air was cold and smelled like cedar.

Amy waited while Dallas lit the butane lamps. Yellow light filtered through the building and she looked around in a haze. Dallas saw her curiosity. "Hand-built," he told her. "My dad and I. One and a half stories of rough-hewn, split lumber and timbers. It's simple enough. The main level is just what you see: living area, a rustic eat-in kitchen, and you'll be happy to know there's even indoor plumbing. Bathroom's over there," he said, pointing to an open door off the kitchen." He saw her look back at the narrow staircase off the living room. "Goes up to the loft," he told her, pulling out a chair in the kitchen and helping Amy into it.

"We built the place a few years ago," he explained. "Dad thought of himself as a pioneer of sorts. Wanted to be self-sufficient, so there's no electricity. The heat comes from the oil stove and the fireplace." Dallas lit a long match and dropped it into the stove. He waited for the oil to ignite, then dropped the lid back down, filled a kettle with water, and placed it on the stovetop to eventually boil. "Dad might have taken the pioneer spirit too far because we originally didn't have running water. Mom made him change that fast." He saw that Amy was still shivering, so he went into the living room and reached into the woodbin for kindling. "Won't take long for the stove and the fireplace to heat the place up," he told her, placing slivers of wood in the fireplace and lighting them. He added small pieces of split wood until flames danced across the hearth. Finally he placed a few logs on the fire.

Amy cringed and looked away. Dallas realized that a *fire* was probably the last thing she wanted to see right now. He stood, wiping his hands on his jeans. "How about some soup?"

"Huh?"

"Cures everything."

Amy was too tired to argue. Her mind was on Gramps. "Maybe he wasn't in there," she said.

Dallas looked down at her. The hospital staff had cleaned her up, but her clothes were torn, scorched, and damp. He disappeared into the storage room behind the kitchen where he rummaged in a box of clothes and returned with a red jogging suit. "Here," he offered it to Amy. "Looks like it'll fit, but even if it doesn't, it's clean and dry." He motioned to the bathroom. "Change in there, if you like," he suggested, putting one of the butane lanterns on the bathroom vanity.

Amy took the jogging suit, looked down at her jeans and shirt, then made her way toward the bathroom. Dallas waited for what seemed an eternity.

"You done yet?" he called through the door.

"Soon," she told him.

A few minutes later he inquired again. "You coming out of there tonight?"

"Ah, maybe," she mumbled. "It was here a minute ago--"

There was a loud thump. He knocked on the door. "Everything okay?" When there was no response, he opened the door slightly and peered around it. She was sitting on the floor, staring at the sweatshirt, naked from the waist up. She looked up at him, then tried to cover herself with her bare arms. Her ivory skin was flawless, her breasts firm and round. Dallas realized that he was gaping at her, so he grabbed the sweatshirt, and pulled it

103

over her head. "Here. Stick your arms through here," he said.

Her arms landed around his neck. "You have nice blue eyes," she told him matter-of-factly. Her eye met his and lingered. "Very handsome…too."

Dallas grinned. "Uh, I think we need to get you dressed. Here, try it again. Stick your arms through here." This time they tangled in the sleeves. He worked the fleece down over her arms. Her skin was silky soft. *She's so beautiful.* He lifted her off the floor. A vivid image of soft white skin and perfectly round breasts involuntarily flashed through his mind.

Amy reached out to steady herself and ended up clutching his shirt. Confused, she looked up. "Sorry, Dallas, drugs do strange things—to me." Her words slurred. "But you've been very…nice." She kissed his cheek and laid her head on his shoulder. "And you're very com-for-ble." Then she stood up and stepped past him into the kitchen.

He sat her down at the table, pushing the soup bowl toward her.

She stared at it. "When will they…know?"

"By morning."

Amy dropped her head into the palms of her hands and closed her eyes. She swayed and almost fell off the chair. He grabbed the flashlight off the fridge and scooped her up. Cursing his bad knee, he carried her up to the loft and laid her on the bed. Gently, he pulled the blankets over her and saw that she was already asleep.

He tidied the kitchen and then stretched out on the big recliner by the fire. He hadn't intended to stay at the cabin, but he couldn't leave her in her current state either. He slept peacefully until a scream woke him hours later. Grabbing the flashlight, he dashed upstairs. Amy was thrashing in the bed, her breath coming in gasps. She called out again. "No! Help him.

104

Help…him." Tears streamed down her face and she struck out at the air around her.

Dallas grasped her wrists and pushed her arms down onto the mattress. She fought him. "Amy, wake up." He dug his thumbs into her shoulders and spoke loudly, "Amy, you're dreaming. Wake up."

Her eyes flew open and she sat up. "Oh Gramps, I'm so sorry," she whispered. She dropped her head onto his shoulder. Tears soaked his shirt. He stroked her hair. "It's okay, Amy. It's okay," he said gently.

Dallas held her until she drifted back to sleep, then covered her and went back downstairs. He picked up the poker and stoked the fire, anger burning in his gut. He knew the fire at old man Hadden's was arson. Somewhere out there were two of the worst creatures known to man. Dallas swore aloud.

He repositioned his chair and sat back down, too angry to sleep. Around dawn he drifted off, only to awaken a couple of hours later with a start. Amy stood over him, wrapped in a blanket, her long golden hair shimmering in the early morning sunlight. He sat up with a jolt, wondering how long she'd been there.

CHAPTER 19

Amy pulled the blanket around her and gazed down at Dallas. She had stood that way for some time, watching him sleep, sprawled out in the armchair. She didn't know a man like this existed. He had saved her life at great risk to his own. The paramedics told her no one else would risk a rescue. It was too dangerous. Why did he do it? They told her the roof collapsed while he was inside, but he still carried her out. Did she thank him? She couldn't remember.

Dallas stirred and sat upright. "Everything okay?" he asked.

Amy nodded and sat gingerly on the edge of the armchair opposite him. "I've been trying to remember if I thanked you," Amy paused, "They said I was crazy to have gone into that burning building, but my grandfather means everything to me." Her voice broke and she took a breath before continuing, "What I don't understand is, why you went in. You risked your life."

Dallas ran his hand through his hair and leaned back in the chair. "I don't see it that way. It was something that had to be done, that's all. A man can't get hung up thinking: *if I go in there this could happen or that could happen.* Hell, nothing would get done in this life, at that rate. You see a window of opportunity, you jump in."

Amy stared at him in amazement. "Well, your window of opportunity looked like a wall of flames to everyone else."

"Maybe."

She hesitated, "I appreciate what you did," she said softly. "More than you can imagine. I can't even fathom the kind of man who would do something like that, especially for someone you hardly know."

He waved her suggestion away.

Still hugging the blanket Amy wiggled deeper into the armchair and tried to collect her thoughts. "I also want to apologize for last night. I think I was a disaster. You must be wondering what kind of weird person I am."

Seeing her discomfort, Dallas slid forward in his chair. "Hell no," he said, his eyes never leaving hers as he searched for the right words. "Not at all. You're a very special woman, Amy. I've seen you over the years and heard you at the odd town hall meeting. You're a quiet, intelligent, self-possessed, woman. And you've got courage. Even though I think you were crazy going in that burning house, I respect why you did it. It took a lot of guts. Not many people, men or women, would have done that."

"Gramps means everything to me. I couldn't leave him in there." Amy swallowed hard.

Dallas nodded, getting up to stoke the fire. Soon flames danced and their warmth took away the night chill. "You know, the situation you're in is tough. And I've got a feeling things will get a lot tougher."

Amy considered that. "If that's true, I hope I'm up for it. Feels like I've been pushed to the brink these past days, and sometimes I've thought, 'I can't take anymore!' but like it or not, I find that I can. I guess that's how you grow as a person, but I don't know whether it's good or it's bad. If it is for the better, it's probably the only good coming out of this situation."

She saw his expression and added, "that is, besides meeting you."

The intensity of his look shook her. She had been living on the edge for days. Her world had tilted and she now resided in a dark and terrifying place. The only time in these past days that she had felt safe or saw light, was in this man's presence. At those moments the world righted itself, and she wanted it to stay that way. She wanted to find Jamie, Gramps, and her twin, and end the violence.

"You are such a good man, Dallas. You have incredible inner strength. What you did for me last night was beyond comprehension. It was astonishing. In this room, now, with you, I actually feel *whole* again." He was strong and confident. A special warmth radiated from him and she wanted to move closer to it, and to him. She wanted that desperately. But something held her back.

His pale blue eyes met hers and she felt her breath leave her, reminding her of the first time he had done that to her, and how uncomfortable it had made her feel.

He reached over and touched her face, his thumb running along her cheekbone. She sat perfectly still. His touch was warm and gentle. He was so close. She wanted—no! He dropped his hand and leaned back, studying her. Then, abruptly he stood and walked over to the cabin door where he plucked his jacket from the coat hook. "We're low on firewood. Water's hot if you'd like a bath."

Amy stood up quickly, the blanket cascading to the plank floor around her feet. Picking it up, she swung it over the back of the chair, and hiked up the jogging pants. A bath sounded good.

The water was warm and soothing and she sank down in the tub as low as she could without dousing the burns on her hands and arms. Tilting her head back, the water swirled around her scalp lifting the smoky odor from her hair. Shampoo and soap were on a shelf above the tub and she made use of them, using her fingertips. Finally she soaked, the warm water caressing her aching muscles.

There was a tap on the door and it opened wide enough for a stack of clothes to make their way onto the bathroom counter, before swinging shut again. She smiled and closed her eyes.

Immediately, her thoughts flew to her grandfather's burning house. How had the fire started? Was it the stove? An electrical short? Or…was it intentionally set? Then she remembered the threat she'd received. *You made a big mistake calling the Sheriff.* Amy sat up so fast water splashed over the lip of the tub. Her breath left her.

Did he see me with the sheriff? Did Gramps pay for that? What have I done?

By the time she was able to regain her composure enough to get out of the tub, the water was cold. She toweled off and inspected the stack of clean clothes: jeans, a blue plaid shirt similar to the one Dallas was wearing, cotton socks, soft bra and—she held them up—French cut panties. The fit was about two sizes too large, but the clothes were clean.

When she opened the bathroom door, she found Sanville's sheriff bent over the oven door, fork in hand, toasting bagels. He looked at her and frowned. "Too big, huh?"

Amy tugged at the jeans, examining the fit. "I guess she's a little shorter and bigger around."

"They belong to my ex. Ellen and I used the cabin a lot after my parents moved back to Texas, so we kept clothes here. When she left me, she was mad as hell. Never came back for her things, so I threw them in boxes and put them in the storage room."

He plucked the bagels from the oven, dropped them onto plates, and pushed them across the small table. Then, he reached around for the coffeepot. "Breakfast is served," he announced, setting a pot of honey beside the toast. "Luckily, I had a bag of bagels in the truck. They were for the office. We each bring something, and donuts aren't allowed."

Sitting at the plank table, Amy found herself eye level with a framed wall photo of a young girl about ten. Her long dark hair was knotted into a sporty ponytail; her cool blue eyes looked right at Amy, and a capricious smile played on her lips. "Your daughter?"

Dallas looked up. "Maya. My ten-year-old. That picture was taken last summer, right after she creamed me at tennis," he said with a grin. "She wants to be a lawyer, or rather, a prosecutor. She says there's a distinct difference. She's fed up seeing criminals go free, so *she's* going to change all that."

Amy smiled. "She sounds like her dad. She must be fun to have around."

"She is, when I get to see her. Ellen doesn't want me interfering in their busy lives. I guess that's my ex's way of retaliating for all the years that I was too busy for them. They each have a new life now, or so Ellen says." Dallas smeared honey over his toast. "Two months after we were divorced, she married a retired English professor. Dr. Do Little. Or Do Nothing. He's now acting father to my daughter."

Amy could hear the sarcasm and hurt in his voice. "You miss them?"

He applied another layer of honey to the toast. "More than you can imagine. There isn't a day goes by that I don't think about Ellen or Maya and the life that we had. Problem was, I put the job ahead of my family for fifteen years. Thought it was the right thing at the time. But it's too late to change that now."

Amy could see pain in his eyes. "Sounds like you still love your wife."

Dallas took a deep breath. "Never was any other woman. Just Ellen. Guess I'm a one-woman-man," he paused, "Or was."

Amy watched him. "Must have been lonely after they left." Amy fidgeted with her plate. "Have you ever gone out—you know—with anyone?"

Dallas shook his head. "Nope, never thought of it." He put down his bagel. "That is, 'till just recently."

Another hot flush gave Amy away. "I don't mean—I mean—that's not what I mean."

Dallas laughed at her discomfort. "I know what you mean, Amy," he said reaching over for her hand.

His touch sparked an emotion so intense that it left Amy speechless. She gaped at him then turned away quickly. What was happening to her? As they cleaned away the breakfast dishes, Amy asked, "Were you born in Dallas, Texas by any chance?"

"That's exactly where I was born. Mom's hometown. Grew up there."

Amy smiled, "And that's where the slight drawl comes from." She ran water into the sink and was about to immerse her fingers when Dallas stopped her.

"I'll wash." He told her. "You don't need those burns in the dishwater." They changed places. "I don't hear a southern drawl. Do *y'all?*" he asked, emphasizing it.

Amy laughed and reached for a towel. When they were finished she turned to him. "I hate to keep bugging you about this, but I was wondering if there's any news about Jamie?"

Dallas shook his head. "Nothing. I called in and talked to Debbie while you were in the tub."

Disappointed, Amy looked down. "If I don't find Jamie soon, I'm going to go insane. I'm so worried about him that I can barely function, let alone think straight."

Dallas pulled the plug on the soapy water. "We contacted Jamie's teacher. She says that Dan called her to say he was taking Jamie on vacation and that they'd be gone a couple of weeks. Same story right across the board. We're keeping an eye on your sister-in-law's house, the clinic, the hospital, and Dan's apartment. The man seems to have temporarily vanished. We checked the outbound flights from Portland airport and we broadcast the tags statewide. No one's seen his Mercedes or his sister's Camry."

Amy gaped at him. "Can we back up a bit? What did you say about Dan having an apartment?"

Seeing Amy's expression, Dallas dropped the washcloth and dried his hands. "You didn't know."

Amy began running her towel back and forth over the same square of countertop. "I guess there's a lot I don't know."

He reached over and put his hand over hers to stop the repetitive motion, and then put his hands on her shoulders and turned her to him. "Listen to me, Amy. You're well respected in Sanville, something your husband isn't. Your designs are outstanding; people rave about them. You're a good mother; I've seen you with Jamie at the rink in the winter, at parades in the summer, at McDonald's, at the park, at the fair, heck I've seen you a lot over the last few years. And I've seen the doc too. God knows, there must be something wrong with that man."

His hands felt strong on her shoulders, and in some way they seemed to transmit his inner strength to her. She put her forehead against his shoulder and he pulled her into him, his arms closing around her, his warmth wrapping her protectively like a cocoon. Dallas stroked her hair and she closed her eyes, his masculine scent filling her nostrils. She tilted her head and looked up. His lips brushed her forehead. Then he pulled back.

Amy stood there, her heart racing. That had felt so good. It had been years since she'd been held like that. But was this right? With Dan's years of infidelities and his walking out on her, was she free to be with another man? She glanced up at Dallas. He was a calm, courageous, dedicated man—a good person in every respect. Any woman in her right mind would consider themselves lucky to be in her shoes. Amy wanted to be with him, but she turned away. She needed air and she needed it now. Stuffing her feet into her sneakers, she said shakily, "Think I'll go for a walk," and she bolted for the door, yanking her jacket off the wall hook on the way by. She jogged down the path and into the clearing where she burst into a full-blown run, her feet flying down the dirt trail.

Dallas caught up a few minutes later, half-running, half-limping. "I thought you said *walk*," *he* complained.

She saw his limp and slowed, remembering the kick she had given him. She scolded herself. *What was I thinking, doing a thing like that?* She touched his arm, "Dallas, I'm so sorry that I hurt your knee. I can't believe I did that. Now you can barely walk."

"Don't feel bad, Amy. These knees got toasted years back, playing football. They were gone long before you threw that kick."

They walked in silence along the wood trail, and then she stopped. "Let's go back."

As they retraced their steps, Amy savored the sound of the forest: leaves crunching underfoot, birds singing in the trees, and a creek trickling. It endowed an overall sense of peace upon her. *How can things be so normal and so abnormal at the same time?* As they wound their way down the slope of the mountainside, a breeze rustled through the trees bringing fresh, cool air, indicating the approach of another winter storm. Amy looked up and saw black clouds billowing above the treetops. The morning darkened noticeably. She resisted the urge to run.

His large hand closed over hers and with that single motion her fears melted. They walked down to the overlook below the cabin and resting their arms on the wooden rail, gazed at the river winding through the ravine below. After a while Dallas said, "I made some calls while you were in the tub. You want to talk about those things now?"

"I want to know whatever you can tell me, Dallas."

"I spoke with Sam, our fire chief," Dallas hesitated unsure how she would react to what he was about to tell her. "They're still investigating the fire and nothing is conclusive, but they did find a body." He reached for her hand and squeezed lightly.

Amy swallowed hard. With a shaky voice she asked, "Where was he? I looked everywhere."

Dallas cleared his throat uncomfortably. "In the living room."

Amy's hands covered her face.

"You okay?"

She nodded solemnly.

"They haven't been able to make an identification; in fact they're not even sure of the gender."

Amy flinched, closing her eyes tight, trying to shut out his words.

Dallas put his arm around her and pulled her close. He continued reluctantly, "They won't be able to use dental records to make the I.D. The victim had no teeth of his own, so that means we'll have to see if we can use DNA or some other means of ID."

Amy said flatly, "Gramps wore dentures."

"I know." But, there's one more thing. Sam expected to find the manual steel wheelchair near the body, but it wasn't there. In fact, it wasn't in the house at all."

"It had to be. He never takes it out of the house. Never."

"Sam said it wasn't there," he repeated.

"That doesn't make sense. If Gramps was in the house, then the wheelchair would've been in there." Amy gripped Dallas jacket and looked up at him. "Maybe the body isn't his; maybe he's still alive. Maybe he got out!" The heavy weight that had descended upon her days ago did not lessen, but until they had a positive identification, she had a small reprieve. Perhaps that was just as well. She couldn't grieve for Gramps right now; it would paralyze her. For now, she had to stay away from her emotions. But she still had one big regret. "If only I'd taken Gramps with me yesterday, he'd be okay now."

"Amy, don't do that. *What ifs* only make things worse."

"I know. You're right," Amy agreed.

Dallas looked down at her, his expression tight. "There's more. The fire was set intentionally. There were gas cans inside the house. We don't have all the details yet, but the missing wheelchair is disturbing. Hadden's a cagey old coot. You just never know."

Amy's head jerked up and she pulled back, looking at him intently. "You seem to know a lot about my grandfather."

Dallas considered how much to tell her. "Hadden and I go back a way. Not only that, we've played cards at the Club almost every week for the past five years. You get to know a man pretty well, playing cards."

Amy smiled sadly. "So true. You ever win?"

"Now and then."

"I seldom have. He'd holler, 'Girl, you're just too damned honest. I can read your cards from the look on your face.' I've been working on that, but I guess I've got one of those faces that shows everything I think or feel."

115

Dallas nodded. "You do, and it's refreshing."

Amy asked, "When was the last time you saw my grandfather?"

"Saturday. Stopped by his place. Figured if you saw somebody who looked like you, it either had to be one hell of a coincidence or the two of you must be related. If it was the latter, then the only person who could shed light on that subject was Hadden."

"And did he?" Amy asked.

"It took some arm twisting, but he coughed up with the story; told me pretty much everything. You were at his house before I got there, so I found him in a dilemma over how to tell you about your twin. He thought he was protecting you. Can't say I blame him, after everything that's happened in the past. One thing's for sure. He thinks the world of you. He may not always make the right decisions for you, but there isn't anything the old man wouldn't do for you."

Amy nodded. "I know that. Gramps and I have always been close." She twisted away from Dallas. "He finally told me about my twin and the truth about my parents' accident. What I don't understand is, why someone would murder my parents simply because of the phone call my sister made to them. All she said was that she was their daughter, and she was alive. Seems like the overkill, if you'll pardon the bad pun."

"I think there's a lot more to it, Amy. I think we're looking at the tip of the iceberg."

"If that was the tip of the iceberg, I'm terrified to think about what's coming down the pike." Amy realized it was time she told Dallas about her twin's visit to Beaverdale, the hospital fire, and subsequent death of Dr. Lamont, and what she learned about OB/GYN, Dr. George Johnstone. She explained that he was the specialist who had delivered Amy and her twin sister, along with at least one other set of twins. She asked Dallas: "Given everything I just told you, do you think it's possible this Dr. Johnstone could have been involved my parent's murder?"

Dallas rubbed his chin in thought. "I don't think it's that simple. I think the hospital fire covered Johnstone's ass. What happened to your parents probably covered someone else's."

CHAPTER 20

White knuckled, Amy gripped the seat as Dallas sped up the coast highway toward Sanville, where his team was attending an emergency. Dallas gave clipped, fast instructions over the radio as he swung the truck into the oncoming lane, passed two cars, dodged back into the northbound lane momentarily, and then angled back into the oncoming to pass another vehicle. A small truck was heading straight for them. Dallas pushed back into the northbound lane, and glanced at her. "You should've stayed at the cabin where you'd be safe—" he said to her before speaking into the radio once more, "Hell no, tell them to leave now!"

Amy gritted her teeth. "Safe?"

"Every time you go out, you're visible to the killer. Please, remember that." He yelled into the radio, "Don't wait for anything. I'll meet you there in ten minutes."

"Dallas, you've got an emergency to look after. Drop me like we planned, and do what you have to do."

"I don't like the idea of you driving back down the coast—" he turned back to the radio, "—send the second unit to Stiller Street—"

Amy pointed to the approaching cross street, "Don't forget to drop me—" then held on as the pickup swerved right, sped toward First Street, and came to a sliding stop beside the Jeep. Amy stepped out, "I'll call you later," she said with relief.

Dallas tossed her a key. "The cabin. Promise me you'll go straight there afterward, and remember, watch your rear view mirror. Make sure no one follows you. If you even suspect you're being followed, call it in, and get lost in traffic. Don't let yourself get trapped," he told her, anxiously inching the truck forward.

Amy nodded and stepped back as he accelerated. She watched the pickup turn the corner and disappear. She started the Jeep and slowly, very slowly, pulled around the corner, and idled toward her grandfather's house.

Gone.

An empty space existed between the two neighboring bungalows. The perimeter of the yard was taped off, as if to protect the few remaining walls and charred remains that littered the foundation. The fire chief's official car was parked along the curb. Amy shuddered and drove away. "Oh, Gramps," she choked, wiping away the tears.

The coast highway was quiet, allowing her time to think. Everything had started with her birth and that of her twin. *Why did they tell my mother that my twin died when she hadn't? What happened to my twin? Was she adopted? Sold? Who took her? Johnstone? Or had he merely facilitated the abduction? He was involved in at least one other apparent death of a twin.* Amy had a litany of questions and no answers. *How did my mom get involved? Did Johnstone target her?* Amy considered a few theories, and then discarded them. Nothing made sense. But she knew one thing: if a doctor tells a new mother that one of her twins has died, that mother would never disbelieve him—especially in those days—when deaths for newborns, particularly in multiple births, were higher.

As Amy pulled onto the private road that wound uphill along the tree-lined street to Somerset Meadows, more questions plagued her: *Why did they want my twin?*

Why just one of us? Why not both of us? Amy parked in the front lot and walked up the long walk toward the sprawling three-story building. The day was cool and sunny. She crossed the vast tiled lobby, questions swirling in her brain. *What kind of life has my twin had? Where did she grow up? Who raised her?*

Amy signed in and walked quickly past the elevator, toward the stairs. She planned to break the news of the fire gently to her grandmother, allowing time for her to absorb the information, if that were possible. Amy wouldn't say anything about Gramps until she knew for sure what had happened to him. How much her grandmother would understand, Amy didn't know.

Cynthia Hadden wasn't in her room. Thinking the staff may have taken her to the day room, Amy returned to the elevator and rode up a floor. It was visiting hours so the day room was crowded. A therapist recognized her and called out, "Hi there! If you're looking for your grandmother, she's outside, on the grounds. Her son came by and asked if he could put her in a wheelchair and take her out for some fresh air—"

"Son?" Fear was audible in Amy's voice.

The therapist paused, "Right. That's what he said."

Alarm bells went off for Amy. "She doesn't have a son! Which way did he take her?"

"Out the West Entrance."

"Call for help!"

Bypassing the elevator, Amy dashed down the stairs, along the corridor to the West Entrance, and outside, her heart pounding in her chest. She paused by the balustrade and looked around anxiously. The day was unusually mild. Patients, visitors, and staff were outside, enjoying the afternoon. Amy scanned the manicured grounds, her eyes resting on various wheelchairs. She spotted a small, white-haired woman being pushed by an elderly man.

Bounding down the stairs two at a time, Amy landed on the walk and ran after them. "Stop!" The old man continued on. "Wait, please," Amy called, catching up to them. She grabbed the wheelchair, brought it to a stop, and swung around to see her grandmother.

Instead, she was looking into the face of a complete stranger. "Oh, I'm sorry—☐ I thought—" The old couple eyed her with alarm. "I thought you were my...I'm so very sorry."

Desperate now, Amy scanned the grounds. Someone yelled a warning near the Main Entrance and Amy whirled around. A lone wheelchair freewheeled down the sloping walk toward the parking lot. "Grams!" Amy bolted across the lawn, hoping to catch the chair before it passed through the open gates and onto the entrance road. An unsuspecting driver would never see it coming.

The chair picked up speed on the downhill run, making it impossible to catch up. She shouted a warning as the chair flew through the gates. Amy saw the approaching car and pumped hard. She was right behind the chair now. Her fingers gripped the handles. The car jerked to a stop as Grams whizzed past the front bumper. Now, she was freewheeling toward the curb. Amy pictured her grandmother flying through the air.

Knowing there was only one way to stop the forward momentum without serious injury to her grandmother, Amy threw herself across the chair; her weight veering it left onto one wheel. Amy shifted her weight quickly, righting the wheelchair a second before it struck the curb.

The sudden impact hurtled Amy onto the sidewalk, landing her hard on her right hip. For some unfathomable reason, Cynthia Hadden remained in the chair. As pain traveled in light waves down Amy's leg, she stared in shock at her grandmother.

The old woman's eyes were clear; they glistened with tears. "Amy. My dear Amy."

The moment of recognition dumbfounded Amy. Struggling onto her knees, Amy reached for her grandmother's shaking hands. "It's okay, Grams, we're fine," she whispered, noticing for the first time the piece of paper her grandmother held. Amy pulled it out of her hand and read the words:

When on the wrong path, one must never lose sight of those one loves.

A man's voice drew her attention, "Are you hurt?"

Amy looked up. A tall, heavy-set man in a lab coat stood over her. His facial features were compressed into the center of a huge face and underscored by a long, jagged scar that ran along his jaw. His cold eyes stared at her.

"I'm okay," Amy replied, standing. Her hip throbbed. Staff and visitors gathered around them. A nurse anxiously checked her grandmother. Amy turned to the nurse. "Please take Mrs. Hadden back to her room."

While the staff re-settled her grandmother into bed, Amy went in search of the therapist who had allowed the visitor to take her grandmother out of the building. He was working on the ward. Amy stopped him. "I need a word with you. Let's go out into the hall." Once outside the ward, Amy turned on him. "How could you let a stranger take my grandmother out of here? Do you realize he sent her freewheeling out onto the street? She could have been killed!"

The therapist was red-faced. "You're right. My sincere apologies. It won't happen again, I assure you."

"Didn't you think to check this guy out before you let him take my grandmother out of the building?"

The therapist grew red in the face. "I feel very badly, Mrs. Johnson. I was busy and I didn't take the time to do that."

Amy wasn't satisfied but told the therapist, "I'm worried this man will come back. Do you remember what he looked like?"

The therapist rubbed his jaw. "Big guy, six foot something, balding. Scar on his face."

"Scar?"

"Yeah, along his jaw."

"What was he wearing?"

"Casual clothes. A plaid jacket and slacks."

The heavyset man in the lab coat flashed across her mind. "You sure he wasn't wearing a lab coat?"

"Only staff wear those, and I know he isn't staff."

An unsettling mix of fear and anger coursed through Amy. "Ever see him before?"

The therapist considered this. "No, I'd remember if I had."

"I guess that should have been your first clue. Meanwhile, if you ever see him again, keep him away from Cynthia Hadden and for godsake call security, me, and the sheriff's office."

On the way back up to her grandmother's room, Amy thought about what she'd just done. At no time prior would she have taken anyone to task, especially a professional. "What's happening to me?" Amy wondered.

When she returned to her grandmother's bedside, Amy could see that, although the older woman's color was deathly, the glaze that had coated her eyes for the last years was gone. The gray eyes were clear and focused intently upon Amy. But the pale lips trembled.

It was Amy who broke the silence. "Who was he?"

Cynthia's eyes flooded with tears and a hand slid across the bedspread, her icy fingertips gripping Amy's as she groped for the words. At last she whispered, "A killer."

CHAPTER 21

Dallas returned to the police station, and taking the stairs three at a time, pushed through the door, whipped past Debbie's desk, then reversed himself and did a double take. The raven-haired thirty-two year old had been his assistant almost eight years and he'd never seen a look on her face quite like this.

"What's wrong?"

She pulled off her glasses and looked up at him, shaking her head. "It's the Johnson case, Sheriff. It's scaring the hell out of me. Amy and I are good friends, so I've spent a lot of time thinking about this, trying to figure it out. So, if you don't mind, I'll just talk out loud for a minute."

Dallas nodded encouragement.

"First, an injured woman shows up at Amy's house and then vanishes. Seems like she's a twin Amy didn't know anything about. The family knew about it and believed the twin died at birth. There's no birth record, or any other record for that matter...and that's just plain weird."

Dallas nodded. "Go on," he said.

"Then, Amy's house is broken into by some thug who threatens to hurt Jamie if she doesn't get our investigation stopped. We've got zilch on that incident. Right after that, Amy's jerk of a husband decides this is the perfect time to dump her. So, he sends over a moving truck, cleans out the house, and absconds with his son on some unscheduled vacation. His sister, Nita, seems to have gone with him. We've got zilch on all of that."

Debbie looked up at Dallas. "Shall I continue?"

"You're on a roll."

"You find out from old man Hadden, the accident that killed Amy's parents was premeditated murder! To top things off, like all this isn't enough, old man Hadden's place gets torched, with him in it. At least we think it was him. Still waiting on that."

Debbie took a deep breath. "So, now my poor friend, Amy, has one single family member left who hasn't been harmed, killed, or threatened. That is until a couple of minutes ago."

Dallas bent over her desk. "No."

"Oh yes. Amy called it in. Some guy with a big scar on his face, got into Somerset and gave Cynthia Hadden a wheelchair ride in front a moving car. Amy managed to prevent the chair from being hit, but she's pretty upset and pissed off. The guy left some weird note."

Debbie rubbed her cheeks with the palms of her hands. "At the rate things are going, Sheriff, I'd say Amy's next. I'm terrified for her."

"You're not the only one. Where's she now?"

"Somerset. She said she'd be staying with her grandmother for a while. Wants to make sure Mrs. Hadden's going to be all right."

"Send Larson out there right away. We need to fingerprint the chair too," Dallas instructed her as he disappeared into his office. He called Amy's cell. Voicemail. He left a message telling her to stay put until he could get to Somerset. Next, he tried Somerset's Chief Administrator. His secretary took the call.

"He's not available right now, Sheriff."

"I need you to get a message to Amy Johnson. I understand she's with Cynthia Hadden. Please tell her to remain at Somerset until I get there. It could be a few hours, but it's important that she doesn't leave alone."

"Yes, Sheriff. I'll do that."

"I'm sending one of my deputies out to investigate the incident. We'll be taking prints from the wheelchair so please don't let anyone touch it."

"I think it might be too late, Sheriff. They put the chair back into the lobby with all the others. I don't know which it is."

Dallas groaned. "Do your best to find it."

He considered the case. It was definitely escalating. The meat cutter, Sven Werner, whose prints were lifted from the Taurus, was a dangerous criminal wanted on a string of violent crimes including murder. Dallas suspected it was either him, or one of his accomplices, who set fire to old man Hadden's house, leaving a charred body inside. If Dallas was right, he was dealing with a cold-blooded murderer who was upping the ante. Deb was right. Amy could be next. He needed to get her out of harm's way until this was over.

Werner was known to work in tandem with an ex-con named Jerry Lee Ray. Ray had served time for racketeering and assault and was wanted for conspiracy to commit murder.

So, Dallas thought, *what do we have? Two, maybe three potential killers that seemingly have no personal reason for the threats or the crimes they're committing. That usually means one thing. They work for somebody. The big question is, who?*

Debbie stuck her head around the door, interrupting his train of thought. "Sheriff, I meant to tell you, your daughter phoned. Twice."

Dallas jumped up. "Damn! I forgot."

"Maya said to let you know that she's at the McNaughton Rink. You can pick her up there."

Dallas grabbed his coat. "It'll take well over an hour to get to Portland," Dallas said, cursing loudly. "It slipped my mind completely. You wouldn't think a man would forget the thing he'd looked forward to all week."

Debbie handed him his hat as he breezed past her desk. Dallas had given her a name to check out. She'd penciled it on a sheet of paper and now sat, twirling her pencil between her fingers. "Dr. George Johnstone," she said aloud. "George Johnstone. Why does that sound familiar?" She touched AutoDial and waited for her mother to pick up.

The rink felt cold compared to the milder evening air outside. Dallas walked to the boards, his eyes following the small figure flying over the ice. Maya moved with amazing grace for a ten-year-old. She was building up speed for the dreaded axel, the jump with one and a half revolutions in the air. Dallas knew the setup well. He had dubbed it the *dreaded splatter,* as Maya seldom landed the damned thing and usually ended up in a bone-jarring heap on the ice. She had explained to him: "It's like jumping off the roof, Dad, but don't worry, I'll get it."

This time she under-rotated. Dallas winced as her right knee cracked against the ice. A second later, almost without losing a beat, she was back up and trying it again.

"Oh mylord." Dallas turned away, hoping with all his heart that she landed it this time, because she wouldn't quit until she did. Bone struck ice a second time. A couple of minutes later, he felt a cold breeze on the back of his neck as Maya flew past. "It's okay Dad," she called out, "I'll get this one for sure."

Grimacing, he turned to look. She was airborne. Steel cut ice and Maya landed it, barely. She glided toward him with a big grin and came to a fast T-stop. "There, that wasn't so bad, now was it?"

If she only knew.

Half an hour later they were at her favorite restaurant ordering enough Chinese food for three people, when his cell rang. Maya frowned disapprovingly as he answered.

"Wayburne."

"You're eating Chinese right?" Debbie chuckled.

"Almost. What's up?"

"Well, I might have something, and seeing as how you're in Portland, I thought I'd run it by you, maybe save you a trip back there."

"Shoot." Dallas noticed Maya was eavesdropping intently.

"I finally found out why *Dr. George Johnstone's* name was familiar. Ran it by my mother and she recognized it right away. He's the OB/GYN who delivered my aunt's twins back in 1980. And guess what, something went wrong during the delivery. My aunt almost lost her life. As it was, one of the twins died. Sound familiar, Sheriff?"

"Where was this? Portland?" Dallas leaned back in his chair as the server put huge platters of Chinese food in front of them. Dallas motioned for Maya to start.

"The first time she saw Dr. Johnstone was in Portland, but she delivered the twins in a Houston maternity hospital."

"Houston?"

"Uh-huh. My mother tells me that my aunt developed complications during pregnancy and Johnstone recommended she go there."

"Got anything on the hospital?"

"I'm working on it. But I did manage to locate Johnstone's wife. That's why I called. It just happens that Mrs. Vera Johnstone lives not too far from where you are right now. I called her before I called you, and asked to speak to *Dr. Johnstone*. She told me in no uncertain terms that he doesn't live there anymore and hasn't for years. I can tell you, she didn't appreciate the call."

"Did you identify yourself?"

"No way. If you've got a pen handy, I'll give you her address."

Dallas jotted it down. "Thanks, Deb." He put the cell back on the table and Maya reached over and turned it off.

"It's our time now, Dad. Work can wait." She lathered her egg roll in plum sauce and looked at him thoughtfully as she sunk her teeth into it. "Big case?"

"A real strange one," Dallas replied, spooning chop suey onto his plate. They ate eagerly and when they were finished they were both surprised to see three empty platters. Dallas checked the time. "Want to come with me on an errand?"

"Sure."

Dallas drove into an older neighborhood of expensive homes. Maya eyed them curiously. "Who lives here?"

"An older lady. Be right back," he told her after parking. He was only a few feet up the walk when he heard the truck door slam behind him. Maya ran to catch up. He threw his arm around her. "You were supposed to wait in the truck."

"If you're going to run errands on my time, Dad, you're going to have to put up with me trailing you around."

Dallas looked at the house. He didn't anticipate any problem, but he could almost hear his outspoken daughter adding her two bits worth. "Okay, but leave the talking to me."

"Sure thing."

The woman who opened the door was in her sixties, well dressed, with a cap of salon-coifed silver hair, flashy diamond earrings, vivid red nails, lots of rings, and an aloof demeanor. Even though she was half a foot shorter than Dallas, she appeared to look down at him. Maya's dislike for the woman was obvious. Her nose wrinkled as she looked Vera Johnstone up and down.

"Well?" Vera snarled.

"Mrs. Johnstone?" Dallas inquired.

"And you are?"

"An acquaintance of your husband, Dr. Johnstone—"

She cut him off. "Don't give me that crap. If you were anything of the sort, you'd know he hasn't set foot in this house for years." She started to close the door, but Dallas blocked it with his foot.

"You a nurse by chance, Mrs. Johnstone?" Dallas could see by her reaction that he had guessed right. "The way I figure it, you'd probably like to keep Dr. Johnstone's business away from your front door?" She gave him an icy glare. "Well, ma'am, the best way to do that would be to give me the Doc's address and I'll be on my way."

The woman was suspicious. "Who are you?"

"Let's just say I'm someone who can bring your past to life."

She regarded him nervously. "What do you want?" she hissed.

"Like I said, my business is with the Doc."

The woman's eyes darted from his face, down to Maya's, behind them to the pickup, and back to Dallas. "He lives on the coast. There's no real address—"

Dallas pulled pen and paper from his shirt pocket and thrust them into her hand. "The directions will do just fine," he said coldly.

She stalled. "I don't think I can—"

"Oh, I'm sure you can, Mrs. Johnstone, unless you want me to make this official."

Her eyes lingered on his momentarily, then she scrawled the directions onto the paper and flung it at him. "Now get away from here," she spat, slamming the door closed a split second after Dallas removed his shoe.

A second before it closed, Maya retorted, "What a bitch!"

"Hey!" Dallas admonished, hurrying Maya off the porch.

"Sorry, Dad, but I couldn't help myself."

A man should never mix family and business, but Maya had a point.

.

CHAPTER 22

Amy stayed with her grandmother long after the older woman had drifted into a troubled sleep. Although Cynthia Hadden had said nothing more, her words, *"A killer"*, echoed in Amy's mind and put cold fear in her heart. It was a profound statement from Grams, under the circumstances.

Her recognition of the man alarmed Amy even more. That meant her grandmother knew who he was. Was he the one who'd drove over her grandfather's legs and threatened her grandmother with Amy's life? Had he driven the eighteen-wheeler that killed her parents? Is that why Grams called him *a killer?*

Was he the one who'd broken into the house, threatening to hurt Jamie? Amy recalled the timber of his voice outside a few hours ago. *Are you hurt?* She couldn't be sure it was the same.

She had looked right at him. *The scar. Where is he now? What will he do next?*

Glancing out the window, Amy could see the sun low over the Pacific. Dallas had left her a message to wait for him. She rummaged in her purse, found the iPhone, and speed-dialed Dallas. Again the call went directly to voice mail. She tried his office. Debbie was on a meal break and the duty officer told her the sheriff was off duty. Then, Amy remembered Dallas saying he would be in Portland today, seeing Maya. Feeling suddenly very alone, Amy dropped the cell back into her purse.

She sat by her grandmother's side a while longer, decided to leave. She'd go directly to the cabin. As long as she wasn't followed from the lot, she'd be fine.

Not wanting to tempt fate by walking into the parking lot alone, she located two security guards and asked them to accompany her to the Jeep. It was quiet outside. No one seemed to take notice as the trio made their way down the walk and into the lot. Amy glanced around, and seeing nothing unusual, she climbed into the Jeep and pulled out quickly, heading down the hill and south onto the coast highway in the direction of Dallas's cabin. No one followed. The sun was low over the ocean. It was one of those clear evenings where the sky burst into reds and oranges, sharing the colors with the surface of the sea.

As she drove, she re-constructed the incident at Somerset Meadows and realized with a shock that it had been a *setup*. *It was staged to scare me, to warn me that they had their eyes on me, and my grandmother.* Amy twisted in her seat and her hands *went suddenly cold.*

Was Dan's disappearance related in some way? What if he and Jamie were caught up in this? After all, the sheriff's office had no leads on them, and that in itself was unsettling.

Feeling increasingly vulnerable, she glanced in the rearview mirror. No one was directly behind her, but there was a car a quarter mile back. Accelerating, she passed an old truck, and swung back into the southbound lane. A minute later the car did the same, making her uneasy. She passed by a brightly lit pullout. No other vehicles were there, so Amy didn't dare stop. She checked her mirror again. The car, now visible under the bright lights, was a black BMW, and it was directly behind her.

Surprisingly, there was very little traffic, enabling her to accelerate and put considerable distance between them. The Jeep dug deeply into the turns. Moments later, the BMW caught up and stayed right behind her.

She was bearing down fast on an old pickup that crawled down the highway. There was no time to brake so she swerved around it, almost shearing the side of the rusty truck as she skimmed past. Before she was clear of the truck, a car rounded a curve from the opposite direction. They were positioned head on.

Amy pushed harder on the accelerator and as she did so, the pickup increased speed, blocking her re-entry into the southbound lane. *Damn him!* The on-coming car loomed just ahead. *Hurry!* She put the pedal to the floorboards and the Jeep jumped ahead far enough for her to squeeze in front of the pickup. It braked sharply, horn blaring.

Heart racing, Amy looked in the mirror. The pickup had lost speed and the BMW remained behind it. For a while she was alone on the road and she told herself the whole thing was an incredible fluke. Then the BMW crept up behind her.

This time Amy slowed down and pulled onto the narrow shoulder, hoping the car would pass. Instead, it dropped back. She reduced her speed to 30 m.p.h. Two cars passed them. The BMW dropped back further.

Amy watched the mirror for another overtaking vehicle. A small car was approaching. She hit the gas and the Jeep fishtailed onto the highway in front of the car. A horn blared. Amy sped south on the snaking highway not daring to slow down until she was certain that she was alone on the road.

The worst section of the coast road was ahead. Both lanes narrowed as the highway cut into the rock bluff high above the Pacific. Two hundred feet below, the ocean surged around the rocks creating a churning cauldron known as The Devil's Bath. The sharp turns forced her to slow more than she wanted, but the BMW did not catch up, and she felt some relief.

As she approached a hairpin curve in the road, an eighteen-wheeler rounded the bend from the opposite direction. It swung wide, encroaching on her lane. Suddenly, it was directly in front of her. Amy braked hard, expecting it to veer back into its lane, but it didn't. It was coming right at her. *They were going to collide!* The image of her parent's mangled car flashed in her mind. *Dear God. No!*

Amy swerved hard left, into the oncoming lane, trying to squeeze between the truck and the rapidly approaching bluff. She prayed no one was coming. For a second she lost control. She clipped the side of the truck, sending the back end of the Jeep into a wild swing. The bumper tore into the bluff going into the curve, and the Jeep skidded crazily. Amy turned into the skid, over-reacted, and ended up sliding the wrong way down the highway. The tires lost their grip on the pavement and the Jeep struck the embankment, the impact spinning it around ninety degrees. It bounced to a stop facing the wrong direction.

Amy watched, horrified as the eighteen-wheeler collided head-on into the mountainside, metal and glass exploding in all directions. It bounced off, careened left, and tilted crazily before breaking through the guardrail. Then, it disappeared silently over the edge.

At the same second a car rounded the curve, horn blaring. The driver swung wide to avoid hitting her. Quickly, Amy re-started the Jeep, backed it around, and pulled onto the thin shoulder, on the ocean side. She jumped out, ran to the guardrail, and looked down.

The truck had impaled itself on the rocks, pieces of cab submerged in the foaming sea. If anyone was inside, there was nothing that could be done now.

A car whizzed by, the back draft blowing Amy's hair across her face. Turning into the wind to pull it from her face, she glimpsed the BMW. It was coming right at her!

Amy grabbed the broken guardrail and flung herself over it, her body flying out over the edge. She slammed into the gravel incline. She dug the toes of her sneakers into the loose rock. They gripped momentarily, then her feet began to slide. Using her knees to stop the downward momentum, Amy tried to pull herself up. Her right foot found a small perch and she used it to propel herself back up onto the rail.

The BMW was still on the wrong side of the road, moving toward her. Tires squealed as an Expedition loomed down upon it. The car diverted back into its own lane too late. The Expedition swerved hard, its side body striking the front of the car.

Using the distraction, Amy raced for the Jeep, dove inside, turned the key, and with tires screaming, she peeled from the scene. She shook so hard she could barely drive.

The Coast Highway curved inland, away from the sea, and descended into the river valley, now shadowed by tall trees and a gloomy sunset. Amy glanced nervously in the rear view mirror. Still no sign of the black BMW. Gripping the wheel with icy hands, she swerved onto the exit ramp, and sped south across the overpass toward the river flats. She was going so fast and was so distracted by what just happened, that she almost lost the Jeep on the curve.

Her heart pounded like a rock in her chest. One thing was clear. She was no longer being warned. She was now the target! A vile sense of danger sent cold fear surging through her bloodstream. It was hard to breathe. *No! This can't be happening.*

A glint in the rear view mirror grabbed her attention—headlights. The BMW! It careened down upon her at perilous speed. Before Amy had time to react, it struck the rear of her speeding Jeep. Amy fought to keep the truck on the road, but it was too late. The jeep shot over the embankment. The road disappeared. For seconds all she could see was the darkening sky. Then the Jeep pointed downward. A wide ditch opened up below. At the speed the Jeep was going, the impact would be fatal!

She threw open the truck door and leapt.

Everything became a blur as her body hurtled through the air. Then she dropped like a stone toward the soft, damp earth on the far side of the ditch. Even so, she hit like a sack of rocks, knocking the air out of her lungs. She panicked, unable to breathe. Pain ripped through her crumpled body, nauseating her. As she lay prone, fighting for air, she watched—like a spectator at a bad movie—as the front end of the Jeep embedded itself into the far bank.

There was an eerie sound of twisting metal. The hood crumpled and flew into the air. Then the windshield blew sending dirt, dust, and glass exploding around the truck. Finally the truck dropped into the muddy ditch, the frame twisted miserably, windows gone.

A strange muffled silence filled her ears. Then blackness. From its depths, she became acutely aware of approaching danger. A car door slammed. Amy lifted her head. The BMW was parked on the side of the road. A man lumbered through the tall grass toward the Jeep. She had to get away. But first, she had to get up. Her knees buckled repeatedly as she staggered into the brush. She wouldn't get far like this; she needed to find a place to hide. It appeared the driver hadn't seen her, so for now she had a small advantage.

Then, in the distance came an angry howl. The sound sent fingers of ice down her back. It was feral; the most terrifying sound she had heard in her life. *Get up. Get away!*

She tried to stand, but her right leg refused to support her. The left one sent hot spikes of pain shooting up her spine. She found a broken tree branch on the ground and used it as a cane. Behind her, heavy footsteps crashed through the undergrowth.

In the twilight she saw a small bluff and limped into its shadow, searching for a place to hide. Nothing. Loping on, she tried in vain to pick up speed. The heavy footfalls grew closer. Too close. She fell behind a stump, pressed her body between the roots, and pulled branches and ground cover over her, hoping the thin foliage would provide enough cover. She held her breath and fought down the panic of being in such a small space. The footsteps stopped. He was close. Very close. She could hear him panting and cursing. She could smell him—acrid and foul.

His hollow voice inflicted a suffocating terror of its own. "Ha! Bitch! Now we'll see what you're made of."

CHAPTER 23

Dallas pulled in front of his daughter's new home—a stately three-story residence on a hedged acreage overlooking the river and valley below. Thick front pillars made Dallas think of the White House. The family name was etched into the entrance post. It may as well have read *money,* as far as Dallas was concerned. "What's it like to be rich?" he asked Maya, driving around the curved drive and parking under the portico.

"Don't start on that, Dad. He's no different than anyone else—"she grinned, "except for the money."

"Yeah right." Dallas reached across to give Maya a goodbye hug. "Next week, same time?"

"No way. You're supposed to pick me up at three, remember?"

"Don't tell your mom."

Maya threw her arms around his neck and squeezed hard. "Love you, Dad."

"Love you too, Munchkin."

Dallas continued around the circular drive and then headed back across town toward Vera Johnstone's house. Something had bothered him when he was there earlier. The entire time he had been on Vera Johnstone's porch, he had sensed a presence behind her. Something wasn't right.

Turning down her street, he looked for a parking place well away from her house and then tucked his

139

pickup between two cars. No vehicles parked directly in front of the Johnstone house, making him think that whoever was in the house with her was either without a vehicle or, it was parked in the garage. He tucked his identification under the seat, as he had no jurisdiction in Portland. Not wanting to be seen in the dark, he turned off the pickup's interior light, got out, and quietly pushed the door closed. He strode down the street, turned up the driveway, and followed a sidewalk along the side of the oversized garage to where it joined the house. When he was at the house earlier, he'd noticed a side window on the garage wall.

Dallas flipped on his flashlight and directed its powerful beam onto the two cars parked in the garage. One was a Jag, the other a Bentley. The Jag's plate wasn't visible from his angle, but he was able jot down the Bentley's license number. It was his bet that the Jag belonged to Mrs. Johnstone, but who owned the Bentley?

Suddenly, the door beside him burst open and he stared down the dark hole of a .38. Two cold black eyes were leveled at Dallas.

"We shoot intruders where I come from." The man spat. His words shot spittle. "Who are you and why are you here?" A bony finger was on the trigger.

The man inspected Dallas coldly and Dallas did likewise. The man panted and his teeth snapped together repeatedly. A tic, Dallas guessed. "You first," Dallas replied taking a step forward.

"Don't come any closer!" The voice was powerful, belying the frail stature. The man was in his sixties, almost completely bald, sloping shoulders, concave chest, thin wrists, and skeletal hands. But the dark eyes were cold and calculating. He pursed his lips. "There's something about you—"

With one quick move, Dallas grabbed the barrel of the gun and yanked it upward, out of the man's grasp.

140

"Yeah, you too," Dallas said checking the clip and pointing the pistol at the man's kneecap.

The bald man looked down at the gun, then back up at Dallas. No fear or emotion showed in the eyes, but his teeth snapped rapidly now. "You won't shoot. I can see it in your eyes. You're Mr. Super Citizen. One of the high and mighty." More spittle. "I have no use for your type." With that, he stepped back through the doorway, into the house. The door slammed behind him.

Dallas stared at the door, his blood running hot. Only a few times in his career had he seen eyes so cold. Dallas had no doubts that the bastard would shoot to kill. Dallas fought an overpowering urge to kick the door down. His target was standing on the other side, waiting. Dallas could feel him there. The thought seared into his brain: *jurisdiction be damned!*

Exercising all the control he could muster, Dallas yanked his handkerchief out, wrapped it around the gun, and slid the pistol into his pocket. He left without looking back.

As he drove away, he pulled out his cell. He'd forgotten Maya had turned it off. He powered it up and called in the tags. The Bentley was registered to a corporation called *CellBIX,* a name that had media coverage attached to it, but he couldn't recall the context.

Next, he talked to Debbie. She sounded relieved to hear his voice. "I've been trying to get you, Sheriff. Amy's Jeep was found in a ditch off the 101, thirty miles south of here. It's totaled--hit the bank pretty hard. Deputy Matson says there was no way she was inside on impact or they'd have found her body. They figure she must have jumped clear before the crash, but they can't find her. A damaged beamer was nearby and the driver's whereabouts are unknown right now."

Dallas cringed. "So both drivers are missing."

"Right."

Dallas cursed under his breath. "Something's wrong with this picture. Both drivers missing? My gut tells me Amy's in serious trouble. Did they call in the dog?"

"They did, but Max is on an exercise over in the Mt. Hood area. Matson told them to get him back here pronto, but it's a four-hour drive. Meanwhile, Matson has our guys tracking without Max. It's dark, Sheriff. You know what that's like."

Dallas cursed, thinking of Matson's long history of serious blunders and mind-boggling screw-up's over the past few years. "Tell Matson not to bugger this one up, Debbie, or I'll personally nail his balls to his front door."

"I'll pass that along."

"If I remember right, Deputy Larson's off duty tonight."

"He's off duty, but I got hold of him a few minutes ago. He's going to head down there as soon as he can."

"Good."

"There's more, Sheriff."

He could hear her flipping through papers.

"An eighteen wheeler went over the bank and landed smack in the middle of the *Devil's Bath*. No word on any survivors, but it's unlikely." She took a deep breath before continuing. "And here's the clincher," She waited a beat. "Are you ready for this? The BMW that was found near Amy's Jeep is registered to Dr. George Johnstone."

"You're kidding."

"Blew me away when that came in."

Dallas told her, "Deb, it's absolutely imperative that they find Amy ASAP. Make sure Matson understands that."

"I will, Sheriff."

Dallas turned onto the overland highway and sped toward the coast. He cursed himself for not being there for Amy. She'd probably given up waiting for him. Deep down, in a place he seldom visited, he was terrified for her. She had become significant in his life. He had feelings for her, but he had no words for those feeling. All he knew was that he had to get to her *fast*.

When he arrived, the accident scene was lit and taped. Looking at the mangled Jeep, he wondered how Amy could have survived, even if she did jump clear. "Jeezuzcusser."

Matson and his deputies were milling around the scene when Dallas walked up. "It's just too dark to waste anymore time looking, Sheriff," Matson explained. "All we're doing is tromping potential evidence. We'll never find her tonight. Not without Max. Better to start fresh in the morning."

A mental vision of Amy running from a possible killer flashed through Dallas's mind. Matson had ignored the order pursue them with haste. "You stupid son of --! You see that car over there?" Dallas pointed to one of the cruisers.

"Yeah."

"Sit your fat ass on the front seat until we're finished here. I'll explain to you later how your future's going to play out."

"But my shift ended half an hour ago—"

"The hell it did." Dallas turned to his men. Smirks from the other deputies disappeared when they saw his thunderous expression. "Anybody else off shift?" He glanced around. No one spoke. "Okay. Let's go."

CHAPTER 24

In the black of night, his shout sent a sickening surge of fear and adrenaline surging through Amy's arteries. He was right behind her! She dodged. Two powerful hands reached out and grabbed her from behind. She flew into the air, hitting the ground a second later. She tried to roll away, but a steel-toed boot struck her ribcage, expelling the air from her lungs and sending pain shooting through her chest. He flung her over onto her back. "Ah-ha, a wild one. I like that," he laughed. Then, he dropped to his knees, positioning them across her thighs, pinning her to the ground under his immense weight, his kneecaps pressing heavily on her thighbones.

She swung at him with her fists, pummeling his eyes with all her strength, in an effort to blind him. Grunting, he grabbed her wrists with one meaty hand. With the other, he fished in his jacket pocket and pulled out a piece of twine. In one quick movement he lashed her wrists and tied a knot.

Amy writhed and squirmed beneath him. *This can't happen. God please! Don't let this happen! Help me to help myself!*

He threw his head back and laughed again, then his face appeared above hers, the scar flashing white against his whiskers, his sour breath hot on her neck.

A rough palm scraped her cheek and she recoiled. "Very beautiful." His hand ran down her neck, applying pressure on her windpipe. "And so fragile."

Amy choked, the blood rushing to her brain. Tears clouded her vision. She knew his hand would bring death. But first it would bring pain and with it, maybe, just maybe an opportunity to escape. His fingers closed over her esophagus and she choked uncontrollably.

He let go. She coughed and gasped for air. His hand began to move again, this time along her collarbone, then down over her left breast. "A body this perfect mustn't be wasted. Waste is sinful." He chuckled and dropped his mouth over hers, his teeth colliding with hers, his tongue pushing against them. Amy clenched her jaw. Her stomach contents rose to the back of her throat and she gagged. He pulled back. "Ah, a little resistance. We'll fix that."

Leaning back, he reached into his breast pocket and produced a long, thin knife. Unsheathing it, he held it up. The blade glinted in the moonlight. "Before my career in Special Security, I was a meat cutter," he informed her, as he examined the blade, stroking it. "and I enjoyed my work immensely." With a single motion the knife sliced through the air and he slit her top from neckline to hem. "I was very good at what I did."

He flicked the knife again, slicing her bra in half, exposing her breasts. "Ah, yes. My cuts are good, clean, very precise." He opened his mouth and dropped down to suck her breast. He bit down hard. Amy screamed, a sound of raw terror filling the night. Tears of pain streamed from her eyes. She tried to push him off with her bound hands. He grabbed her wrists and flipped her arms over her head, pinning them there with one hand. With the other he drove the knife deep into the ground beside her cheek, then he grabbed her other breast, and twisted hard.

Amy writhed, her screams forming a conduit for the pain—an escape route for the agony he imposed on her. Deep inside, beneath the pain, she could feel the burning desire for revenge.

Panting, he released her wrists and reeled back onto his knees to unzip his jeans. He struggled to lower them, his eyes boring into hers, perspiration beading his forehead, his body emitting a nauseating stench. He threw his weight onto one knee and lifted the other in an attempt to drop the jeans down his thighs. Amy watched and waited. The second the pressure let up on her legs, she twisted free and scrambled, crab-like, across the ground. When she managed to get her legs underneath her, she ran.

He groped for the knife, yanked it out of the ground, and staggered after her. His jeans slipped to his knees, restricting his movement. He stumbled and went down. "Bitch. I'll get you!"

Amy fled through the brush, running on adrenaline and raw fear, her feet flying under her. She dared not look back. She needed every precious moment of time and every ounce of energy to escape him.

The evening was silent except for the sound of her feet pounding the dry earth, her raspy breaths, and her thumping heart. For a while she thought she was free of him. Then, a cry broke through the darkness. "Whore, you can't escape me. I'm coming!"

Hoping her numb feet wouldn't fail her, she ran down an embankment, tumbled a few feet, pushed herself upright with her bound hands, and continued downward. She could hear him above her now. Breathless and exhausted, she ducked beneath a rocky ridge and froze.

He stopped above her and called out. "I know you're there."

WINTER'S DESTINY

She held her breath. The silence was absolute. There was not a breath of wind. Somewhere below, a river flowed. But around her, nothing moved.

Not even him.

She heard his boots bite into the dirt as he paced back and forth on the trail above her. He stopped. The minutes ticked by. Then, suddenly, he was on the move. She could see his dark form cutting diagonally along the bank above her. He stopped again, turned, and then worked his way back to the top. When she thought he was beyond hearing range, she crept in the opposite direction, continuing downward, slowly and carefully, taking care not to make a sound. One snapping twig or rustling leaf would give her away. Placing each foot softly, one below the other, she descended in a crouch toward the river.

Growing colder, she became aware that she was exposed from the waist up. To zip her jacket she had to free her hands, so she put the frayed rope to her lips and tugged at the knots with her teeth until they loosened. The rope fell away and she zipped her jacket before continuing slowly down the bank. She could hear the river now and guessed she must be about thirty feet above it. There would be no cover down there, so she would have to move quickly. She traveled a few more feet and peered down. Below her, the river glistened platinum in the moon's rays.

When the moon slipped behind the clouds, she darted around a large outcropping of boulders. The movement was too quick and her foot slipped between two rocks, dislodging one. It crashed downward. She froze, the sound deafening to her. He'll hear it! She listened for his footsteps. Nothing. *Where is he?* She had to get out of there!

Amy bolted down the incline. If she could get to the riverbank, she could gain speed. Even if he spotted her, she was sure she could outrun him.

147

Suddenly the earth broke away from underneath her. A small landslide of mud, sand, and rock cascaded down the final fifteen feet, to the riverbank, taking Amy with it, depositing her at the bottom in a heap of mud and rocks. The moon broke clear of the cloud cover, swathing her in brilliant white light.

A large boot landed beside her and an ugly laugh sent terror through her heart. She leapt back. He grabbed at her, but she was faster this time. Twisting away from his grasp, she fled across the bank.

Quicker off the line than she thought he'd be, he caught up with her, threw his arms around her and lifted her off the ground. "Got you now, Bitch."

Amy let fly with both arms and legs and gouged his eyes with her fingernails. As he dropped her, she drove her right knee into his groin. He howled like an animal and released her. Amy bolted across the bank.

He roared with rage and stumbled after her. Leaping into the air, arms wide, he tackled her, driving her to the ground. They rolled across the bank toward the river's edge. Amy could see the water fast approaching. *Good... or bad?* Good, she decided if she could break free of him when they hit the water. *Bad if I can't.*

Suddenly, they were completely immersed in the icy, fast flowing river. The shock caused him to release her. His feet found the rocky bottom and he struggled upright, chest deep in water, choking.

Amy tried to swim away, but he grabbed her long hair and dragged her back. She broke the surface and saw his face in the moonlight, eyes wild, saliva and river water running from his mouth.

He's going to kill me!

He lifted her out of the water, threw his head back, and shrieked in outrage. Then he pushed her into the river and held her there.

Amy was a strong swimmer and could hold her breath a long time, but she knew he wouldn't let her resurface. She kicked and fought his grasp. He pushed her deeper. Her lungs were bursting; she needed to breathe! *I can't hold on any longer. I can't.* She could see nothing, only blackness, then Jamie's sweet face appeared. She tried to reach for him, but he was too far away. She tried again, but he disappeared. Suddenly, she was drifting. Jamie reappeared above her and she tried once again to touch him. She needed to feel him, to know he was okay. She swam toward him, breaking the surface of the water, her starving lungs inhaling air and the river. Gasping and choking, she drifted downstream. She looked around her and saw that she was free of her assailant. He was gone. But the river current had caught her, forcing her downstream.

The current flowed faster as it dropped toward the gorge. Above her was the highway overpass; ahead was the open sea. In a few minutes the incoming ocean would surge upstream and meet the out-flowing river in a head-on collision of forces. Many people had been caught in the powerful undertow and drowned. She had to get out. *Now!*

But the river hurtled her into the mid-stream. Choking, Amy kicked hard and pulled with long, strong strokes in the direction of the bank, hoping to find a back eddy. She gained about ten feet, but knew at the rate she was moving that she would never make it. Using every muscle in her body, working each one to its limit, drawing on all her body strength, she swam for shore. She had to get there before she was carried into the gorge. There, the constriction threw the river into a frenzy of standing waves, overfalls, and powerful undertows. She could never fight them. They would sweep her away like a piece of driftwood.

CHAPTER 25

The night was silent except for the odd footfall and crunch of leaves. Occasionally the moon threw white light across the landscape, but when it didn't the team crept along, relying on their powerful searchlights. They moved systematically through the scrub, taking care not to destroy the subtle clues left behind. Whether it was a footprint in the soil, a hair caught on a branch, a leaf bent backward—each small clue created a trail for them to follow. Often they wasted many precious minutes on the wrong path and had to return to the last point and try another route.

Frustrated by their slow progress, Dallas unclipped his radio. "Where the hell is Search and Rescue?"

"ETA thirty minutes, Sheriff."

"That's what you said thirty minutes ago. Tell SAR that all they have to do is follow our yellow markers. When K-9 gets here, tell them we've got personal items from the vehicles so Max can pick up each scent. We need these guys here yesterday." Dallas re-clipped the radio, stopped in his tracks, and looked around. "We haven't seen anything for a good five minutes. We're going the wrong way."

A team member replied, "Maybe Sheriff, but we're doing a heck of a lot better than we did following Matson. He had us going the other direction entirely. No wonder we didn't find any trace of them."

"When it comes to Matson everything's a wonder," Dallas grumbled. "The real problem is that the entire SAR team *and* the K-9 unit went to Mt Hood for an exercise. Somebody's supposed to stay behind in case of an emergency."

Deputy Larson, who'd caught up with the team said, "When do we ever have an emergency, Sheriff?"

"Well what do you call this, a night hike?" Dallas barked in frustration and retraced his steps. The small footprints they were following belonged to Amy. The large imprints were made by a man's heavy boots. Dallas fought down the bitter taste that rose to the back of his throat. Judging by the size and pressure of the boot prints, he guessed her pursuer to be well over six feet and probably a good two hundred and seventy-five pounds. *Werner.* The markings indicated both of them were on the run. Amy was running for her life from this killer. Her only hope would be to outrun Werner, then use the darkness and groundcover to hide.

Dallas feared he and his deputies were too far behind her and much too late. Flashing his light across the ground he battled an impulse to race after her. He caught sight of a clearing on his left and moved quickly to it. Each of the deputies turned their lights onto the ground in front of Dallas. "Lordlovin..."

"Looks like he caught up with her, Sheriff." Larson commented.

Examining the impressions and markings left on the ground, Dallas could see there had been a struggle. He squatted down and shone his light over the area. *No blood.*

"Look over here, Sheriff."

Dallas stood. Two small footprints were visible. Two larger ones had stepped on them. "She's on the run again. Let's go."

With a dire sense of urgency Dallas pressed on, using as much speed as he dared without losing the trail.

Again he fought the desire to run, knowing that if he did so he would lose her trail instantly in the darkness. The minutes ticked by with excruciating slowness as they followed the footprints to the ridge.

Dallas didn't want to think about what had happened to Amy in the clearing. Instead, he concentrated on the fact that she had escaped the attacker and was once again on the run. His gut told him this man would kill her the second he caught her.

They had to catch up *fast!*

Larson interrupted his thoughts. "They went down the bank, Sheriff."

Dallas shone the light over the rocks unable to see which way she went. The team moved with care trying to sight a clue as to the direction. Suddenly a howl—angry and feral—shattered the night.

Dallas stepped off the ridge, half-running, half-sliding down the embankment, sending rocks rolling ahead of him. A second howl split the air.

Drawing his gun, Dallas scrambled down the bank. A second later he saw movement in the river. A large man broke the surface, dragging an object up with him.

Amy!

Never slowing, Dallas leapt down onto a rocky ledge as the attacker shoved her underwater and held her there.

"Freeze!" Dallas shouted. "Stand up with your hands over your head. NOW!" He aimed the barrel of the gun at the man's heart. "I said *now!*" He moved the gun a hair and fired a warning shot.

The man lurched sideways and disappeared into the river along with Amy.

Dallas catapulted off the ledge and raced down the grassy bank, his eyes on the slight figure drifting near the surface. She was almost midstream. He couldn't swim fast enough to catch up to her. The only hope was to run along the riverbank and beat her downstream.

Racing against time and distance, his feet barely touching the ground, arms pumping, lungs bursting, he fought to out-run her. Her head came up and her arms started to move lethargically. Suddenly, she saw him and started swimming toward shore.

Dallas looked up. The gorge was only twenty feet away. No time left! He threw off his heavy belt and boots and leapt from the bank into the cold river. The frigid water tore his breath away, but he was close to her. He grabbed her arm and started back to shore, but the current caught them. Suddenly they were flying downstream.

Into the rapids.

They were flung feet first into an overfall. It sucked them under and held them momentarily, then spit them out. They surfaced gasping for air. Amy had Dallas's shirt in her fist, but the forces against them were so powerful, the shirt was yanked out of her hand.

They were separated! Dallas felt it instantly and reached to catch her. He missed and dove for her, his hand clenching her belt. The deadly pull of the undercurrent caught them both and dragged them beneath the boiling surface. They somersaulted and tumbled, all the while being pushed deeper and deeper.

Amy slipped from his grasp again. Dallas felt his lungs bursting. He knew if they didn't surface soon, they'd drown.

His shoulder struck a boulder and Amy flew into him. He grabbed her as a strong upsurge of water catapulted them toward the surface. A second later they broke through next to a snag of logs and tree branches. Coughing, choking, Dallas knew this was their last chance.

He grabbed hold of a thick log and pushed Amy up over it. Exhausted, choking, their lungs full of river water; they clutched it, their strength gone. Dallas knew they had to keep going. "Work your way toward shore," he shouted over the roar of water.

With painful slowness they dragged themselves along the half submerged trees, the current pulling at their legs, trying to suck them back into the main stream.

Overwhelmed by cold and exhaustion, Amy slipped under water. Dallas caught her and pulled her back up, prodding her. "Come on, Amy, you can do it," he gasped. "Do it for Jamie!"

Deputy Larson appeared on the shore, followed by the rest of the team. They waded into the river and dragged Amy and Dallas the last few feet to shore.

Amy collapsed onto the ground. Dallas took the survival pack and a warm jacket from Larson. "Here," Dallas told her, stripping off some of her wet clothes. "Put this on before you get hypothermic." He pulled her to her feet.

Amy collapsed against him, her cheek pressed against his shoulder. She could barely stand. "Forget hypothermia," she said through chattering teeth. "I need a hug."

The hike back to the road seemed to take forever. A dry jacket helped, but wet jeans and the chilly night air prevented them from warming up. Dallas was cold to the bone. He couldn't see Amy's face in the dark, but he could feel her shaking as he half carried her slowly up the path.

Not far from the river, Max bounded toward them, followed by his handler, Greg. "We gave up on the markers, Sheriff, and followed the racket. Could hear you guys a mile away," Greg told them. "SAR is right behind us."

"I'm real glad you could make it," Dallas said sarcastically.

"Ah, come on, Sheriff, you know we go to Mt. Hood every year. It was just bad luck that we were needed here. It's never happened before." He looked at Amy. "You find both of them?"

Dallas shook his head. "The perp either swam away or got washed out to sea. Personally, I hope it's the latter. My guys are checking the riverbank. They've got his sweater, so Max can use that scent to pick up the trail, if there is one. Keep me posted. I'll be at the hospital."

Amy stopped walking. "No, I don't need the hospital. That monster didn't get a chance to rape me."

"You should be checked over anyway. The Jeep's totaled. You could have head or internal injuries."

"I jumped before the Jeep hit. Landed in the bog. I'll be okay, Dallas, really. The worst part is the cold."

"I agree with that. Keep walking," Dallas told her. "Search & Rescue aren't far away. They'll have dry clothes and hot packs."

CHAPTER 26

Less than an hour later, Dallas pulled off the 101 at the Coastal Pacific Resort and Spa and stopped outside the office. The truck heater was blasting and even though Amy had changed out of her wet clothes into a pair of drawstring pants, T-shirt, and fleece shirt provided by the Search and Rescue team, Dallas could see that she wasn't able to get warm.

"What are we doing here?" she asked.

"We've got to warm up. I'll be right back." The cold, wet jeans clung to him. Desk clerk Ira Florence found them fascinating. "Fly fishing, were we, Sheriff?"

"River rafting, Ira. In the dark. Sans raft. Give me one of those rooms with a spa."

"Sure thing, Sheriff. Just scrawl your damp Henry on the bottom line and the honeymoon suite's all yours." She slid the registration form and a key across the counter.

Dallas pushed the key back to her, "I don't want the damned honeymoon suite, Ira, just give me a room with one of those big, hot baths."

"Spa. We don't call them baths anymore." Ira glanced at the woman sitting in the sheriff's truck. "Here, take it, Sheriff. No extra charge." She held out the key. "Nobody deserves it more 'n you."

Inside the suite, Amy and Dallas found themselves staring into a huge spa built into a private glassed-in solarium, adjoining the suite. "It's the best way to warm up in a hurry," he told her turning on the taps. "You go first."

When there was no response he turned to look at her. "Amy?" Her pale skin had taken on a bluish hue. Her lips were chalky, her eyes bloodshot, and her hair fell in long, damp clumps down her back.

"No, you go ahead," she answered absently. She gazed into the adjacent bathroom, her eyes fixed on the tiny bottle of mouthwash that protruded from a basket of bath condiments. *He* had put his tongue against her lips and teeth. The vile taste still lingered. "I need to clean up." She left Dallas and walked into the bathroom. She popped the lid, and tipped the contents into her mouth, rinsing until the container was empty. Then she plucked the soap bar and shampoo from the basket, and walked around the corner to the shower. She felt...*filthy*. The fast flowing river had removed all traces of mud and sand, but not the feel of *his* hands on her skin. *The bastard!*

Shedding the clothing she'd been given, she turned on the shower, and stepped in. The lukewarm beads of water felt like needles on her cold skin. She stood directly under the showerhead and closed her eyes, soaking up the warmth and the feeling of *him* running off her. She shampooed her hair and scrubbed her body with soap, cleansing *him* away. Thank God she had the strength to fight him off.

Amy knew she was lucky to be alive. He was close to drowning her when Dallas fired his gun. What a strange feeling that had been. She had seen Jamie. *No...can't think about Jamie. Not right now.*

It was a long time before she finally turned off the water. Reaching for a bath towel, she wrapped it around her slender body and padded back into the solarium. To her surprise Dallas was sitting on the planter, still in damp jeans, staring at the tub, and looking like he was deep in thought. He looked up. On their hike back to the highway Amy had told him, in detail, what had transpired from the moment her Jeep struck the mud bank to the struggle in the river. She could almost see him going over it in his mind now. "Why didn't you go in the spa?" she asked. "You look frozen."

Dallas had filled the tub with warm water. Steam drifted over the surface. "Ladies first."

Amy shook her head at the simplicity of his response, yet it spoke volumes about the man who had waited in cold, wet jeans while she showered. Sitting tenderly on the tile surround, she swung her legs into the tub, immersing her feet. "It's quite hot."

Dallas tested the water. "It's comfortably warm," he told her. "Go ahead. Get in. Add more hot water as your body adjusts to the temperature." He turned to leave, but Amy caught his hand. He looked down at her questioningly. She recognized his intense look. Those blue eyes were searching again. His hand went to her cheek. She reached for it and held it there. The towel slipped to the floor.

His eyes traveled down her body.

Amy stepped into the tub. "Come on," she whispered. Amy tilted her head to look up at him and he saw angry red bite marks on her right breast.

"That son of a bitch!"

She glanced down, and seeing the teeth marks, scooped warm water over the raw flesh. "He'll pay for that, Dallas, I swear."

Sitting on tile surround, he reached out and lifted a wisp of hair from her forehead and studied her intently. Amy watched him. The tenderness of his expression tore her breath away. She grasped his wrist and tugged him toward her. "Dallas. Come in the water. Get warm."

"I'll shower first," he told her and disappeared into the bathroom.

158

Dallas returned a few minutes later, and plucking a washcloth from the rack, he slipped into the oversized tub to sit behind her. As he slid his legs around each side of her, the warm water rose to his chest. He lifted her hair over her shoulder, and dampening the cloth, he ran it tenderly over her skin. Cupping the water in his hands, he trickled it across her small shoulders and down her arm. He could smell the flowery scent of her hair and pulling it back, he ran his fingers through the fine silk, then let it fall, like a curtain down her back, before lifting it over her shoulder.

Amy closed her eyes and leaned back against him, allowing his touch to caress her. She was no longer cold. A new warmth flooded her body. She felt his cheek touch hers and his arms close around her. She turned, her lips touching his jaw, her fingertips reaching up to stroke his cheek. He pulled away.

"Timing's bad, Amy." he said getting up.

Amy grabbed his arm. "Timing?" she repeated, her eyes searching his. "How can you say that? If you hadn't pulled the trigger the second you did, I wouldn't be here. The bastard would have drowned me. And, if you hadn't dragged me out of the river at the exact moment that you did, I'd be floating out in the Pacific by now. Your timing is perfect. I'm alive."

She tugged on his arm until he sat back down. He swallowed hard and looked away. Amy waited for him to look back at her.

"The river had turned dangerous by the time you jumped in. You've risked your life for me. That's twice counting the fire. It's almost incomprehensible that you'd do that once, never mind twice." Her voice was choked with emotion. "You gave me another chance to live, to be with my son," she whispered, "and to do so much more with my life than I have. You're a brave, selfless man, Dallas. And I'm so grateful…"

She half-turned, her gray eyes intent upon him. "When I was in the river, I promised myself that if I got out...I would find Jamie and start a new life."

Amy reached up and put her hands around his neck, drawing his face close to her own. She kissed him softly.

Turning to face him, she felt his hands pressing on the small of her back, pulling her into his embrace. His lips brushed her cheek, and her lips. Suddenly, she was being lifted out of the water. He let her feet touch the bath mat, and with gentle strokes, dried her with one of the thick white towels. Then, he carried her to the bed and placed her gently on the duvet.

His body, muscular and lean, pressed against hers, his hands caressed her, and suddenly she drifted into a strange new world of sensations. Her body reacted to his touch in ways she never believed possible. She wanted him.

They became one and the move tore her breath away, launching her into a world of color, emotion, and sensations not of this earth.

Afterward, near dawn, she slept nestled in the crook of his arms, her cheek against his chest, his heart beating in time to her own. She dreamed that she found Jamie.

CHAPTER 27

Amy awoke to find his pale blue eyes gazing at her. "Morning," she whispered sleepily.

"You're beautiful," Dallas murmured, his eyes never leaving her face. The morning sun filtered into the room, dancing over the golden strands of hair and across her translucent skin. He stroked her hair, wondering what was happening to him. He had loved Ellen and believed himself incapable of ever loving another woman. But now he found himself looking at the face of a woman who had captured his heart. How exactly had this happened?

Dallas placed his lips gently over hers. A strange mix of emotion flooded through him. He wanted to protect her, to care for her, and to carry her away to a safe place where no harm could come to her. He wanted to be with her every minute. He craved her touch, her smile, and her embrace.

Suddenly, he was walking new terrain and contending with emotions, desires, and needs foreign to him. He thought he knew himself, but he realized that a man could never really know himself. Things change, and before you know it, a man finds himself in uncharted territory wondering if his body and mind are betraying him or whether he's at a crossroad, with a new life waiting for him.

"What are you thinking, Dallas?"

161

He pushed a lock of her hair off her face. "I'd like to spend the whole day here, with you."

She smiled. "I wish that were possible. Maybe we should plan that for a day down the road, when things are normal again."

Dallas sat up. "Hm. Normal. What's *normal,* I wonder." He sat up. "Hungry?"

Amy slipped out of bed. "Now that you mention it, I am."

He watched as she walked to the shower. She was exquisite. Her long straight back gave way to a tiny waist that rounded out over the soft curve of her hips. A single tress of long, wavy hair cascaded down her back. She moved gracefully on slim, shapely legs. Her arms were slender; her hands and fingers delicate. She half turned and smiled at him. His eyes traveled back up her body, along her neck, to the perfect structure of her facial bones. Her beauty was breathtaking.

While they dressed, Dallas said to her, "I don't understand how your husband could leave you."

Amy shrugged.

"Do you love him?" Dallas asked.

She looked up in surprise. "I did, in the beginning." She thought for a few minutes. "Dan changed a lot after Jamie was born. He pulled away from me. Time passed and after a while, my feelings for him began to diminish." Amy sat down on the bed and put on her socks. "Our marriage mutated into a routine. At some point Dan's career, his personal life—and it seems his sex life, were fulfilled outside our home. *Home* to Dan had become a place where he stored his things, including Jamie and me." She looked away, thoughtfully. "The other night, when Dan left me, I should have felt a huge sense of loss. I admit, I felt a lot of things, but *loss* wasn't one of them. In fact, I felt relief. That really surprised me."

162

Dallas was thoughtful. "Did you know him for long before you were married?"

"Couple of years. We met at university"

"Did he introduce you to his family?"

Amy rubbed her eyes. "His sister Nita, of course. She's the only family he has."

"Where are his parents?"

"They were killed when Dan was a teenager."

"Like yours." It was a statement, not a question.

Amy looked up at Dallas. "Yes."

"That gave you a common bond."

"Yes, I suppose."

"Did Dan ever talk to you about his parents?"

"No. He didn't like to talk about them."

"And he probably didn't like you talking about yours either."

Amy stayed very still. "What are you saying, Dallas?"

"Did you ever meet any of his other relatives, you know, cousins, aunts, uncles?"

"No," she said hesitantly.

"Friends from his childhood?"

"No," Amy repeated.

"Didn't that strike you as unusual?"

"Not really. A tragedy like that is devastating. It kind of knocks you out of orbit. Nothing in your life is normal after that, so how do you judge what's *unusual?*"

Dallas sat down, his forearms resting across his knees.

"Dallas, what is it? "

He was silent, his thumbnail rubbing his brow. Abruptly he stood. "Let's go for breakfast. I'm starved."

"I can't go out dressed like this. I look like a vagabond."

Dallas laughed. "You look just fine." He pulled her toward him and kissed her, "In fact, you look wonderful."

They walked through the state park and down the boardwalk, the sun-bleached wood shifting ever so slightly under their weight. They stopped to watch the breakers roll onto the beach. Rays of morning sun bounced from the mist that hovered above the break line, creating a rainbow. Above, gulls circled, their cry audible over the roar of the sea.

"This is one of my favorite places," Dallas told her, putting an arm around her shoulders. "I came here a lot after Ellen and I split up. There's something about the place." He rested his right foot on the log bench. "Did a lot of thinking right here. We'll have to come back, Amy, when things settle down.

Amy noticed his introspective look and wondered if he was recalling the insights he had gleaned here.

Finally, he said, "Ellen was my whole life. I couldn't visualize a future without her."

"*Time*," Amy told him. "It changes everything. No matter how great the loss, time heals us enough so that we can *feel* again."

He turned her around and put an index finger under her chin lifted her face to his. "The strange part is, what I feel now, for you, I never felt with Ellen."

Amy reached up and touched his hand. "I know. I kind of feel that way too. I co-existed with Dan. After he left, I thought back over our time together and realized our relationship as man and wife had disintegrated completely. I'd stopped loving him, but he had to leave me before I could face that fact." The breeze blew her hair across her eyes. She brushed it away. "I have feelings for you that overwhelm me, but my life is in such a mess right now--"

"I know." Dallas guided her back onto the sandy boardwalk. "You're doing great, considering."

They walked, arms around the other, to the door of *The Sunset Café, a* small beachfront restaurant on the sand. They climbed the driftwood steps to the wide covered balcony and pulled open the weather-beaten door. "I met Nita here for lunch once," Amy told Dallas as he led her across the shiplap floors to an alcove overlooking the bay. They squeezed around the small table for two and sat down.

Dallas slid the vase of fresh flowers to the side of the table. "Were you close to Nita?"

"Not close, no. She and Brandon weren't able to have kids of their own, so they wanted Jamie to stay with them as often as possible. I was never was happy about that, but Dan insisted. I never did spend much time with them. Occasionally, Nita and I would go shopping together, or to a cafe. Once in a while she and Brandon came to supper. That's about it. She's not a warm, fuzzy person. In fact, she's so tainted, it's hard to have a normal conversation with her."

Dallas looked at Amy thoughtfully. "Did Nita ever discuss her parents?"

Amy shrugged. "No, she and Dan were alike that way. Neither of them would open up." Amy adjusted her chair so she could see the ocean. "But that's not an unusual response."

"What about you? Is it hard for you to talk about your parents?"

"Depends. After they died it was a long time before I could function like a normal human being. Talking about it takes me back to that dark time. I don't like going there unprepared."

The waitress brought them two Ship's Logs that served as a binder for the menus, and Amy realized that she was famished. They ordered Captain's breakfasts and coffee. She looked at Dallas and tilted her head. "Why all these questions about Dan's parents?"

"I'm trying to work things out."

The waitress put a carafe of coffee and cups between them and returned a few minutes later with their breakfasts. Dallas reached for the salt, shaking it furiously onto his eggs and hash browns.

Amy watched in amazement. "Wow."

"What?"

"Don't you ever worry about high blood pressure...or worse?"

"Hell no. Blood pressure's not even on the list." he said digging in.

Avoiding the salt and pepper altogether, Amy picked up her fork and took a bite of bacon. "What's on the list then?"

Dallas laughed. "Getting shot, or stabbed, or totaling the Yukon in a chase, you know, stuff like that," he told her.

Amy nodded, "I guess they would take priority. How long have you been Sheriff?"

"Fifteen years."

She saw the pride in his expression. "You love your job, don't you?"

"Most of the time."

They ate in silence and when they were finished, Dallas reached for her hand. "There's something you need to know about your husband, Amy. I've been trying to find a gentle way to say it, but there isn't one."

Amy stiffened. "What, Dallas?"

"In my line of work coincidences don't exist. When I found out that a Dr. George Johnstone was your mother's OB/GYN, I got that old feeling in my gut."

Amy nodded, "I know. It bothered me too. But both versions of the name are pretty common."

"How about two OB/GYNs with almost identical names?" Dallas suggested.

"It's seems pretty unusual," Amy agreed.

"All right. I'm going to say this straight out, so here it is: your husband, Dan Johnson's birth certificate reads, Daniel Oliver Johnstone. His name was legally changed when he was seventeen."

Amy fell back in the chair and gaped at Dallas.

CHAPTER 28

Dallas pulled up in front of a local family clothing store and outfitters. Amy looked at the display in the window. After what she'd just heard about Dan's name being changed, Amy was in no mood to shop. She looked at the storefront. "Let's go, Dallas. I don't feel like buying clothes right now."

"Go on," he encouraged, "You need something to wear."

She tugged at her jeans and coat. "I won't be long." She grabbed new jeans, sweaters, a bra, panties, socks, and a pair of sneakers, and was back in the truck in twenty minutes.

Dallas was shocked. "That must be a record."

Amy dropped the shopping bags into the rear seat and reached for his arm. "Dallas, I've got the feeling you know more than you're saying."

He started the truck. "Well, I can tell you this. I was in Portland yesterday, seeing Maya. While I was there, I learned that Dr. George Johnstone's wife, Vera Johnstone lives there. So, I dropped by. She's not exactly the warm, fuzzy type, either, even though she used to be a nurse. Anyway, to make it brief," he said, pulling out, "she confirmed that Dr. George Johnstone is her ex-husband, so while I was driving back, Deb did some checking for me. Vera Johnstone is Dan's mother—"

Amy finished the sentence: "And they're both very much alive." Amy drummed her nails on the door panel. "All these years I believed that Dan, like me, had lost his parents."

"If it's any concession, not having known Vera Johnstone is a real plus. She's one cold, calculating piece of work. It's a wonder Dan turned out as well as he did."

Amy speculated, "If she was a nurse, she could have assisted her husband with child births."

"Very likely. The two have been separated some time, but I did persuade her to tell me where her husband is. Turns out, he has a place down the coast, near The Caves."

Amy's eyes widened in surprise. "He's here, on the coast? I wonder just how much Dan and Nita have seen of their supposedly *dead* parents over the last seven years." Amy wound her hair around her finger and gazed out the window. "No wonder you were asking me questions about Dan's parents." Thoughtfully, she asked, "Do you think Dan and Jamie are staying with Dr. Johnstone?"

"Possible. My hunch is Dan's close by. Doesn't look like he flew anywhere and he's not the kind of man to drive far. I figure Nita and Brandon are also at some prearranged location, close by."

The surprise showed on Amy's face. "All they'd have to do is go where nobody knows them, and presto, anonymity."

Dallas pulled up in front of his apartment. "We're still missing the key to this puzzle. That key is the piece that will open the doors and give us answers. I have a few theories, but nothing concrete." They sat quietly for a few minutes, each deep in thought.

Amy's brain was whirling. "Dallas," she said, "Do you realize the implications? We know that Dr. George Johnstone delivered my twin and me. So how in godsname did I happen to marry his son. And to top that, none of us knew it, except Dan's family."

Dallas shook his head. "I couldn't figure that either. It's something your going to have to ask Dan."

Angrily, Amy rapped the truck door. "I don't know why, but I feel like I was setup and used by all of them."

As they hiked up the stairs, Dallas warned her, "I'm a terrible house keeper. I was going to say, make yourself comfortable, but it's such a mess, I don't think that's possible." He unlocked the door for Amy.

She stepped inside and looked around, aghast. Newspapers were stacked on the table, clothes were strewn across the back of the chairs and over the couch, she groaned aloud at the sight of the takeout containers and dirty dishes that littered the countertops and filled the sink.

"I know. I need to hire a service," Dallas said, closing the door behind him.

"I should design a little house for you," Amy said. "A place you could enjoy coming home to. Then you'd be motivated to keep it tidy because you'd be happy living there."

Dallas smiled. "Sounds nice. I bet you draw houses in your sleep,"

Amy's face brightened a little. "I actually do. I was born to draw houses and landscapes. I started putting images on paper at the age of two and I can remember drawing floor plans in my head before I started school. I'm one of those people who are *compelled* to do what I do. I get the greatest sense of fulfillment from designing buildings that suit their setting and make their owners happy."

"Well you've sure left your mark."

Amy's eyes lit up. "You haven't seen anything. The residence I'm working on right now will redefine West Coast living. That is, if I ever get back to work and get it finished. The budget is over twenty million dollars."

Dallas whistled. "Twenty million. What does the owner do—rob banks?"

Amy laughed. "A cop's suspicious mind. He's a scientist of some kind. But to look at him, you'd never guess he has a dime."

"Hmm. Since when can a scientist afford a twenty million dollar house?"

Amy poked him. "There you go again. He's owns some big bio-pharmaceutical company. It trades on the NASDAQ."

"No wonder prescriptions cost so much," Dallas grumbled, reaching in his pocket. He pulled out a key ring. "Here's the apartment key," he said, pulling it off the ring. "In case you go out. Which I hope you won't. No point in me telling you again how dangerous that is."

Amy assessed him. "If you're going to Johnstone's place, Dallas, I'd like to come."

He shook his head. "Sorry, Amy, that's not possible. I'll call you later," he said, pulling her into his arms.

CHAPTER 29

Amy located the stacking washer/drier set in Dallas's apartment and threw in the damp clothing she had worn the day before. Touching them triggered vivid, terrifying memories of her encounter and near rape. She could still smell *his* sour breath. The memory of *his* hands made her skin crawl. His teeth biting into her breast was excruciating. Her body ached from head to toe, and the memory haunted her.

Pouring soap into the dispenser, she dropped the lid, and turned the dial to the heavy-duty cycle. She didn't want a trace of *him* left behind.

Wearing one of Dallas's shirts, Amy padded back down the hall into the living room. The apartment was a stark contrast to the tidy, cozy cabin Dallas loved so much. The small area appeared to serve him while he was working. It wasn't home.

She went to the scarred desk in the corner of the living room where Dallas kept his laptop. She put her fingernail on the lid and tapped it. Her laptop hadn't survived the accident. While she considered using Dallas's, she noticed a scrap of paper with the name *VERA JOHNSTONE* printed neatly across the top. Below, was an address in Portland. Amy held the paper in her hand, her mind whirling. Vera Johnstone. The woman could give Amy answers to her growing list of questions.

Amy changed into her new clothes, grabbed her jacket, her battered purse, and iPhone, which one of the deputies had salvaged from the Jeep. She took care to lock the door behind her and walked stiffly down the wooden stairs. The car rental agency was only two blocks away.

Amy rented a Sportage SUV and then headed across town to see Walt Marshall, an old friend of her grandfather's. Walt collected guns and she needed some protection. The *monster* was out there somewhere and she didn't want to fall prey to him again without being able to defend herself. The hard part was, she hated guns. She'd never even allowed Jamie to have a toy gun. When Nita bought him one, Amy tossed it in the trash.

"What kind of gun do you want?" Walt asked skeptically.

"Something small that'll fit in my purse." *And hopefully I'll never have to use.*

He pulled out a 32-caliber semi-automatic Beretta and handed it to her. Amy took it reluctantly. It was small and cold in her hand. "It's the right size, but is it easy to shoot?"

"Sure. No kick either. Good little weapon for a lady."

"I need bullets too." Amy could barely believe she had just said that. And if you could show me how to load it, and what to do with it, I'd appreciate it." *So I don't shoot myself, or worse, the wrong person.*

"Sure thing." Walt ejected the magazine from the pistol, showed her how to load the bullets, and re-inserted the empty clip, "Now," he said, "Just remove the safety, aim, and pull the trigger. And just so you know, you can carry the gun on your belt, but if you put it in your purse, you're supposed have a license to carry a concealed handgun. You can get one at the Sheriff's Department."

Great.

Walt finished by telling her, "And one more thing. Don't tell a soul where you got this thing."

I won't even tell anyone I've got it. "Don't worry. I won't. Thanks, Walt."

Almost two hours later, Amy was in Portland looking at a gray Tudor home. As she parked, one of the three garage doors lifted and a Bentley backed down the drive. As it whizzed past her window, she caught a glimpse of the driver--an older man with wire-framed glasses on a beak nose. Pale hands and bony fingers gripped the wheel. It was difficult to see him through the car's tinted glass, but he looked naggingly familiar.

Amy went to the front door and rang the bell. A moment later, Vera Johnstone, appeared, flashing bracelets, rings, and long earrings.

"Alesha! What are you doing here? You're supposed to be—never mind. Come in." She stepped aside. Surprised by the woman's reaction, Amy walked into a vast vestibule. *Alesha. Gramps said her twin's name was Alesha. Dallas had also mentioned that a woman named Alesha Eickher had rented the Taurus. So, I know for certain I have a twin and her name is Alesha.*

Vera Johnstone motioned Amy into the huge kitchen. French doors looked out over a blue kidney-shaped pool sparkling in the sunlight. A circular Jacuzzi spa formed the shallow end. Vera motioned to a chair. "Sit, if you want. Tell me why you're here, Alesha."

Amy stood where she was, noting Vera Johnstone's brisk manner, aloof demeanor, and unpleasant attitude. "Why are you surprised to see Alesha, Mrs. Johnstone?"

The woman's mouth dropped. For a moment, she was speechless. Then her eyes narrowed and she looked Amy up and down. She said flatly, "You're Amy."

"Where's Alesha, Mrs. Johnstone?"

"None of your business." The woman grabbed Amy's arm and tried to maneuver her toward the front door. "Get out of here. You're not welcome in my house."

Amy pulled away. "It is my business. She's my twin. And from what I hear, you helped deliver both of us, thirty-two years ago, in Beaverdale."

"You've got no proof of that."

"What did you do with my sister, Mrs. Johnstone? Did you sell her?"

Vera guffawed. "You've got to be kidding. You don't know anything. And it's going to stay that way."

"What about Dan. Does he know?"

"There's nothing to know. Now leave." Again Vera tried pushing Amy out of the room.

Amy twisted away. "Take your hands off me, Mrs. Johnstone. Don't ever touch me again." Amy moved an arm's length away from the woman. "I came here for answers and I'm not leaving without them."

"Haughty aren't we? Too bad Dan had to settle for you."

"And how is that?"

"Water under the bridge."

Amy could see she was getting nowhere. The woman was too sure of herself. She had no intention of talking. Amy looked around for photos, anything that might give her some insight. She stepped into the dining room and glanced around. Sitting in a polished display case was a beautiful Ming vase. Amy recognized it's worth immediately, opened the glass door, and plucked it off the ebony shelf.

Vera followed her into the dining room. "Hey, what are you doing? Put that down!"

Amy turned slowly back to Vera. "Is Dan here?"

"Of course not. Give me that!"

"Where is he? And where's my son, Jamie?" Amy watched the woman closely. She could see from the blank look on the woman's face, Vera didn't know.

"How the hell would I know? I've never laid eyes on your son. Haven't seen mine either, for years."

Amy could barely imagine a mother saying that. "Obviously you've seen Alesha."

"Except for a few days ago, it's been years. I have no interest in her."

Amy was sure that was the cold truth. She needed to try a different tack. "Why was Dan's name changed?"

"Why do you think? We didn't want anyone making any connections. Particularly you."

Amy took a breath and exhaled slowly. Then she lowered her voice, "What happened to Alesha after she was born?"

"Ha! You must be kidding. You think you can just walk in here and demand information from me—NO! Don't!"

Amy raised the Ming vase above her head.

"Don't let go, for godsake! It's worth a fucking fortune. All right! We took her to the facility in Paraguay."

"Paraguay! A facility. What kind of facility?"

Vera's eyes were glued to the vase. "A bio-developmental research center. George, the greedy bastard, got suckered into the whole damned affair. We wanted out. Figured the less we knew the better. We didn't ask questions."

Amy was appalled. "Are you saying my twin spent her life in some institution in South America?"

"Apparently."

Amy studied Vera Johnstone. She and her husband had abducted her sister. And they were likely well paid for it.

"Don't judge me." Vera spat out. She reached up for the vase, but Amy leapt back. She knew she wasn't going to get much more out of this woman, Ming vase or no Ming vase so she had to choose her final

176

questions wisely. If she could find Alesha, she might find Jamie. "Where's Alesha now?"

The woman grew impatient. "Who knows? The only reason I found out she was here, in the U.S., was because they called me last week. They said Alesha was hurt. George, the stupid bastard, was drunk. So they demanded that I attend to her. Like I wanted any more to do with any of that whole damned mess."

"Where did you do that?"

Vera said flatly, "My ex-husband's clinic."

Amy's eyes widened. "Are you saying your husband, George Johnstone is still a practicing OB/GYN?"

"Old quacks die hard, but I doubt he actually works anymore, the worthless drunk."

"Where's the clinic?" Amy asked.

Vera Johnstone grew angry. "That seems to be the fifty million dollar question these days. It's down the coast, by The Caves."

Amy knew the area. She'd been on the design team for The Cliff House, which was near The Caves. Hopefully, Dallas would find it. "Who asked you to help Alesha?" Amy asked.

"You know, the goons who work for Helmut."

"Helmut?" Amy's thoughts flew to the project she was working on. The owner's name was *Helmut*—what was his last name? Amy couldn't recall. She asked, "Helmut who?"

Vera Johnstone had let his first name slip out. She'd realized it immediately and held back, calculating the risk.

Amy kept the vase held high and stared her down. "Last chance."

"Eickher."

The Ming vase slipped from Amy's grip.

CHAPTER 30

On the road back to Sanville Amy tried to put the pieces together.

Helmut Eickher!

No wonder the name was familiar. Her current project, the twenty million dollar house she was designing, was for none other than Helmut Eickher, a man she had met only once, briefly. She remembered the project manager saying the owner had specifically requested Amy. But *why?*

Meanwhile, she now realized it had been Helmut Eickher that she had seen back the Bentley from Vera Johnstone's garage. Now, Amy understood why he had looked familiar. *But why was his car parked inside Vera Johnstone's garage? Was he staying with her? Were they friends, or were they a couple?*

Amy tried to figure out why Helmut Eickher's *goons,* as Vera Johnstone had aptly named them, were so intent upon harming Amy and her family.

So, who exactly is this Helmut Eickher?

According to Dallas, a woman by the name of Alesha *Eickher* had rented the Taurus. *And why does my twin have Helmut Eickher's surname!*

Amy rubbed her eyes. She was tired. No, way beyond tired…exhausted. The road blurred and the SUV slipped onto the shoulder. She swerved back onto the asphalt. Her body screamed for rest, but her mind wouldn't allow it. The need to find Jamie was a driving force pushing her on relentlessly.

Amy forced her thoughts back in time once more. *Mom and Dad were killed right after Alesha's telephone call, sixteen years ago. Soon after, two men attacked Gramps at his cabin and drove over his legs. Then, they threatened Grams with my life. Had those brutal, horrific crimes been committed by Eickher, or his goons, sixteen years ago?*

Now, sixteen years later, the cycle is repeating itself. Like the last time, Alesha has appeared. And once again, our family is in the middle of a nightmare: Dan has left, taking Jamie with him; Nita and Brandon are nowhere to be found; Gramps' house was burned down, likely with him in it; Grams was pushed in front of a car; and the only reason I'm alive is because of Dallas.

What horrific evil surrounds this man, Helmut Eickher? What is so important that he will murder to protect it?

The digital clock on the dash read 8:15 p.m. If Dallas had returned to the apartment, and found her gone, he'd be worried.

Pulling out her iPhone, Amy put in his cell number. He answered on the first ring.

"Amy! Where are you? I've been going crazy worrying."

Amy was taken aback by the concern in his voice. "It's been a long time since anyone besides Gramps has told me that. I went to see Vera Johnstone. I'll tell you about it when I get back, but there's a name I was hoping you could checkout. It's Helmut Eickher." She spelled it. "He backed his Bentley out of the garage just as I arrived. Thought I recognized him. It seems he's the owner of the design project I'm currently working on."

"The twenty million dollar one?

"Exactly. You were right to be suspicious."

"Describe your client."

"Thin, short, late sixties, bald…thick glasses…" she hesitated, "and dark eyes. They're black, but they're so—"

"Cold."

"Yes." A chill went through Amy as she recalled the way he'd looked at her when they'd met. "I only met him once. I work with the project manager. The project itself is owned by a corporation."

"Not CellBIX by any chance?"

"Yes, that's it." Amy said with surprise. "How'd you know?"

"Saw the Bentley parked in Vera Johnston's garage, yesterday. Ran the tags. Car's registered to a company called CellBIX."

"CellBIX," Amy repeated thoughtfully. "Vera told me that she and her husband took my twin Alesha to Paraguay right after she was born. They took her to a bio-medical research facility there. Considering Alesha has Eickher's last name, do you think there might be a connection between the facility and CellBIX?"

"Could be. We'll see what we can find out."

"Another thing," Amy told him, "I think the meat cutter and his friend work for Eickher."

"Kind of figured that," Dallas said, "But what I don't understand is, why Eickher chose *you* to design him a house. We're missing something."

Amy agreed. "I can't figure that out either." Amy changed the subject, "By the way, did you find George Johnstone?"

"The directions were a dead end. Literally. We spent hours looking, but no luck. I'm on my way back to the apartment now."

"Me too. See you soon, Dallas."

CHAPTER 31

Turning off the highway at Sanville, her mind still reeling from her encounter with Vera Johnstone, Amy missed her turn and found herself near Nita's house. On impulse she turned down the street, switched off the headlights, and let the Sportage roll along the curb until the house was visible.

As Amy expected, the building was dark, most of the blinds drawn. What she didn't expect was to see Nita's Camry on the drive.

A narrow shaft of light moved inside the house, near the entry. The front door opened and Nita stepped outside, dragging two huge suitcases. She locked the front door, deposited the luggage into the trunk of her car, backed down the drive, and drove off.

Without switching on her headlights, Amy followed about a block behind. When they reached the main road, she turned on her lights but stayed well back. Nita turned into Burgers'nMore, pulled up to the take out window, and a couple of minutes later, parked on the side of the lot.

Amy made her move. She jumped out of the SUV. A second later, she swung open the car door and slipped into the passenger seat of the Camry.

Nita's eyes grew large as they settled on Amy. "What the—"

Amy turned toward her. "Put your burger down and start the car."

Reluctantly, Nita pulled from the lot.

"Now, head for the 101."

In shock, Nita did as she was told. "Where are we going," she asked nervously.

"To your father's house."

Nita glanced sideways at Amy, her initial surprise passing. "I don't know what you're talking about."

Amy was suddenly furious. "We're talking about your father, George Johntone! Who's not so dead after all. And you're mother, Vera Johnstone, also very much alive and who has all the warmth of a glacier."

Nita shrugged. "So you found my parents. So what?"

"You're father sold his soul thirty-two years ago. He abducted my twin and took her to some bio-medical research facility in Paraguay. "What was that about?"

"Never heard about that," Nita said stubbornly.

"Your parents are criminals, Nita. Both of them."

Nita swerved into a pull off. "You've flipped. All the stress, like Dan said." Nita taunted. "You don't even sound like yourself."

"Could be," Amy agreed, trying to calm down. "Stress has a strange effect on a woman, especially when her child has been kidnapped."

"You stupid, ignorant woman," Nita spat out, "you were doomed the day you married Dan. You inserted yourself into the middle of a lethal situation. There's no way out now. You'll never see Jamie again." She turned on Amy. "I knew it would come to this. Why do you think I spent every minute I could with Jamie, for the last five years? I knew everything would come to a head, and then you'd be out of the picture. Someone would have to raise the boy. I knew he'd be mine one day."

Amy could barely breathe. "So, you stole my son?"

Nita stared at Amy. "I didn't *take* Jamie. Dan's *giving* him to me. Being Jamie's loving aunt, I'm the logical choice as surrogate mother."

Amy almost choked. "Just like that? You can't have a child of your own so you're stealing mine?"

"It's not *stealing*. Like I said, Dan's *giving* him to me."

"Well I didn't give him to you, Nita. Jamie is my flesh and blood. *My* child. Nothing will ever change that." Amy wondered why she'd never seen Nita for the kind of woman she really was. "You'll never be Jamie's mother, Nita. And time won't change that. Jamie is a part of me, and that bond will never be broken. Even if you lathered him with love and affection for the rest of your life, it wouldn't make any difference to Jamie. You'll always be his Aunt Nita. Nothing more."

Nita sneered, "You always had everything. Everything: beauty, brains, money, career, and on top of all that, a wonderful little boy. It made me sick to look at you. Well, things have changed. You'll never find Jamie. Now, get out of my car!"

Amy lost it. "You snide, self-righteous, pompous, sick excuse for a human being!" Amy grabbed Nita's hair and yanked her around to face her. "Being the barren woman that you are doesn't condone kidnapping. I want my son and I want him now!"

Amy was furious. "You're a viper, just like your mother." Amy glared at Nita. It was clear she had no intention of telling Amy where Jamie was. There was only one thing left to do. Amy slipped the Beretta from her purse. Her eyes flashed to Nita as she thrust the barrel toward her.

Nita jumped. "A gun! My god! You really have flipped. What are you going to do? Shoot me with that thing?"

"You'd be hard to miss."

"You'll never do it. Not with all you've had to say about gun violence."

"You've put yourself between my child and me, Nita." Amy pointed the Beretta at Nita, "and there's no room for you!"

"You stupid bitch!" Nita spit. Your life's not worth a damn. You're on borrowed time. So, by default I get Jamie. Now, get the hell out of my car."

Amy let off the safety. "Where's my son?"

"You wouldn't dare!"

The explosion was deafening. Amy sat in stunned silence, her ears ringing, the gun shaking in her hand. Nita's eyes were popping, her mouth agape. Neither woman said a word.

Amy recovered first. "Just be glad I missed. Start the car."

Nita swallowed hard. "You're crazy!"

"Start the car." Amy leveled the gun again.

"No! I don't care what you do. I'm not taking you to Jamie."

The second blast seemed to blow out Amy's eardrums. But that soon proved untrue. Nita's scream rang in her ears a second later. The driver door flew open and Nita bolted out onto the highway.

Amy walked around the car and slipped behind the wheel. Rain dripped in through the holes in the roof. Turning the car around, she headed back to Sanville making a call on the way.

"Sanville Sheriff's Department. Is this an emergency?"

"Not yet," Amy replied.

"What's the nature of the call?"

"I want to report a woman wandering down the US101 about five miles south of town. I'm a little worried. She doesn't seem all there."

"Do you have a description?"

"Short, dark hair, swarthy skin, white sneakers, no coat, and she's ranting at the top of her lungs."

CHAPTER 32

Dallas opened the apartment door and flipped on the lights. He didn't bother to call out to Amy. It was too quiet. She wasn't there. Disappointed, he kicked off his shoes, and dropped his cell, keys, and pocket coins onto the kitchen table and headed for the shower.

With hot water pelting his skin, his thoughts drifted back to Amy. Each passing day she grew more distraught about Jamie. The need to find her son and to resolve the nightmare that had taken over her life was pushing her to close to the edge. It had numbed her senses and sent her body into overdrive.

Worse, the danger to Amy's life increased every passing hour. The key, at this point, was Dr. George Johnstone, the OB/GYN who delivered her and her twin, but finding the man was proving difficult. It was no surprise that Vera Johnstone's directions were faulty. Yet, Dallas felt that he and his team had been close. Dallas had returned to Sanville frustrated and weary.

Meanwhile, where was Amy? She should have been back by now.

Several possibilities came to mind as he stepped from the shower and toweled off. Once dressed, he called the car rental agency down the street. Bingo. She rented a blue 2011 KIA Sportage.

Dallas retrieved his keys, coins, and cell phone from the table, noting he had missed a call while he was in the shower. It was Debbie. He called her back.

"Helmut Eickher, Sheriff. No birth records or any other vitals, social, or driver's license within the US, but I did some digging. He's listed as a shareholder of CellBIX along with Vera and George Johnstone, and a Doris Eickher."

"Interesting. Thanks a lot, Deb." Dallas hung up, tipped a can of chili into a bowl, and stuck it in the microwave. Next, he pulled a loaf of Tuscany bread from the freezer and opening the microwave, he retrieved the heated chili and put in the bread.

Carrying the bread and chili over to the table, he had just sat down when the phone rang again.

"Something just came up, Sheriff," Debbie told him, "An anonymous call came in concerning a woman seen wandering down the 101, just south of town. Dispatch sent Larson to check it out. You'll never guess who he's bringing in. And, I might add, she's madder than hell."

Dallas ground his teeth. He hated these *you'll never guess* routines. "Spit it out."

Debbie continued, "Nita Williams. Larson says she frying mad and she's accusing Amy of trying to kill her. According to Nita, Amy fired a gun at her. And not once, but twice!"

"Twice," Dallas repeated dully, trying to visualize Amy with a gun.

"What was Nita doing on the highway?"

"She says Amy hijacked her car."

The whole thing sounded bizarre to Dallas. He couldn't even visualize Amy with a gun, let alone her shooting anyone. "When Nita comes in, hold on the statement. I'll look after that." Dallas clipped the cell to his belt, and headed out the door, his uneaten supper still on the table.

Nita was being escorted inside the building when Dallas arrived. By the time he joined her in the interrogation room, she was steaming. "I want Amy

Johnson arrested. She's off her rocker! Tried to kill me!"

Dallas sat down on an old metal chair, leaned back, and put his feet up on the empty chair beside him. He waited her out.

"I want that woman charged with...with...attempted murder and grand theft!"

"Theft of what?"

"Don't mock me, Sheriff. She stole my car."

"I drove by your place on my way here. Your Camry's parked on your drive."

The door opened a crack and Debbie poked her nose inside, motioning Dallas over to the door. She whispered, "The Camry on Nita's drive? There are two bullet holes in the roof."

Dallas's eyebrows shot up. Debbie gave him a strange look and left.

Nita pounced. "What was that about? You find her?"

Dallas ignored the question. "Amy Johnson is your sister-in-law."

"So?"

"Any idea why she'd do what you just described?"

"She's gone mad. That's reason enough."

"Give me another reason, Nita."

Nita slammed the palms of her hands down on the table. "What do you mean, *another reason*? I'm the goddamned victim here, Sheriff, remember? I'm not supposed to analyze why the woman's gone off the deep end."

Dallas met her gaze and held it, his cool blue eyes boring into hers.

Nita turned away. "You're not going to get away with playing mind games with me, Dallas Wayburne." Nita yanked out a chair and collapsed into it, her cheeks flaming. "Get out your pen and start writing up the charges."

187

Dallas slouched in his chair, but his eyes never left her.

"You hear me, Sheriff?"

Dallas sat up slowly and leaned forward until his face was only inches from hers. He spoke quietly. "I'm only going to say this once, Nita, so listen up. In about two minutes Deputy Larson is going to come through that door and read you your rights. You'll be charged with the kidnapping and the abduction of Jamie Johnson." His voice was hushed, but it filled the room.

Nita stared at him, aghast. Dallas continued, "You are going to be taken to a cell downstairs where you will remain until your arraignment. The State will ask for the maximum sentence—they don't take kindly to kidnappers." Dallas stood and walked to the door.

Nita's eyes followed him. "You can't be serious!"

Ignoring her, he put his hand on the doorknob, and pulled open the door.

Nita jumped up so fast the metal chair flew out from under her, clattering against the concrete floor. "Wait! I didn't take Jamie. You've got it wrong."

Dallas stood still, his back to her.

She continued, "Dan, Brandon, and I have been staying with our father. Jamie's with all of us, sort of. Dan promised we'd get Jamie when things settled down. But that hasn't happened yet."

Dallas turned. "And where exactly is your father's place?"

Nita appeared to consider her options. "You can't hold me, Sheriff. I haven't done anything."

Dallas stepped out the door.

"Wait!" Nita called to him. "I'll explain how to get there, but you have to let me out of here, Sheriff. I hate this place."

Dallas ripped a piece of paper from his pad. "Start writing." When Nita was finished, he read them over.

"These are the same directions your mother gave me. It's a dead end."

"It looks that way. In fact, my father had the architect design the house so it can't be seen from the drive. Amy can show you. She was working under his architect at the time."

Dallas was surprised. "Are you telling me that Amy helped design your father's house?"

"Yeah. Real joke's on her. She didn't know she was designing a house for the doctor who delivered her."

"And her twin." Dallas finished the sentence.

Nita smiled slyly. "And her twin."

"The same twin who was abducted by your parents." Dallas added.

Nita sat back in her chair. "I refuse to get into that. That's in the past. Before my time. You got questions for my father, you ask him."

Dallas studied her. "Who else is at this house besides you, Brandon, Dan and Jamie?"

Nita studies her nails.

"I can come back in the morning."

"No! I want to get out of here," she said, hesitating. "My father is there along with his nurse-assistant, Maria. There's also a security guard. Dan and Jamie are there, of course. I think Alesha might still be there, although I'm not sure. Or, they may have flown her back to Paraguay. And then there's Helmut and his personal bodyguard, Francisco."

Dallas leaned across the table and looked her in the eye. "Helmut Eickher?"

She nodded. Nita brushed her dark hair from her face with trembling fingers. "You've heard of Helmut Eickher?"

Dallas sat down. "Tell me about him."

Nita hesitated, her reluctance obvious. "He owns a cellular research company that makes him a fortune. He also runs some research facility in Paraguay and a

189

smaller one in Germany." She shuddered. "He's a scary guy. Unstable, volatile. Dan doesn't trust him; thinks Eickher's going to turn on us because we know too much. So, Dan's made arrangements for us to leave the country."

"Who's *us*?"

"Besides Dan, there's Alesha, if she's still there, Jamie, Brandon, and me. And my father."

"Dr. George Johnston, the infamous OB/GYN?"

"Seems like you know a lot about this already." Nita looked at Dallas, expecting an answer, but when none was forthcoming she asked: "Can I go now, Sheriff?"

Dallas pushed his chair back and stood up. "You have to do better with these directions. There are a lot of lives at stake."

"Okay, okay!" Nita finally said, "It's what people used to call the Cliff House. You know, down by the caves."

CHAPTER 33

The moonless night swallowed the ocean and the shoreline. Hammering over the potholes, the SUV raced along the narrow road in spite of the enveloping darkness. Fighting impatience, Amy tried to concentrate on driving as she sped down toward home.

Dan's call had come just as she had parked Nita's car on her drive. "Meet me at the house in half an hour," he said tersely and hung up.

Amy was anxious to get there, her hopes high on the possibility of Jamie being with him. She thought about the last time that she'd been with her son, his flaxen hair silky against her cheek, his big gray eyes dancing with curiosity, his sweet scent... *Stop!*

Instead of torturing herself, Amy decided to plan her approach so she wouldn't be seen. Once she reached the house, she'd stay hidden until she found Jamie. Then she'd grab him and run for the SUV with the intention of being long gone before Dan realized Jamie was missing.

When she was close to home, she extinguished the headlights, and allowed the Sportage to coast quietly along the last eighth of a mile. A hundred yards from the house, she nosed it into the brush until the SUV was obscured from the road. She pulled her house key, penlight, and the Beretta from her purse and put them in her pockets, then tucked the purse under the seat, locked up, and crossed the road to the vacant lot next to the house.

A cold, stiff wind blew off the ocean, swaying shrubs and tree branches, making it hard to decipher human movement in or around the unlit house. No sign of Dan's Mercedes.

Crossing the lawn to the front porch, she climbed the steps, nervously scanning the dark corners. With shaky fingers, she inserted the key into the lock and cautiously pushed the door open.

Amy peered into the dark entrance hall and stepped inside nervously. The house didn't feel like home anymore. She used to cherish its serenity, security, and above all, the overwhelming sense of belonging it gave her. This house had been more than home and hearth, this was where her soul had lived, where she'd shared her life with a man she had once loved, and where she'd raised their only child, the small being she cherished.

She glanced quickly around. A dusty odor overrode the usual rich smell of woods. She stood nervously in the dark foyer absorbing her surroundings, trying to understand the strange sensations. The joy that had once filled each room with love had been leached away by the events of the past week. All the warmth was gone, leaving behind only a cold, damp sense of foreboding.

She closed the door, switched on the small flashlight, and tiptoed down the hall into the vast, vacant living room. The high walls that once sheltered them protectively now loomed above her. Amy cast the flashlight across the room as she tread softly over the wood floors toward the bank of windows.

Amy looked across to Cape Peril and the lighthouse that had, for over a century, flashed its powerful strobe intermittently across the ocean, warning unwary sailors away from the rocky cape. Maybe she should have paid heed to the warning. For a second Amy thought she saw a small flicker of yellow light, perhaps from a flashlight, behind the lighthouse, but after watching a few moments, decided she must have imagined it.

She watched for a few minutes, and then her eyes traveled beyond the back deck to the gardens she'd planted years ago. They were impossible to see in the dark, but that didn't prevent her from feeling an enormous sense of loss. Thinking of the gardens reminded her of the hopes and dreams she'd also planted here. Like seeds placed lovingly in rich soil, she had nurtured and protected them, believing that as the roots spread deeply into the ground, her hopes and dreams would grow and blossom, prospering from the love that she gave.

Suddenly cold, she turned around and cast the penlight across the room, thinking how much things had changed since her departure a week ago. *Was it just a week? If felt like eons.*

Like a ghost re-living the past, she drifted through the main floor of the house. In the hall, outside the study, her flashlight rested upon a wall photo taken in the park last summer: Dan, smiling his million-dollar smile, his arms around her and Jamie, creating the illusion of a happy family on a beautiful summer's day. So deceptive. How could he have maintained the charade so long, without her knowing? *Because I refused to see reality. That's how. I was so damned afraid of feeling any more pain and being forced to do something about it, that I existed in a bubble.*

She wandered listlessly into the study. Her real work seemed a world away from her current existence. Even though she loved architecture, it would become meaningless without Jamie. She couldn't live without him.

Glancing out the study window, she thought of the night that had launched this morbid chain of events and wondered what had become of her twin. *Is she still alive? Will I ever have the chance to meet the sister who's virtually identical to me in every way?*

Amy looked down at the desk, the thin beam from her flashlight illuminating the stack of bills. She expected to see the letter describing Dan's indiscretions, but it wasn't there. She re-positioned the light for a closer look and shuffled through the bills. Gone!

Dan?

Had he arrived ahead of her? Had he found the letter and taken it with him?

Turning in thought, the flashing green light on the answering machine caught her eye. Distracted, her finger went automatically to PLAY, but her thoughts were on Dan. There were several work-related messages. Then, a gravelly voice caught her attention. It was the spike-haired woman Amy had talked to in Beaverdale.

"Hi. Remember me? You left your card and said to call if anything came up. Well, something came up. An older woman came to my door this afternoon. Said her name was Doris Eickher. Anyway, she had a photo of the woman you were looking for—or maybe it was you, who knows? Anyway, she told me that the photo was actually of her daughter. Believe me, this woman was totally stressed. She was going on about how her daughter's life was in danger, and how she had to find her quickly, and so on. I would've thought she was nuts if I hadn't met you and your sister, no pun intended. I gave her your phone numbers. Well, anyway, just thought I'd let you know."

Amy replayed the message, listening intently, imagining this woman, Doris Eickher, holding a photo of Alesha, filled with the same hope and desperation that drove Amy day and night—the need to find her endangered child.

Amy played the next message. Then, there was a long pause and she heard tiny breaths and a soft cry.

Jamie! Her heart leapt in her chest as his voice filled the room. "Mommy." There was a sniffle, then, "—come get me, Mommy, pl-e-a-se." He hesitated a minute, then added, "I'm not lost. I can see the caves from my room—"

A male voice shouted in the background. Then there was a click and the machine went silent. Amy hit RE-PLAY, her mind racing, fear for Jamie forming a painful rock in her chest. She listened to his voice again, hearing the fear, and the loneliness. When the tape ended, another voice, this time behind her, sent Amy leaping into the air.

"Smart kid."

Amy whirled around. Dan was barely visible in the dark doorway. She turned the penlight on him. "Dan!" Her heart was crashing in her chest.

Blinded by the beam of light, he groped for the light switch and flipped it on. Light flooded the study. "For crying out loud, Amy!"

Amy looked behind him. "Where's Jamie?"

"He's safe, which is more than I can say for you," Dan said, stepping toward her.

Amy retreated, her hand flying to the Beretta in her coat pocket. "Don't come any closer."

Dan took another step, "Come on, Amy—"

She pulled out the gun and aimed it at him pointblank. Dan froze in surprise. "What the hell—"

"Don't come any closer. Where is he, Dan?"

Dan reached for the gun. "Put that thing away before it goes off. Have you gone mad?"

As his hand shot past her face, Amy inhaled a strange mix of antiseptic and bacterial soap. It spiked a memory of the break-in—the gloves—that strange smell. "*You!*" She pointed accusingly, recalling his mottled complexion—a result of his allergy to wool—and the stocking cap that had covered his face. "It was *you!* *You* broke into our house. *You* threatened me with Jamie's life! How could you do that? Your own wife and son! *Why?*"

Dan shook his head. "I was trying to warn you Amy, to scare you off, for chrissakes. The way you were going, you were going to get yourself killed. You still are."

"Why would that bother you?"

"I'm still your husband, that's why!"

"That's a little hard to believe, all things considered. Do you have any idea what's been happening? What kind of hell I've been living? Gramps being burned alive in his own house. Grams being pushed in front of a moving car. Me being run off the highway, chased down by an animal, nearly raped, and drowned. All the time I just wanted to find my little boy." Her voice shook with anger, but her expression changed when she saw the truth in his face. "You knew, didn't you, Dan? You knew what they were doing to me."

He became still. "Not the details. Look Amy, you're in terrible danger."

"And why is that?" She asked, breathless.

"They're going to kill you. Trust me, we don't have much time. You've got to come with me now, while there's still a chance to escape." He pleaded.

Amy took a step forward, the gun wavering dangerously. "Come with you?"

Dan jumped back. "No! Don't! Amy, listen, I know you think I'm a jerk for running out on you—"

"*Jerk?* You were unfaithful for years! You took my child! You left me alone to fight for my life! *Jerk?* How about a disloyal, unfaithful, narcissistic bastard." Amy's voice echoed shrilly through the near-empty house. The gun shook violently in her hands.

"Take it easy, Amy. Take it easy!" Dan's eyes were glued to the semi-automatic. "Believe me, I never thought it would turn out like this!"

"I lived with you for seven years. Seven years! And never once did I guess you were with other women. Nor would I have thought you capable of abandoning me to killers!"

Dan swallowed and looked away.

Amy paused to catch her breath, fighting for control. They stared at each other in a cold silence. She reached deep inside herself, to find some sense of calm. Finally she whispered, "Your father, Dr. George Johnstone took a tiny newborn baby from my mother. He lied to her and told her the infant had died. Then he and your mother flew that tiny baby to some facility in Paraguay, of all places."

"Yes, that's right."

"You knew all this?"

Dan looked down. "Yes."

Appalled, Amy studied him. Her voice rose angrily. "Tell me, Dan, why did you marry me? Was it some kind of sick setup? Considering everything your father did or knew about… the kidnapping of my sister, the death of my parents, and everything that's happened, why would *you, son of George & Vera Johnstone,* marry *me?*"

Dan pressed his lips together, his face ashen, his voice a whisper. "Alesha."

Amy's mouth fell open. The name hung in the air between them. "Alesha?" Amy murmured in disbelief.

Dan looked at her, his expression pained. "Yes. Alesha." He closed his eyes. When he spoke again, Amy could barely hear him. "I loved her from the first moment I saw her… when we were just kids." His voice was a hoarse whisper as he explained. "My dad used to take me with him on business trips to Paraguay. When I saw her for the first time, she was just eight. She was standing there with the other kids in the facility—"

"Facility?"

Dan took a shaky breath. "She lived in a huge research facility in Paraguay along with sixty-seven other kids of various ages."

Amy groaned, her arm falling to her side, the gun heavy in her hand.

Dan cleared his throat. "Alesha stood out from all the others. Not just because she was so golden, so beautiful, even as a child, but because she was so, so..." He struggled for the right word. "*Vibrant.* It took me two years to work up the nerve to go up and talk to her. The second I did, that was it for me. She has a brain that sears paper and a presence that melts your heart. She makes people laugh when they wanted to cry. She has a spirit that soars. Alesha is special. Like no one on this earth." His eyes were glassy, distant. "She is life itself. She's magical..." His voice faded away.

Amy was stunned. When she found her voice, she asked, "And then?"

Dan ran his hand over his face. "Then she got in trouble. When she was sixteen she raided Eickher's files and found out who her real parents were—"

"My mother and father."

"Yes." He shifted his weight miserably and continued, his voice choked with emotion. "Eickher was outraged about that. He arranged to send her away to Germany, but when she and her bodyguard landed in Miami, Alesha took off. They found her in Portland a few days later, drugged her, and shipped her to Eickher's satellite facility in Germany."

Amy winced. "She came to Portland. That must have been when she called my mother."

"That's right." Dan paused for a while, struggling with the last part of his story. "Afterward, they told me to forget her," he hesitated, "but I couldn't. I could never forget Alesha."

Amy felt hollow. Empty. "So when you couldn't have her, you settled for me."

Pain filled Dan's eyes. "It wasn't like that. I withdrew so badly that my father finally told me about you, in the hope of reviving me, I suppose." Dan looked at her strangely. "You see, the first time I saw you the same thing happened to me all over again." He expression grew tender. "You were walking across the campus, your long golden hair blowing in the wind, your movements so graceful. Your beauty was absolutely breathtaking. I stood there mesmerized, watching you. I was so awed I could hardly breathe." Dan reached out for Amy, "By then it had been years since I'd seen Alesha, so it was a shock to see this exquisite young woman with a different name: Amy." He touched her cheek. "I loved you, Amy, the same way I had loved Alesha. Only—"

Amy stepped away from his touch, finishing the sentence for him. "Only I wasn't Alesha."

Dan dropped his arm. "No. You weren't. I began to see that right after we were married, but it wasn't until Jamie was born, and I saw you as a *mother,* that I knew I'd made a mistake."

"And you still love her."

"I've always loved her. I always will."

A huge piece of the puzzle suddenly crashed into place and for the first time Amy could see part of the picture. Dan had, in many ways, been caught in the same web that had brought tragedy and sorrow into her life. He too had been born into a situation that had taken over his life. But there was one big difference. Dan knew about his parents' and about Amy's past. And he had kept it hidden from her. "You lied when you said your parents were dead to hide your father's horrific involvement with my family."

"It was best you didn't know."

Amy stared at him coldly. "Who is Helmut Eickher?"

When Dan looked up, she saw that his face had aged, lines etching deeply around his eyes. "He owns, amongst other things, an international company called CellBIX. They do cellular research. The man's a scientific genius gone amuck. His obsession is cellular research, and along those lines he's made millions. Aside from that, he believes that by creating a group of elite, super-intelligent beings, that he can place some of them in positions of power around the world and control them."

"How does that involve twins?"

"From the late 70's to the 90's Eickher targeted pregnant women with high IQ's, like your mom, who were expecting twins. He figured he could slip one twin away, explaining it as a death, as long as he left the mother with the other infant. Of course, he never did any of this personally. Just arranged for it."

Amy concluded, "That's where your father came in. He coordinated everything for Eickher, delivered the babies, and transported them—my twin and all the others, to some God-awful facility in Paraguay, to be raised like lab rats."

Dan closed his eyes, his face haggard. "Back in 1979, Eickher made my father an offer. Dad refused, but Eickher found his weakness. Money. Still, my father resisted until Eickher convinced him it was in the interests of humanity. Finally the right sum of money was put on the table and my father relented. Dad told me that he had planned to do just one delivery to make the man happy, but after the first one, Eickher had him. Dad couldn't extract himself and because my mother had assisted him, she was trapped as well."

"And the trap snared all of us." Suddenly Amy heard a sound. Something foreign. Something odd. Her scalp prickled and she tensed.

Then an explosion rocked the study.

CHAPTER 34

Dan yanked Amy through the doorway and together they dove onto the hallway floor.

The shotgun blast exploded the study window and blew a hole right through the back wall, detonating a lethal spray of glass shards, drywall, and wood chips in a deafening blast.

Dan and Amy belly-crawled along the floor, and then scrambled to their feet, Dan yelling, "Out the kitchen door. *Run!*"

A second explosion blew the front door to pieces. Amy bolted for the French door in the kitchen, crashing hard against it. Locked. Dan reached around, twisted the lock, and pushed her onto the porch. "The beach. Hurry!"

As they raced for the staircase leading down to the beach, another shotgun blast followed them. Amy could hear Dan's heavy breathing behind her as they tore down the rickety staircase. Knowing they were targets on the stairs, Amy twisted her body over the wooden rail, and with a push, flung herself off. She landed on the packed sand with a heavy thud. A second later, another shot rang out and Dan hit the sand beside her.

"Keep going! Run!" he shouted.

The surf was up, leaving only a slender strip of damp, hard-packed beach. The frigid wind whipped the

201

tops off the waves sending an icy white froth racing up the sand. They spurted toward the cape, adrenaline pumping, the roaring sea preventing them from hearing their stalkers. Where were they?

There was a spitting sound and the sand by Amy's feet exploded. Instinctively she dodged right. The shot had come from the bank, high above them.

"They're up on the bluff," Dan yelled, "Run for cover." He reached for her arm, pulling her toward a rock outcropping. The night was so black Amy could see nothing in front of her. Suddenly her right foot hit the end of an old log and she pitched forward into the sand. Dan stopped, scooped her up, and pushed her ahead of him. "Keep going—don't stop!"

Another deadly spit of the gun. Dan spun around. Something warm and wet spurted across Amy's cheek. Dan grabbed his chest and fell forward onto his knees.

Amy put her arms around him and tried to help him up. "We have to keep going, Dan, or they'll pick us off like birds." She put his arm over her shoulder and using her hip, leveraged him onto his feet. Her hands were slippery with his blood. Dan lurched forward, his chest heaving, his breath ragged.

With his weight resting heavily on her, Amy staggered the last few feet, toward the bluff, her feet now sinking into the dry sand, her knees giving out repeatedly. Only a few more feet and they'd be under the cover of the bank.

Another shot, so close to Amy's leg that sand peppered her jeans. She tried to run, but Dan was too heavy and he was slipping from her grasp. Just a few more steps. Finally, with the outcropping protecting them, she took one last step, landing heavily, beneath the overhang. Dan fell beside her, moaning and gasping for breath.

She couldn't see his face or his wound and didn't dare use her penlight, as it would expose them. She trailed her hand across his damp jacket until she felt his wet shirt beneath. The coppery scent of his blood mixed with the salty mist from the sea and lingered sickeningly in the damp air, before being carried away by the wind. Then, another cold blast of wind hit her, and with it came the knowledge that Dan was dying. "Hang on, Dan. I'm going for help!" Amy found his hand and pushed it down hard over his wound. "Press down here."

Instead, Dan reached out and grabbed her arm, stopping her. "Amy, I'm sorry,...so sorry—" he gagged and, turned his head to spit out the blood that filled his mouth.

All the alarms were going off for Amy. His time was short. "Just rest. I'm going—"

"No!" His voice was suddenly stronger. "I'm a doctor, if I know anything," he coughed, "I know when it's over. You can't help me, Amy, but you can save yourself. Go before these bastards get both of us!"

Amy pushed the handle of the Beretta into the palm of his other hand. "Here. If they find you, kill them."

Dan shoved it back into her hand. "No," he choked, "You'll need it. And Amy," he coughed, "use it!"

Amy held onto him, her heart beating wildly in her chest. A damn broke. Sorrow flooded through her like a swollen river. She wanted Dan to live! He had fathered their child. He had made love to her. They had laughed together, cried together. They had shared their lives with each other, and for a while they had shared their love for one another. She pulled free of his grasp and pressed his hand back over his wound. "I'm going for help, but I'll be back, Dan. I promise."

"Amy," he whispered hoarsely, "I was a stupid fool. So wrong—" He writhed as a spasm of pain tore through him. "I'm so sorry," he said, his voice raspy now. "Amy, I love you. Always have."

Tears filled her eyes. She squeezed his arm. "Please Dan, before I go, tell me where Jamie is."

He tried to sit up. "Cliff House, by the caves. Be careful, Eickher's there...he's dangerous, he'll kill you. Amy...go! I'll try to keep them here...if...they find me."

She squeezed his hand. "Don't die. I'll be back."

CHAPTER 35

The meat cutter was certain the bullet from his silenced revolver had struck Dan Johnson, but looking down onto the beach from high ground, he could see nothing in the black void below. Thanks to the crashing waves, he couldn't hear anything either. Damn! What satisfaction could be had from striking the prey when you couldn't see the hit? He nudged Jerry Lee Ray. "I'm going down there. You stay up here. If anyone shows up, you know what to do." Without taking his eyes from the beach, Jerry Lee raised his shotgun skyward in acknowledgment and spit a wad of tobacco into the night.

Leading with his revolver, Werner descended the beach staircase, his eyes scanning below him for movement. He didn't relish the thought of becoming the target. That would be unseemly, considering the position he had earned in Eickher's Special Security Task Force.

Werner had seen the woman with a gun, so he proceeded accordingly: meaning he would blow a hole right through her the minute he spotted her. Not that he wouldn't like a piece of that sweet little ass of hers first, but with things heating up like they were, there was no time for life's small pleasures. Unless... he glanced up at the spot where he had left Jerry Lee Ray...unless, he made it quick.

As for Dan Johnson, if there were anything left of him, it'd be easy enough to finish him off. The guy was a pussy and an ass. Werner's orders were to stop the woman and take her to Eickher, but what the hell.

Blind in the intense darkness, Werner stumbled across the sand to the spot where he thought he had dropped Johnson. Kneeling, he ran the flat of his hand over the sand in a semicircular motion until he felt a moist, sticky substance. Swiping the substance with his index finger, he brought it to his nose and sniffed.

Yeah! Fresh blood. He sampled it. *Thick, rich, coppery arterial blood.* He had him. Well, almost. The man had managed to walk away, but he couldn't have gone far.

Using his hand to follow the moist trail of blood, Werner duck-walked up the dark beach toward the bluff, the gun poised in front of him. When he felt the wind bounce off the rock face, he knew he was close, even though he saw nothing in front of him but black space.

Suddenly, a man's scream filled the night air. The shriek was so deep, so primal, that it stunned him momentarily. A body flew into him, knocking him backward. Excruciating pain sent yellow light flashing across his vision. A rock-hard object struck his temple almost knocking him out. It pummeled his skull again and again, nauseating him.

Werner squeezed off a shot, but it went wild. Anger surged through his veins like poison. Nobody drops Werner. Nobody!

With a mighty yell he heaved himself up off the sand, threw both arms around his attacker, and pitched the man onto his back. Werner landed on top of him, his left hand around a slippery neck, his right pushing the barrel of the gun into the hollow of the attacker's cheek. The scent of warm, fresh blood wafted up his nostrils. *Johnson.*

The meat cutter laughed. "So, you've got balls, after all. A little late, don't you think?" Werner sniffed the air. "You're dying. I can smell it." He laughed again, his thumb pressing down on Dan's windpipe. "But I can prevent that. Ha! I can make it so you die of asphyxiation instead. How does that sound? It would give me great pleasure to render assistance as you exit this world. I'll witness your transition to the underworld. I'm sure they're waiting down there with bated breath. Or is it bad breath?"

Dan died before Werner had the opportunity to take his life. As his final breath expelled from his collapsing lungs, Werner reached excitedly for his flashlight. Sensing the woman was long gone, and he was in no danger from her gun, he flicked on the flashlight and signaled upward to Jerry Lee Ray not to shoot.

Werner wanted a peak at his handiwork. Ah, yes. Very good. How he loved his work. He slid off Dan. Enough! There was more work to do. He had to nail the Johnson woman before she got away. He owed her one. "Hmm-m," he mumbled, rubbing the scar on his chin. "Maybe two." She was a livewire, that one, a nice little challenge.

He stood and waved his light at Jerry Lee Ray, this time signaling his intention to continue toward the cape. Then he turned the light down the beach, in search of the Johnson woman. Seeing nothing, he shuffled down the beach, toward the compact sand, where he could move more quickly. As soon as his boots bit into it, he started to jog and with the aid of his light, made fair time.

Speed was of the essence if he was to catch her, as she had a considerable lead. If he remembered correctly, the only place along the bluff where she could climb back up was near the Cape Peril lighthouse. That meant she was trapped on the beach, as long as he caught up to her in time.

The cold wet wind, heavy with spray from the huge rollers, saturated his hair and clothing, drained off his body heat, and bit into his skin. The waves seemed to be running continuously higher up the beach, sending their icy wash over his boots, soaking his feet, and slowing him down. His wool socks were wet and his feet sloshed inside his leather boots. "Son-of-a-bitch," he cursed, moving higher up the beach. He needed to pick up speed.

Why was it that the elements always conspired against him? No matter what the assignment, he was in constant conflict with nature. It was the story of his life!

A powerful gust of wind tore open his jacket and whipped salt into his eyes. He rubbed them, trying to clear his vision. At that moment the moon broke through an opening in the clouds, exposing the beach.

A movement caught his eye a hundred yards ahead. Something darted into the shadows and he swung his flashlight in that direction, triumphant that he had nearly caught up to the woman. Searching the ridge, he saw no sign of Jerry Lee Ray. Good, there was time for a little pleasure. Heat surged to his loins. He licked his lips and smiled. He could taste her already.

CHAPTER 36

Amy picked her way along the rocks, her eyes moving back and forth between the Cape Peril's flashing light and the light that hunted her, from behind. Another few hundred feet and she'd reach the old rope ladder leading up to the lighthouse. Then, it would be a race for the SUV. She cursed herself again for leaving her iPhone behind. Dan needed help. So did she for that matter.

The trip down the beach was taking too long.

She broke into a run, her feet sinking into the sand, her arms outstretched in the dark, to prevent her from running headlong into the uneven rock face of the bluff. The clouds parted and suddenly she was exposed and vulnerable in the moonlight. A beam of light swung across her. Feeling like a duck in a shooting gallery, Amy bolted.

The balls of her feet sinking into the sand, legs pumping, she glanced back. He was coming up fast from behind and was gaining on her. She wouldn't make it to the rope ladder unless she picked up a lot of speed.

She raced down the beach onto the hard-packed sand so she could run faster. A bullet hit the sand beside her. She sprinted, lungs heaving, heart pounding, her eyes fixed on the spot where the ladder should be. Glancing back again, she heard her pursuer closing in,

209

not thirty feet behind. He fired another shot.

Looking toward the ocean, she wondered if she could escape through the waves. White-capped rollers towered steeply, then crashed ferociously onto the beach. No chance. No one could swim through that. Not even her.

Her muscles burned, her breaths were dry spasms, and the ladder was still about twenty feet away, barely visible in the cool moonlight.

A loud, haunting laugh whirled around her, and a powerful hand gripped her arm, flinging her around. *It was him! The meat cutter!* She bounced off him, her eyes locking onto the ugly diagonal scar. She grabbed the small gun out of her pocket and tried to shoot. Oh, no, the safety. She struck his face with the barrel as hard as she could. In the moonlight she saw feral anger flash across his eyes.

"Bitch!" He swung back, his hand snapping her head around, knocking her to the ground. His boot flew at her ribcage. She saw it coming and dove for the leg, wrapping both arms around it. She held on tight. He stumbled backward in surprise. His balance lost, he came crashing down beside her. Amy jumped to her feet and started to run. His hand snaked out and grabbed her ankle, yanking her down hard onto the beach. The gun went flying.

He leapt on top of her. Amy rolled sideways, her hands flying at his face, her nails gouging his eyes.

"Rotten bitch," he shouted, dropping his gun and grabbing her arms. Amy fought like she'd never fought in her life, arms, legs, feet, and hands flying, punching, and kicking. Her gun was gone. So was his.

They rolled into the icy water. Cold seawater washed over them, dragging them back toward the open sea. If it caught them, they'd be sucked out by the undertow. She looked toward the ladder. If she could get free of him for just one second, she might have a chance.

His huge head rose above her face. Amy went for his eyes, but he moved and her nails dug into the soft pockets of flesh beneath his eyes. He howled, his hands flying to his face.

Leaping from his grasp, she stumbled up the beach fighting the suction of sand and water, trying to outrun the giant roller that was rising up behind her. Her shoes bit into the sand and with a Herculean effort, she sprinted for the ladder.

Panting and shouting, he clawed at her jacket, his fingers catching a fold. He pulled, but Amy kept going.

Out of the corner of her eye, she saw something huge and dark looming toward them from the sea and a new fear gripped her as she realized what it was. *Oh, no! Not again. Not now.*

A curling wall of black water was speeding toward the beach, sucking up everything in front of it. Suddenly the sand receded beneath her feet and she stumbled.

"Bitch, I'll get you." Werner took advantage of the slip and grabbed for her. Anticipating him, Amy pulled her shoulders back, allowing him full grip of her jacket. With an eye on the wave that loomed toward them, she pulled herself free of the jacket and raced for the bluff.

The motion slowed him. He ended up with her empty jacket. With an angry shout, he threw it in the air and stumbled after her. The watery sand beneath his feet was traveling seaward so fast, it pulled his feet from under him. Cursing loudly, he staggered forward once more, oblivious to the danger that was almost upon him.

Amy grabbed for the rope ladder and pulled herself up, her hands and feet working the rotting rope, fighting for height. Suddenly the ladder swung out from the wall, lifting her feet off the rungs. She dangled, legs clawing the air.

Looking down, she saw the big man's face grinning up at her as he flung the rope ladder into the air, in an attempt to dislodge her.

Amy's hands slid down the rope, her feet flailed. She looked seaward. A scream escaped her lips as the huge wall of water rolled toward them.

Werner saw it, latched onto the ropes, and planted his feet onto the first rung.

The ladder stilled suddenly. Amy put one hand over the other, her feet flying up the rope. She gained five feet, ten, then fifteen, the rope burning through her skin. Her eyes registered the final seconds as her body fought for height.

Werner's eyes widened in horror.

Huge, curling, and ugly, the Sneaker Wave exploded against the bluff, impaling him on the rocks, pulverizing bone and muscle.

It struck with so much force that the water climbed the bank, riding up to Amy's chest, slamming her against the bluff. She wrapped her arms and legs around the ropes and held on. The back surge came, dragging her down the ropes. Her hands, arms, and legs slid along the braid as the sea retreated. Amy held on, her hands bleeding, her body shaking violently with the effort.

Then it was over. She collapsed against the bluff face, her arms and hands raw, salt water biting her open wounds, blood seeping from her facial cuts. Finally, she looked down.

The wet sand sparkled in the moonlight. There was no sign of the human being that had hunted her, nor the Sneaker Wave that had crushed him against the rock face and carried him out to sea.

Her legs felt like water as she wobbled up the old ladder to the mossy ground above. She knew she had been too long getting help for Dan and as she climbed onto the bank beneath the light station, she was overcome with grief. It snuck up on her, catching her unaware. Tears streamed down her cheeks as she staggered unsteadily along the cracked concrete foundation of the lighthouse.

Rounding the corner, she walked into the short steel barrel of a shotgun. A tall, emaciated man, spat twice before he spoke. "I watched what you did. You planned the whole escapade to sucker Werner. No loss though," he growled, "He was a real prick. Well, it's your turn now, Missy," he said poking the barrel of the gun hard into her ribs. "Turn around."

Amy turned, her mind racing. She needed an escape route fast.

"Now, walk your fancy ass over to the edge. Keep going. That's it. You're almost there. Now look down and tell me what you see."

Amy swallowed hard. If she jumped, she'd probably end up a quadriplegic, but she *might* live. If she didn't jump she would die.

"I said, what do you see!"

Amy flinched. "The beach."

"Well now you're going to see stars—"

Amy sunk into her knees preparing for the jump. There was a deafening explosion and the thought that tore through her mind was that she was too late. But no shell struck her. Shaking, she turned around.

Jerry Lee Ray was sprawled face down on the ground, his shotgun still clutched in his right hand. Twenty feet behind him, was a man with a gun.

CHAPTER 37

At first Amy thought it was a trick, but the husky voice changed her mind.

"I'd give my eye teeth for one those hugs of yours."

"Gramps!" He was leaning on the open truck door, the smoking gun still in his hand. She limped over and threw her arms around his bony shoulders. Pressing her cheek firmly against his stubby whiskers, she whispered. "You don't have any eye teeth."

He slid the gun behind the truck seat and sat down hard on the truck seat. "Don't have any dentures either. Left them in my living room with the bugger who tried to give me a barbecue."

Amy pulled back and looked at him. "I kept wondering if you might have made it out." She squeezed him tight and said into his ear, "I'm so glad, Gramps, so glad."

He pointed to the body on the ground. "Well, Girl, someone had to send that son of a bitch to his maker."

Amy looked back. Gramps was right.

He caught her hand. "Come on now, let's get over to the house. We're targets out here."

Amy shivered in her wet clothes. He was right again. They were standing targets. But she couldn't go with him. She had to go back to Dan. "Do you have a cell?"

"You know I don't use those things"

"Is that your van?"

"Temporarily."

"Can you go over to my house and call an ambulance? Dan's been shot. He's down on the beach. I need to get back down there."

"That's not a good idea, Amy. Too dangerous. Wait for the cops."

"I can't wait, Gramps. He's dying and I'm not leaving him down there alone."

Gramps took off his warm fleece-lined jacket and put it over her shoulders. "You're getting too damned headstrong, Girl. Here. Put this on." He reached for his pistol and handed it to her. "And take this."

She pushed it away. "There's no one down there but Dan. You keep it. Who knows what could happen next."

Working her way back down the rope ladder, Amy landed on the beach and ran to the outcropping where she'd left Dan, her penlight a frail beam of light leading the way.

He wasn't there.

She widened the search area, wondering if he'd moved to a safer place. Nothing. She cried out, "Dan, where are you? Dan!" The only sound was crashing waves. She searched up and down the beach. Exhausted, she slumped down on a damp log and stared at the huge rollers marching into the bay. The rogue wave that had saved her life and pummeled her lethal attacker, had taken Dan to his final resting place. She dropped her head in her hands and cried for him.

A while later, a strong hand gripped her shoulder and she looked up. Dallas knelt beside her and put his arms around her. She collapsed against him and pressed her face into his chest.

He held her until the tears stopped. Then he lifted her to her feet and took her back up the staircase to the house.

CHAPTER 38

After showering and slipping into clean jeans and a warm sweater, Amy combed her wet hair into a ponytail, and started downstairs. As she descended the stairs, she became aware of sounds emanating from the kitchen. There was the clatter of pots and pans, the sound of rummaging, and the voices of two men attempting to cook something. Near the bottom step she stopped and listened, a smile playing at her lips.

Gramps: "You think there's any bread?"

"Try the breadbox."

There was a loud crash. "Damn, rice of all things"

A moment of silence, then Dallas said, "Hellndamnation. It's everywhere."

"Well, don't stand there, Wayburne, start frying the eggs. I'll sweep up."

There was a clatter of pots, the fridge door closed, and a moment later Amy heard Dallas say, "Never could crack eggs. How do I get out the pieces of shell?"

"Scramble the works."

"Hey, what's that? Something's burning. Oh no. The toast!"

Another silence. "Scrape off the black part. She'll never know the difference."

Amy heard scraping sounds and then Gramps yelled, "You watching those eggs, Wayburne? They smell scorched."

"Yup. What now?"

"Put the top part on the plate and the burned part in the sink."

Things were quiet in the kitchen. Then, Dallas said, "Looks like the dog's breakfast."

Amy threw her head back, and erupted into laughter. Out of the corner of her eye she saw Dallas and Gramps pop out of the kitchen.

With a worried frown Gramps yelled, "She's lost it."

Dallas added, "Too much pressure."

Amy caught their words and collapsed on the stairs in uncontrollable laughter.

Both men watched in alarm. Gramps said, "What're we going to do? She's a goner."

Dallas chuckled and reached out to help Amy up. "Nah, they say laughter's the best medicine." He wiped the tears from her cheeks. "Hey, Babe. We got food on the table."

Amy burst into another gale of laughter.

Eventually, she made it into the kitchen and, trying not to notice the rice on the floor, she sat down. There, on the table was *the meal.* The toast was limp and in a post-burn state. The eggs smelled scorched. Amy picked up her fork and as Gramps and Dallas watched expectantly, she stabbed the eggs, desperate for a diversion. It was probably the worst meal she'd ever tried to eat, but it was made with love. Through the kitchen window, she saw red and blue flashing lights over on the point. "It's become a regular crime scene around here lately," she said flatly.

Dallas reached across the table for her hand. "How're you holding up?"

She smiled. "Well, to tell you the truth, I feel much better now. You two in the kitchen are a cure for anything." Amy became serious. "When this is over, I'll let myself grieve for Dan. I can't do that right now or it'll be the end of me. I have to stay sharp and keep my wits about me if I want to get Jamie back." She looked at her grandfather with his old steel wheelchair angled toward her. "Besides, I have a lot to be thankful for. I was a second from being shot in the back when Gramps came to my rescue," she told Dallas. Amy reached out for her grandfather's hand. "Don't know what I'd do without you two. For a guy in a wheelchair you sure get around. And speaking of getting around, how did you get out of your house while it was burning?"

"It was a close call, I'll tell you," Gramps replied loudly, "Some big thug broke in while I was watching TV. Guess he thought I'd be easy pickings, with my bad legs. So this guy comes in throwing gas around the living room, tosses a match to it, and goes after me with a tire iron. I wasn't going down without a good fight. He misjudged my upper body strength. Got my hands on the tire iron and I made it out. He didn't. Kind of figured, with my wheelchair missing, you and Amy would figure it out."

Amy exchanged a look with Dallas and shook her head. She decided it was best that Gramps didn't know she went inside the burning house to look for him. Satisfied that Dallas understood, she turned back to her grandfather. "What happened after that?"

"Charlie next door heard all the yelling and came over to see what was going on. He helped me out, and took me to the hospital. Then, they airlifted me to Portland."

Amy motioned for him to lower his voice. "Is that where you've been these last few days?" Amy asked, perplexed.

"Well, I was trying to get out of there. The docs said I had a concussion, smoke inhalation, cracked ribs, stuff like that, but frankly, I couldn't take the place any longer. Checked myself out a few of hours ago. Got the van from the rental company and headed over here, looking for you. Instead, I saw the window blasted out of the study and the front door blown to pieces. Heard a shots from out on the bluff and got over to the lighthouse just in time to send the miserable bugger to his maker before he blasted you in the back."

Dallas said, "And now we've got another murder to deal with. You're going to have to turn over your gun, Art. You realize that, don't you?"

"Figured as much."

Amy had listened quietly and then she said, "Gramps, did it occur to you, when you were in the hospital, to call me? I thought you died in the fire. Would it have been too difficult to ask a nurse to make the call, if you couldn't?"

Gramps dropped his head and said softly, "Sorry, Girl."

A heavy silence descended over the three of them. Dallas looked at his watch. "We'll need to get statements from each of you. Do you want to do it now? Tell me what happened here, in detail?"

Amy began with Dan's phone call a couple of hours earlier. When she was finished, she stood up and walked over to the counter to pull a tissue from the box. "Dan and I were standing in the study when a gunshot blasted out the window. Or rather half of the study." Amy wiped her eyes and looked up at Dallas. She explained the rest and finished by saying, "I left Dan down on the beach thinking I could get him help. Poor Dan. He didn't have a chance." She put her head in her hands.

Dallas went over and put his arms around her and held her. She looked over at Gramps and then up at Dallas. "Jamie left a message on my answering machine. I taught him to memorize our phone number in case of emergency. So, he called here and said that he isn't far away. He can see the caves from his window. I think he's at The Cliff House. I want to go there now and get him."

"Smart little guy," Dallas said, pushing a stray lock of hair from her eye. "But getting him isn't going to be simple. Eickher's at The Cliff House along with Doc Johnstone, his nurse, a security guard, a bodyguard, and possibly your twin, Alesha."

"And maybe Eickher's wife," Amy added, recalling the message from the spike-haired woman. "How do you know who's down there?"

Dallas replied, "Nita. She was trying to have you charged. Which reminds me, do you have a gun?"

Amy screwed up her nose. "Not anymore. It was probably carried out to sea."

Dallas's cell rang. He pulled it from his belt. "Wayburne." He listened, and then said, "Okay, I'll be right over." He looked at Amy. "I have to get over to the lighthouse." He touched her cheek. "I'll be back as soon as I can. Hold on a little longer."

Amy watched him step out the French door and disappear. She squeezed her eyes shut and threw her head back. "I can't wait, Gramps. Jamie's down there. God knows what happening to him." She whirled around and looked at her grandfather. "Dallas could be tied up here for hours. I need to go get Jamie out of there *now*."

Gramps turned the chair toward the back door and the wheelchair ramp. "I'm coming with you, Girl."

CHAPTER 39

The sheriff's Yukon and a police car blocked Dan's silver Mercedes. Without explanation to the deputy who was standing outside, Amy opened the passenger door of the Mercedes and helped Gramps into the seat, collapsed the wheelchair, stowed it in the back, and jumped into the driver's seat. She turned the wheel hard left and drove out over the lawn. "I worked on The Cliff House during my first year with the firm," Amy told Gramps. "The parking area is monitored by cameras. If they see Dan's Mercedes, they won't suspect anything. It gives me a better chance of getting inside."

Raindrops splattered the windshield and Amy flipped on the wipers. Looking at the speedometer, she was amazed. She would never have been able to take the curves this fast in her Jeep.

Gramps seemed to read her thoughts. "Dan always knew how to live. Tell me, what part did he play in all this?"

Amy tried not to break her concentration. "A pawn, like me. His father, Dr. George Johnstone, spelled with a T, was Mom's OB/GYN. Along with his wife, Vera, they delivered my twin and me…and a lot of other infants. Dan was their son and Nita is their daughter."

"*Johnstone*. Kind of wondered if there was a connection, the name being so close. Wish that I'd

221

looked into that years ago. What's the rest of the story?"

Amy turned off Lighthouse Road and sped through town toward the coast highway. She let her grandfather grasp what she was saying before continuing, "Your other granddaughter, Alesha, grew up in a research facility in Paraguay. From what Dan said, I doubt that she ever lived a normal life."

Gramps sat silently for a long time. "Poor girl. What a life, living like that in Paraguay of all places. The end of the earth. Think for a minute, what this Helmut Eickher, has done to our family: the deaths of Sharalynn, Dave, and now Dan, the hurt and threats to all of us, burning down my house, sending killers after you, is there anything I missed? Who knows what he did to the other families. The man's a psycho."

Amy wasn't going to tell him what happened to Grams, nor her previous run-in with the meat cutter. Not now anyway. They drove in silence for a while, then Gramps said, "We're heading into the lion's lair and neither one of us have a weapon."

CHAPTER 40

Doris Eickher sped toward The Cliff House. That morning, she had followed in Alesha's footsteps and gone to Beaverdale where a woman with spiked hair blew smoke in Doris's face and gave her Amy's number. Doris tried to get up the nerve to call but couldn't bring herself to do it. Finally, she had decided to go to George Johnstone's house. Sooner or later Helmut would show up there. Doris knew that when he was in the U.S., Helmut split his time between The Cliff House and Vera Johnstone's bedroom. His visits weren't frequent, but they were often lengthy.

Clutching a map, Doris had gone up and down the coast highway, turning down every road near the caves. Now, she was on a washed out track that ambled through the trees. Worse, it was climbing in elevation. Where was the sea?

She wiggled higher in the seat struggling to see over the wheel and through the torrential rain that defied the wipers. The road turned sharply left and suddenly she found herself in a well-lit parking area. Three cars were parked in front of a high concrete retaining wall, but there was no house or building in sight.

She parked her rental next to the Bentley and sat for a moment, wondering if she was in the right place. She picked up the old flip style cell phone and keyed in the first few digit of Amy's number, then stopped. There

223

was so much to tell the young woman, but she couldn't do it on the phone. She needed to meet with her. But first, she had to find Alesha.

When Doris stepped out of the car, her feet sank into a mulch of wet leaves. The wind tore the umbrella from her hands and the rain drenched her. "Such a miserable climate," she grumbled aloud, making her way to a recessed area in the corner. As much to get out of the weather as anything, she hurried toward it, and was surprised to find herself in front of two black metal doors. An elevator! To one side was a two-button panel with a red light and a thin slot for a key card. She felt in her purse for her ring of keys and pulled it out. On it was her key card. Each of them had one for the elevators at the facility. She wondered if Helmut & Johnstone would have used the same code. She slid her card into the slot and the light turned green. She could hear the elevator coming up the shaft. There was a whirring sound and the door slid open revealing a large brass-walled interior. She stepped inside. The door closed and she stared at the four buttons. She pressed *Main Level* and the elevator descended.

Stepping out, she found herself in a vast atrium filled with potted trees and plants. In the center was an oval pond teaming with Koi. She disliked Koi. A staircase curved dramatically toward the skylight, four stories up. Opposite her, was another staircase, leading down to the floors below. Doris realized she had parked on the roof. George Johnstone had always boasted his house was impossible to find. This must be it!

No one seemed aware of her arrival. In the distance she heard a man's voice lecturing, admonishing. It was the same voice that had ruled her life for almost forty years. Yes, she was at the right place.

Doris reached into her purse and pulled out the handgun she had bought when she arrived in Portland. It felt powerful in her hand: an equalizer. She had never held a gun before, but she knew it would be needed to persuade Helmut to release Alesha. Forty years with the man had taught Doris that she held no power of persuasion with him.

Doris knew that Alesha's unscheduled departure from the Paraguayan facility would enrage Helmut to the point where he would likely immobilize Alesha, as he'd done in the past. Nothing made Doris angrier than Helmut treating her beautiful daughter like a prisoner. It broke Doris's heart to think of it and it was this deep concern for Alesha that had brought Doris to Oregon.

As she listened to Helmut's voice, she thought about all the years she had cared for the man, served him faithfully, jumped to meet his every need, and loved him. Yes, she had loved him. As a doctor, she had worked her lifetime to advance his research. She had been loyal in every way for almost four decades. And for what? What had he given in return? Love? No! What she had mistaken for Helmut's apparent love had turned out to be his best effort at assimilating an emotion he couldn't fathom. He was incapable of love. He was incapable of feeling for others. She knew that now.

But he had proven to be quite capable of pleasing another woman. His affair with Vera Johnstone had sizzled for ten long years! Anger and humiliation rose like bile in the back of Doris's throat. She swallowed hard.

Doris had watched Helmut's obsession with his research grow, and his sanity wane, over the last decade. She grew to understand that her husband was psychotic. Recently, his violent episodes had become more frequent. She was tired of walking with a fresh limp or wearing makeup and sunglasses to hide bruises and black eyes. What hurt more was seeing the same thing happen to Alesha. That was intolerable.

Helmut had to be stopped.

Doris left the atrium and walked into a cavernous room with a wall of glass. Luxurious leather sofas and chairs, a thick rug, and rich dark wood, made her think it must be the living room. Following the sound of his voice, she crossed the rug and entered a wide hallway leading to another room. Doris leaned against the doorjamb and listened.

"Where were you going, boy? Were you trying to escape?" Helmut laughed without mirth. "Well? Speak up. What's that? I can't hear you."

Doris heard a tiny voice and her heart ached. "I want to go home."

"And how were you going to do that?" Eickher shouted.

"Don't know."

Doris peaked around the doorjamb and saw a little, platinum-haired boy of five or so, staring forlornly up at Helmut. Helmut walked over to a wall panel and flipped an intercom switch. "Maria, where are you? What's taking so long?"

"Alesha isn't in her room, Doctor."

"What?" The force of his voice made the child leap into the air. "The door was supposed to be kept locked."

"I know." She replied. "Maybe someone forgot."

"And who might that someone be? You, perhaps? Find her. Quickly!" Eickher looked at the boy accusingly, bending forward until his long nose touched Jamie's. "Did you unlock Alesha's door?" he demanded.

Jamie stepped back nervously, shaking his head, his gray eyes wide with fear.

"Answer me!" Helmut's hand swung at the child's face faster than Doris could react to prevent it. The boy flew against the wall, his small body dropping onto the floor. He scrambled quickly to his feet and backed away from the scientist. Eickher raised his hand again.

"Stop!" Doris screamed, aiming the gun at Eickher.

The scientist froze, his teeth snapping nervously. "Doris..." was all he could manage, his eyes bulging at the sight of the revolver in her hand and the wild look in her eyes.

With the gun pointed at Eickher, Doris sidestepped to the boy, extending her hand to him. "Come here, child," she said tenderly. When she felt his small hand in hers, she maneuvered him out of Helmut's reach. Then she lashed out at her husband, "Now, let's see how brave you are, Helmut Eickher."

CHAPTER 41

Torrents of rain pelted the windshield as Amy maneuvered the Mercedes up the narrow, mucky track. She hoped that she had remembered correctly how to get to The Cliff House, as it had been a long time since she'd been there. Emerging into a parking area, she slid the car next to a Lexus. The parking area and high concrete retaining wall triggered a memory. She recalled that the property was registered to an offshore company. The owner remained strangely anonymous throughout construction. He had hired a local firm to manage the project. Because of its unusual location and design, the house had been dubbed *The Cliff House*.

Amy turned to Gramps. "Wait here. I'm going to try and get inside. If I remember correctly, the elevator is access-coded, so I'll probably have to use the emergency exit down the side of the house."

"What house?"

"We're on the roof."

"You're not going in there alone. I'm coming with you," Gramps hollered, grasping her hand.

"I'll be using the stairs, Gramps, and I remember the floorplan, so I can move around quickly in my search for Jamie and Alesha." She couldn't see her grandfather in the dark, but she could feel the tension in the grasp of his hand. "Don't worry, I won't be long. As soon as I find Jamie and Alesha we'll be out of there."

"Let me tell you, Girl, that'll be no small feat, if Eickher's in there." The old man reached into his jacket. "Wish I hadn't given my gun over to Dallas."

"If I run into trouble, I'll improvise. Besides, I'm no damned good with a gun. I found that out on the

228

beach." Amy pulled her hood over her head and stepped out, grabbed the tire iron out of the trunk and handed it to her grandfather. "Here, use this if you need a weapon. It worked for you once. Keys are in the ignition. Be back soon."

The storm was raging. She followed the concrete wall around a corner to a hidden set of concrete stairs that descended two flights down the side of the building. She was met with a wall of wind and driving rain. She tried the door at the first landing. Locked. She hurried down to the next level. The door handle turned, but the door itself was jammed. She pulled and yanked until it came free and opened inward.

She slipped inside, water streaming from her clothes. If anyone noticed the puddle she was leaving, they'd immediately suspect an intruder. More reason to hurry. She saw that she had entered on the guest level. The floor was quiet, so she tiptoed cautiously, passing open doors, and glancing inside unoccupied rooms. One of these rooms had to be Jamie's or possibly Alesha's. The owner's suite was one floor down and staff accommodations were in the basement.

Amy slipped past the open staircase and continued working her way toward the end of the hall, checking rooms she passed by. Each was being used, but was unoccupied. Sweat trickled down her back, and her hands felt cold and clammy. She couldn't afford to be seen. If she were caught, all would be lost.

She came to the last room. The door was closed. Putting her hand on the handle, she pushed it open. Unlike the others, it was dark inside. She stepped in for a better look. The second she did so, she felt a presence. The door closed and a cool hand flew over her mouth, yanking her head back.

Amy whirled around.

The voice stopped her cold. "Who are you?"

The voice was identical to her own. Amy's response was little more than a whisper. "Alesha?"

A light snapped on, blinding Amy. Suddenly two arms flew around her and she felt an embrace like none she could remember. Her heart flew into her mouth as the warmth from a body identical to her own, held her. Amy dropped her cheek onto her sister's shoulder and put her arms around her, pulling her close. Half a lifetime had separated them. They had lived in two different worlds, on two different continents, neither knowing the other, yet at this moment they were one. It was as though two halves had finally come together to create a complete whole. For the first time in her life, Amy understood why there had always been an empty spot in her heart that no person could ever fill. At this moment it was flooded with a pleasant warmth that pumped through her body, energizing her, and restoring her soul.

Alesha pulled away first and Amy found herself staring in amazement at her twin. Her face was identical: prominent cheekbones, small nose, same full lips, broad forehead, and pale skin. She wore her fair hair long and tied back at the nape of her neck. Looking down, Amy was even more surprised to see that they were wearing almost the same clothes. Their eyes met and both women smiled. Amy was the first to speak. "We're identical. It's amazing."

"I've waited all my life to meet you," Alesha whispered excitedly. "I found out about you accidently, when I was five years old. Doris let it slip. From the moment she told me about you, I wanted to meet you, to be with you, to grow up with you." Alesha hugged Amy again, tears misting her eyes. "I used to drive Doris crazy for information. Helmut had to give me updates to keep me happy—"

Amy was shocked, "What? How did he accomplish that?"

230

Alesha shook her head. "He said you were the control. He watched your growth and milestones so he could compare them to mine. He said there'd never be another set of twins as beautiful or as intelligent. He reveres us. Holds us up as the optimum specimens of *near* perfection. Of course, being *women*, we would never be *perfect*. He has this sick dream that one day soon, he'll have his way with me, resulting in me giving Helmut a *boy*. The idea makes me physically ill. I'm afraid of what I'd do to him if he ever got close to me in that way. In his eyes, that second generation *male* child will be the crowning glory of his life's work."

Amy was appalled by what she was hearing. "Alesha, he's responsible for our parents' murder. He needs to be put away."

Alesha was staring at Amy, horror etched into her expression. "He's cruel beyond words. He strikes out when he's angry. He's beaten poor Doris so badly she couldn't walk for months and sent me flying more than once. But I've never thought of him as a murderer."

Amy grew worried. "We can talk about that later. We need to find Jamie and get out of here."

"You're right. Is Dan in the parking lot?"

"Dan?"

"Didn't he bring you here?"

Amy hesitated. "No. It may have been his intention, but we were attacked at our house. One of Eickher's thugs shot Dan." Amy remembered Dan's words as he spoke of Alesha. *I loved her.*

Alesha was so still Amy wondered if her sister had gone into shock. "Alesha?"

"Is he going to be okay?"

Amy shook her head. "He died from the gunshot wound."

Alesha wiped her eyes, and then she said shakily, "We have to get out of here. Dan and I had planned to leave tonight. I told him I wouldn't go without you. He was supposed to talk you into coming with us. Dan unlocked my door before he left so I could come down the hall and get Jamie. We're standing in Jamie's room." Alesha pointed to a bag of clothes. "I had warm clothes for each of us. Dan had planned for Jamie and I to leave by the emergency exit at the end of the hall. Meanwhile, Dan was supposed to have already picked you up and be waiting down the road from the parking area. Then we'd be off to the Portland airport. The whole thing was quite simple, but Eickher must have suspected something. Jamie has disappeared."

Amy lost her breath. "Oh no." Amy felt her heart beating in panic. She had to find Jamie and get him out of there! She opened the door and stepped into the hall. At that moment a large woman appeared on the landing. Alesha pulled Amy back into the room so they wouldn't be seen. When they checked a minute later, the woman had disappeared down the stairs.

"That's Maria, Johnstone's nurse and assistant," Alesha whispered. "There's usually a security guard, Sven Werner—mean, ugly guy— but he's been off the last few days.

Amy's eyes widened. "Did he happen to have a scar on his jaw and drive a BMW?"

Surprised, Alesha said, "Yes, he does, but the BMW is Dr. Johnstone's. How did you know?"

Amy cleared her throat, "Long, nasty story. But he won't be back."

"Good, but meanwhile, Francisco, Helmut's bodyguard, is covering for him. We can't just go down there. We need a new plan."

CHAPTER 42

The Yukon fishtailed as Dallas rounded a sharp curve on the coast highway. He was southbound for the area around The Caves. Peering through the bucking wipers, he wondered how far he was behind the Mercedes. He was certain Amy was headed to what Nita had described as The Cliff House. Dallas had heard of it, but couldn't place it. He felt in his shirt pocket for Nita's directions and flipped on the interior light.

The Yukon swung wide on a curve, the tires hydroplaning, the back end of the truck sliding off the highway. Slower would be safer, but he couldn't stomach the thought of Amy walking into that house alone.

Dallas plucked the radio from the console. "I'm about three minutes from the turnoff and my rear view mirror is still black. Where the hell are you guys?"

"Mile Marker Fifty-five, Sheriff, and we're sliding around like we're on ice. Rain's so bad we're almost blind. Matson's right behind us."

"He was supposed to stay at Cape Peril."

"He bores easy, Sheriff. The detectives are still there."

Dallas cursed under his breath. "I'm coming up to the turnoff now. It's damned hard to see in all this rain, so make sure you don't miss it. It's a hundred yards

233

past Mile Marker Ninety-two." He flipped off the siren and lights. "It's Code 2. Don't go announcing your arrival." Dallas worked the Yukon up the narrow, pot-holed track. "Road's more like a wagon trail. It's awash and as slippery as oil."

CHAPTER 43

The security room was located on the lowest level of the six story Cliff House. Squeezed into the windowless room was a bank of monitors, a large desk, and one swivel chair. Slouched on that chair was Francisco Mandez, staring at the monitor bank, his feet on the desk. He downed the last of his vodka, and then raised the empty glass to the single overhead light. The bottle on his desk was empty.

His feet hit the floor with a thud. There was another bottle hidden under the passenger seat of the Bentley, but that meant another trip up to the parking area, something he didn't look forward to on a night like this. Oh, how he missed Paraguay. Not just for the weather, he missed the facility, which had been his home since Doris had plucked him off the streets fifteen years earlier.

He staggered around the desk and took another cursory look at the bank of monitors. He was Eickher's bodyguard, but they had assigned Francisco to fill in for Sven Werner, the security guard who had been off the past few days. Francisco hit a toggle, causing the exterior camera to pan the upper lot, and seeing nothing but rain bubbles on the camera lens, he shrugged and proceeded up two flights of stairs to the atrium elevator. Pulling a thin key card from his shirt pocket, he slid it into the slot below the elevator button, and waited impatiently for the elevator doors to open.

It was then he heard angry voices coming from the other side of the house. One unmistakably belonged to Senior Eickher. The other belonged to a woman. He could swear it was Senora Doris. But how could that be? She never traveled. For that matter, she seldom left the facility for more than a day or two.

Deciding to investigate, he tiptoed across the living room, into the adjoining hallway, and stopped. In all the years he had served the Eickhers, he had never heard Doris raise her voice to anyone, let alone to the boss. The fact that she was now tearing into the man, gave Francisco a huge sense of satisfaction. He backed around the corner and listened unabashed, as her wonderfully perfect English exploded through the room. If only he could speak like that!

"So, you've locked Alesha in a room like a common prisoner. How could you! Where's the key? Good. Put it on the table and step away." Francisco heard nothing for a few minutes so he moved closer and peeked around the corner. Doris continued speaking. "You have a lot of nerve, Helmut Eickher. You're like a runaway locomotive thundering down the wrong track. Your research is being done for the wrong reasons and your ideals have taken a wrong turn. To top it off, your sex life is with the wrong woman. You've insulted me. You've humiliated me. You have been—" she looked down at Jamie, "Cover your ears, Child." She cast a searing look at Eickher. "You've been screwing Vera Johnstone for years. We are finished, Helmut! Now turn around and walk out that door. Yes, that's right, down the hall, and keep your hands on top of your head where they won't get into trouble!"

Francisco backed out of sight, and then stuck his head around the corner for a look. A strange trio crossed the living room, lead by Eickher. Doris and the boy followed.

Why was Senior Eickher—a man who gave orders, who never took them—why was he doing as he was told?

Then, Francisco saw the gun. It was pointed at the senior's back. Worse, the Senora's finger was on the trigger! What to do? Francisco was paid to protect the Eickhers, but not from each other.

He watched dumbfounded. Doris ordered, "Open the door." Reluctantly, Eickher opened the patio door. Wind, rain, and the roar of the ocean blasted into the room. Doris yelled above the din. "It's time for you to drop out, so to speak, Helmut, before you do any more harm in this world."

Eickher looked behind him into the stormy void, then back at Doris. "Be reasonable, Doris," he shouted, "I am a man, after all."

"Yes, I'm sure Vera Johnstone will vouch for you in that regard. But it's not just your body that's gone off the rails, Helmut. The brain that operates your body is faulty and corrupt. I used to believe in you and your plan for a better world. But it's no longer betterment you are trying to achieve. It's control. You dream of having the universe at your fingertips. And I won't be a part of that. Nor will l allow you to continue."

Eickher stepped toward her, his jaw snapping. "Doris think!" he implored, spittle flying with his words. "Everything's in place. We have twenty-five super-brains strategically positioned around the world. We have another twenty integrated into government. Twenty-two more are at our facility, devoted to research and the continuance of our project." He rubbed his bony hands together and his beady eyes gleamed. "Our cellular research is bringing in a fortune and our shares on the NASDAQ are going steadily up. Our patent will bring in billions of dollars! Nothing can stop us now. The world is ours!"

Doris smiled sadly. "Oh, Helmut, you have two eyes, but you don't see what's in front of them. You stole sixty-seven infants from their families and left behind tears and heartbreak. You've spent thirty-two years worrying about being caught by the FBI for that ongoing crime. Only you and God know what other horrific crimes you've committed over the years. And, as far as our young adults are concerned, you might remember that I was the one who worked with those gifted children every day. I knew which ones would promote goodness in the world and which ones would not. And you'll remember that I was the one who controlled their test results."

A look of realization changed Eickher's expression. His eyes turned ice cold, his jaw snapped wordlessly, and his hand opened and closed as rage set in.

Doris continued, "Yes, Helmut. The lead group—those you had selected for strategic positions-- showed dangerous inclinations. I adjusted their test result accordingly. I wanted to ensure they'd remain at the facility where I could watch over them. So you see, Helmut, the project's finished. No more controlled births. And your big dream—for Alesha to have a child, *the boy child* you could sculpt into ultimate perfection? That will never happen. She would never have let you plant your twisted seed in her body, and I would have made certain of it. You've done enough damage. Now, let's see if you can depart this world like the man you believe you are. Step back!" Doris waved the revolver. "And on your way down, you can recall all those lustful nights with Vera Johnstone."

Eickher backed out onto the balcony, the wind whipping his clothes. When he felt the rail against his back, he looked below to the crashing waves, then back at Doris.

Suddenly, Maria's deep throaty voice boomed across the other room.

"Put the gun down!"

Turning her head in surprise, Doris saw the large woman bearing down upon her. Out of self-preservation she swung the gun in the woman's direction. Maria's left hand locked around Doris's wrist.

Another voice yelled, "Take your hands off her!"

Helmut, Doris, and Maria froze. Shock registered on all three faces. Francisco angled his head around the corner for a look. Standing not ten feet from him were two Alesha's! He shook his head trying to clear the illusion. He had always known vodka could destroy a man. This was the proof. He closed his eyes, and then opened them slowly, praying his double vision would disappear. But no! There were two. Both had blonde hair tied into a knot at the napes of their long, pale necks. Hail Mary, one of them was enough to make any man weep, such was their beauty. But two!

He longed to touch them, to be certain they were real, to reassure himself that it wasn't the vodka eating into his brain.

Eickher was the first to recover. He dove back inside and grabbed Jamie by the arm. "Come here, boy." Then, he pointed a shaky finger at Alesha and Amy, and shouted to Francisco, "Don't stand there man, grab them. Lock them up!"

Francisco took a faltering step in their direction. He had never been permitted near Alesha at the facility. She was *the Golden One,* the privileged one. Everyone called her *The Angel of Light.* And—she was Doris's child.

As he stepped hesitantly toward the two women, they warned him away. The closest one held up her hand. There was a hypodermic needle between her fingers. Francisco's eyes bugged. He hated needles.

"Can you imagine what's in this syringe, Helmut?" She tipped it toward him. "Humalog." She put the thin needle tip against her sister's carotid artery. "Injected directly into the carotid artery means coma and death.

Without Alesha there will be no ultimate conclusion to your project. And you can't risk loosing that, can you? We're leaving, Helmut. With Jamie. Don't try to stop us, not if you want Alesha, to live."

Eickher's eyes darted between the two women. He pointed to the second woman and ordered Maria, "Shoot her."

Maria looked down at the gun, her fear of Eickher obvious. Shakily, she raised the barrel in the direction of the twins.

Doris gasped and pushed her small body in front of the weapon. "No!" she cried, "you are not going to shoot our child, Helmut. And who knows which one she is."

The twins moved slowly toward Jamie, the far one speaking first. "The only hope you have to complete your project, Helmut, is to let the three of us leave."

"Enough!" Eickher's black eyes burned like hot coals against his colorless skin. "How dare you threaten my project. I don't need Alesha's acquiescence for completion, just her body," he spat, jaw snapping. "No one can stop me!"

He grabbed the gun from Maria and lowered the barrel until it was aimed directly at Jamie. There was an intake of breath around the room. Alarm showed on the twins' faces. "I won't allow my project to be perverted by anyone. Decades of work and sacrifice are at stake." He pulled Jamie in front of him and looked from one woman to the other, his beady eyes settling on the twin holding the needle. "But I do need Alesha. So, I think we can put an end to all of this silliness and determine which one she is." He put one hand on Jamie's shoulders and shoved him in front of the two women. Holding the gun at the child's back, he said, "They say a child always knows his mother." He gave Jamie a nudge with the barrel of the gun. "So, boy. Which one's *your mother*?"

CHAPTER 44

Amy held her breath, willing her emotions to stay in check, even though she was on the verge of screaming. She wanted to dive for Jamie and push him to safety, but Eickher's finger was on the trigger. She couldn't risk a shot going off and hitting her son. She hadn't been this close to him in over a week. She wanted to scoop him into her arms and hold him. She wanted to hug him and to feel his small body against her breast. She wanted him away from Eickher and out of danger. But she had to wait for the right moment.

Jamie's large gray eyes took in each detail of the women's faces. Precious seconds ticked by as he touched their hands and looked carefully at each of their faces. Finally, he stepped between them, and with his back to Eickher, closed his eyes and turned to each woman in turn. He inhaled. Then he turned back to the scientist and looked up at him defiantly. "I don't know."

Eickher's voice became sugary. "Of course you do, Boy. Take your time. Look again. All you have to do is point to your mom, and then you can go home, like you wanted," he crooned. "So, which one is she?"

Amy watched Jamie, her heart in her throat, her eyes darting to the gun. She could see from his expression that he knew, but he wasn't going to give her up to Eickher. He was so brave.

Eickher cocked the revolver. "Enough time wasted. There's one final way to find out." He put the barrel of the gun to Jamie's temple.

Gramps, who'd wheeled his chair silently into the next room, whipped the wheelchair around the corner, and yelled, "Freeze, you bastard!"

Amy and Alesha dove for Jamie, knocking him away from the gun. At the same second, Doris threw herself at her husband, sending both of them sprawling across the floor. Amy scooped Jamie into her arms and ran for the stairs, followed by Alesha.

Francisco dove for the gun, but missed. George Johnstone walked into the room and seeing the mayhem, yelled, "What the hell—"

There was a struggle for the weapon. A shot rang out and Johnstone fell to the floor. Everyone froze.

In the sudden silence, Eickher heard the two women racing up the stairs. With the .38 in hand, he stood and bolted after them.

As he ran for the staircase, he passed in front of the wheelchair. Gramps was ready. The second Eickher came into range, Gramps whipped out the tire iron and sent him sprawling.

CHAPTER 45

Out of the corner of her eye, Amy saw Eickher go down, but he still had the gun and he could shoot again. At the next landing was an emergency exit. She remembered it opened onto a balcony. Was it a dead end? No, she recalled a narrow staircase leading down to a trail. Amy rushed up the stairs toward the door.

Carrying Jamie slowed her, but she didn't dare put him down. When they got to the landing, Alesha reached around her, and threw open the door. Amy rushed out, into the driving rain, pulling her jacket around her son. Alesha slammed the door behind them.

Amy pointed down the steps. "Eickher will be right behind us and he's still got the gun. There's a trail down there. If we take it, we'll be out of sight. Hurry!"

Panting, they ran down the concrete steps and dashed into wet overburden. Amy reached into her coat pocket for the penlight she had used earlier on the beach. She turned it on to see where she was going. Alesha pushed her on. "Don't stop."

A few minutes later, her breathing ragged, Amy ducked under a cedar tree and let Jamie slide off her hip. Alesha dug in her bag for his jacket. She knelt down. "Here. Put this on," she told the boy, "quick, before you get soaked."

He looked at her, his soft gray eyes inspecting her. "Thanks, Auntie."

243

Amy knelt beside him and pulled the hood over his head. To Alesha she said, "He has no trouble figuring out which of us is his mom and which is his aunt, even in the dark." She pulled Jamie close and hugged him tightly. "I missed you so much, Sweetheart." She whispered, "And I love you more than ever."

Two arms found their way around her neck. He kissed her cheek. "Love you, Mommy. I knew you'd come."

Worried, Alesha stood up and looked behind them. "No sign of Helmut yet, but it'll only take him a couple of minutes to figure out what we did. When he sees the trail, he'll probably stop for a jacket and a light. He'll be behind us in no time."

Amy looked in the other direction. The trail was a wide, needle covered passage through cedars and firs. "If I remember right, this is the old trail to The Caves."

Alesha nodded. "I think you're right. Francisco mentioned it to me the other day when they let me out for air."

Amy said thoughtfully, "The bad news is, I don't know of a way to double back up to the parking area. All we can do for now is keep going and hope Eickher gives up on us."

About ten minutes later, the trail reached the edge of the cliff. Amy shone the penlight down. Fifty feet straight down, an angry ocean lashed the rocks. The forest which had sheltered them from the wind and rain, was behind them. The roar of the ocean and the driving rain made Amy step back, pushing Jamie behind her. She swept the light along the ridge to have a look at the terrain. The landscape was small brush and moss covered rock. She turned to Alesha. "The trail gets quite treacherous from here. With all the rain, it's going to be pretty slippery. It would be crazy to go on, especially in the dark."

Alesha glanced back. "Still no sign of Helmut," she said. "We passed a small clearing back there. Why don't we see if we can get out of sight and out of the rain for a while."

They huddled together behind a huge rotting cedar stump. Alesha said, "At least we won't be seen from the trail." Cedar boughs from surrounding trees protected them, minimally. She retrieved the small blanket from her bag.

Amy was taken aback. "That's Jamie's favorite blanket."

"Dan brought it to the house so he could sleep. I knew Jamie loved that blanket so I packed it," she explained. "Thank God I did." She spread it over them. Amy held Jamie on her lap, trying to keep him dry.

Suddenly, a bright light and a loud voice made them jump. Eickher stood in front of them. "Aha!" he yelled, "I hate to be the bearer of bad news, but we have to keep moving. I saw the sheriff back there," he snapped. "Come on. Up! Up! Let's go."

The voice sent fear coursing through Amy. She knew the trail was dangerous, but Eickher was lethal. Now they had to deal with both.

CHAPTER 46

Dallas jumped from the car and threw on his raincoat. He couldn't wait for his team. Following the concrete wall to its end, he found a set of hidden stairs and had just started down when a man ducked out a door below him. "Hold it!" Dallas shouted, pulling his weapon.

Francisco put his hands over his head. "No, no. Don't shoot! I was checking to see if they came back."

"Who?" Dallas motioned him over to the stairs. "Put your back against the wall."

"The Senoritas and the boy. They were running from Senior Eickher. He has a gun."

"Who are you?" Dallas asked suspiciously.

"Francisco Mandez. I work for Senior Eickher. I am hired to protect him, but right now I think it's the senoritas that need protecting."

"Where did they go?"

"Come, I show you." Dallas followed Francisco inside the house, down two flights of stairs, and out onto a balcony. Francisco pointed to the narrow staircase. "At the bottom, there's a trail. I followed it a few days ago. It goes to the caves, but it gets very dangerous, so I came back. It is too thin. I don't wish to go again."

"You mean, narrow?"

"Si. Narrow. Sometimes it slides away."

"Did you actually see Eickher go down this trail?"

"Si. I was right behind."

"And the two women? You're sure they went this way?"

"Si. They came out here. Where else could they go?"

Dallas looked around. He had a point. "Who's inside the house?"

"Senoras Doris and Maria," he hesitated, "and an old man in a wheelchair. He had a tire iron and he come just when everything go wrong and the gun go off."

Dallas rubbed his eyes in frustration. "The gun went off. Anyone hurt?" Dallas asked, silently cursing Hadden and trying to picture the scene.

"Dr. Johnstone. He was shot."

"Did someone call the Paramedics?"

"Si. And Senora Doris is a doctor. She is with him."

Dallas couldn't wait any longer. "Okay, go back inside. My men will be here any minute."

Dallas sprinted down the trail, his radio in hand, and gave them the heads up on the situation inside the house; then he said, "Get SAR out to The Caves. The chopper too. Make it fast. I'm headed down the old trail from The Cliff House."

CHAPTER 47

They picked their way along the steep, slippery incline, Amy leading, followed by Alesha and behind her, Jamie. Eickher was last, the revolver in one hand, Jamie's jacket collar clutched in his other, forcing the boy to walk along the outer edge of the trail. If anything happened to the scientist, the child would go over the edge. That was Eickher's protection in case the women got ideas of overpowering him. It would also prevent the sheriff from taking a shot at him from behind.

Before going after the women, Eickher had stopped for his raincoat and had seen the sheriff's Yukon pull up on the surveillance monitor. He had to assume the sheriff would be behind them soon, if he wasn't already.

Eickher needed to figure out which woman was Alesha and then get off the trail, out of the area, and out of the country, for that matter. The gun he was holding had gone off inside the house. From what he saw, Johnstone was probably dead. The bullet had blown away part of his skull. There was no way Eickher was going to allow himself to be arrested and tried for murder in the U.S.

He knew Alesha disliked heights, so he kept his eye on the two women, watching to see which one of them would show signs of that phobia. Not that it mattered at the moment. He scanned the bluff above him and below him with his powerful flashlight and then shut it off. It was sheer and steep in both directions. There was no way off the ledge right now.

The night was black and the going was painfully slow. Gusting wind and driving rain made the passage almost impassable. So far, neither woman showed any particular fear of heights. Of course, that would change with first light, when the steep drop became visible. As soon as Alesha showed herself, he'd get rid of Amy. The architect had learned too much. A little slip over the edge and that problem would be solved.

He needed the boy though. Alesha loved the child. She had the same ridiculous weakness for children as Doris, so the boy would prove valuable. He'd use the child to manipulate Alesha. Damned incorrigible woman. She got worse every year. But he still needed her to give him a son so he could finish his project. The sooner he did that the better. The thought of taking Alesha to bed excited him. His heart raced as he imagined her perfect body naked against his.

The penlight ahead of him caught his attention. "Keep that light down," he yelled, "or I'll take it away and you can find your way in the dark." Insolent, he thought, the both of them. Last thing he needed was the sheriff seeing the light.

CHAPTER 48

Dallas recalled the trail from years earlier, when he'd used it to hike down to The Caves. A nasty piece of work. When The Cliff House was built, public access to the trail was cut off, so a new access was built a few miles up the highway. Last he'd heard, it was almost unusable in winter due to storms.

Ahead of him, a flickering light was visible intermittently. It diminished, and then reappeared further along. Dallas couldn't see the foursome in the dark, but he knew they would be inching along single file. The last thing he wanted to do was to agitate Eickher, prompting the man to fire his gun or send someone over the edge. Dallas stayed back, hoping that with the coming dawn, he might get a clear shot at the scientist. Truth was, from this distance, he needed Larson's rifle.

He pulled out his radio. "I can't get close enough to risk a shot. Send Larson out with his rifle. And tell him to grab my coil of rope out of the Yukon. Any word on the chopper?"

"A no go, Sheriff. Too windy."

"What about SAR?"

"On their way. I'll keep you informed. Things inside the house aren't good. Johnstone took a head shot. He didn't make it. The four witnesses say Eickher pulled the trigger."

"That explains why he's so damned determined to get out of here." Dallas said.

"Hey, Sheriff, what's all the noise? Where exactly are you?"

"Still on the trail. Worst place in the world on a night like this."

CHAPTER 49

Early morning light filtered through the low cloud cover, giving the group the first glimpse of the precipice they were descending. It was a sheer drop from the trail to the ragged rocks that were now thirty feet below them. The sea hurtled itself over the pinnacles, sending spray up over their feet and onto the trail, which had diminished to about a foot in width. One slip would lead to certain death.

Amy felt Alesha's grip tighten on her shoulder, warning Amy that her sister had a fear of heights. Amy stole a glance over her shoulder and saw Alesha's eyes wide with fear. Did Eickher know about this phobia? If he did, he'd recognize it in Alesha immediately. If that happened, Amy knew her life would become instantly worthless.

Amy glanced back at Jamie. He looked up at her with large, frightened eyes and reached his hand out. "I want to walk with you."

She gave him a small smile. "Soon, we'll change places soon."

"I want to change now," he said, trying to pull away from Eickher

The scientist yanked the child hard. "Stop it!" Eickher still gripped Jamie's jacket. The gun hung from his other hand.

Furious, and helpless to do anything about it, Amy turned back around. She didn't want Jamie to talk for fear he'd call out, *Mommy* and give her away.

Eickher shouted, "Keep moving!"

"We can't go much further," Alesha told him, "The trail's almost gone!"

Amy could hear panic in her sister's voice and reached for her hand, squeezing hard, hoping Alesha understood the warning. *Don't give yourself away.*

Putting one foot ahead of the other with extreme care, Amy continued forward. She tried to remember how far they were from the caves. When she was working with the design team on The Cliff House, she and a couple of co-workers hiked the trail during the summer months. If her memory served, they now were about a hundred feet from the caves.

Rounding a corner, Amy stopped dead. Her right foot was only inches from the edge. The trail had disappeared, taken out by a slide. She looked down into the boiling sea. Alesha's fingertips dug deeper into Amy's shoulder.

"Why are you stopping? Get the lead out!" Eickher yelled.

"Trail's gone. It's been taken out by a slide." Amy called back.

He peered around Alesha, frowning. "Jump!" he ordered.

Amy swallowed and looked down. The ledge on the other side was just as narrow. There was no way of getting a run at it. Amy thought she could make it, but what about Jamie? Worse, Alesha would never get across. In desperation, Amy looked around. A tree limb would bridge the gap, but there was nothing like that at hand.

Anger ignited within Amy. They had reached a dead end to this treacherous journey. To have gone this far in these conditions was incomprehensible. To go further, was sheer insanity. To send Jamie across that gap was to put his young, precious life in peril, and that made Amy sick. She looked back at Eickher. He had put the gun away, but he still held onto Jamie. A small movement of the man's hand and her child would go careening over the edge. Either way, her son was in extreme danger.

Eickher's cold dark eyes bored into her. He seemed to read her thoughts. With deliberate slowness, he placed his other hand on Jamie's shoulder and looked down into the boiling sea below. He spat through his teeth, his jaw snapping. "I wouldn't hesitate to send the boy over. He'd be gone in a heartbeat."

His words chilled Amy to the bone. She was trapped. There was no way out of their predicament. She asked Alesha, "Do you still have that blanket?"

Alesha passed her the bag and Amy pulled it out.

"What are you waiting for? Get your ass across there." Eickher yelled.

Amy didn't answer. Instead, she folded the blanket lengthwise and turned to Alesha. "I'm going to jump. When I get to the other side, I'll throw you one end of the blanket. Stand on it. It'll act as a safety net for Jamie." Amy undid her belt. "Put this around Jamie, then take yours off and attach it, so it works like a safety line." Alesha's eyes grew wider. Amy tried to reassure Alesha and spoke into her ear "You'll be fine. Just don't look down."

Amy prepared for the jump. She closed her eyes and told herself she could do it. She *had to do it.* Taking a step back, then one forward, she sunk down into her knees, and leapt. Mid-air she thought she was going to fall short.

Her right foot landed on the ledge. She grabbed for the rock wall to stop her forward momentum so she wouldn't continue right over the ledge. "Oh, thank God," she whispered, bending over to catch her breath.

When she turned around, Alesha's eyes were riveted on Amy, her sister's face ashen. "Put the belts on Jamie," Amy reminded her.

As Alesha did so, Jamie's gray eyes locked on his mom's. For a second Amy thought he was going to call out to her, *Mommy.* She winked at him like she usually did when she wanted to tell him *it's going to be okay.* He seemed to understand.

"Hurry it up. This is taking too damn long, you aggravating whore." Eickher hollered.

When Jamie was ready, Alesha picked him up and set him down in front of her. The moment she took Jamie out of Eickher's control, the scientist put the gun to the back of her head and cocked the hammer. "No tricks," he said harshly.

Amy unrolled the blanket and tossed it to Alesha. "Put both feet on it." Amy did the same thing, creating a sling over the gap. She prayed that it would not only act as a safety net for Jamie, but also block Alesha's view of the drop-off, so her sister could help Jamie make the jump and then take the leap herself. Amy leaned out over the gap. "Okay, throw me one end of the belt."

"Come on! Come on!" Eickher looked anxiously behind him.

Alesha sent an end of the belt over to her. Amy knew it wouldn't hold her small son for long, but she only needed it for a split second. Amy braced herself against the rock wall. "Okay, when I yell, *'Now,'* throw Jamie into my arms."

Alesha swallowed and nodded. Amy was glad to see her sister's concern for Jamie was overriding her fear. Amy looked at her son. His big gray eyes were fixed on hers. "Okay, Jamie," she told him, "When I say, *'Now'*, you reach out and grab me." The boy nodded. "Ready? *Now!*"

CHAPTER 50

Dallas had his Glock trained on Eickher. Now that it was light, Dallas had a fair view of the foursome, even though they were some distance away. What was unfolding on the bluff was sheer insanity. A dark anger burned in his gut. The man in his gun sight wouldn't hesitate to send Amy, Alesha, and Jamie to their deaths, if it benefited him to do so. Conversely, Eickher kept the three of them close because he needed them, for now. And he was right. So far, there had been no chance for Dallas to fire his weapon.

Eickher would have seen Dallas's flashlight following at a steady distance, so the scientist had to continue moving forward in the hope of finding an escape route.

Dallas watched Amy's preparation for the Jamie's transit across the gap. He knew that Amy was one of those women who would sacrifice her own life for her son's. If the child slipped away, Amy would go with him. Not many times in his career had Dallas felt so incapacitated. There was nothing he could do to help her, to protect her, or to remove the danger she was in. With the steep bluff above the trail and a sheer drop below, there was no alternative route for Dallas to take, to reach them. If he did anything to alarm Eickher, the man could send any one of them flying over the edge, Jamie in particular. Dallas watched one of the sister's take Jamie from the scientist. Maybe Dallas would get his chance; he leveled his Glock on Eickher. In a split second, the scientist put the barrel of his revolver at the back of the woman's head.

He knows I'm here. He's covering himself, knowing I won't shoot as long as he has a hostage in jeopardy.

Dallas could only watch, wait, hope...and stew.

CHAPTER 51

Alesha looked down and froze.

Amy saw her sway with vertigo and called to her, "Focus. *Please.* We have to get Jamie across." Her sister seemed to hear and understand. She nodded and keeping her eyes on Amy, lifted the boy up.

"*Now!*" Amy shouted again.

Alesha pushed Jamie toward his mom. Amy reached as far as she could, but couldn't reach him. "You need to throw him to me. I have the belt. I'll grab him." Amy wrapped the belt around her wrist and leaned out a little more, hoping her feet would stay planted on the ledge.

"Hurry up, you brainless bitch! This is taking too long." Eickher yelled.

It was a knee jerk reaction. Alesha threw Jamie into the air. The boy reached for his mom. Amy grabbed him mid-flight but misjudged the affect of his weight hitting her as she leaned over the precipice. When she caught him, her body dipped low over the gap, knocking her off balance. Amy knew she had to correct fast or they'd both go down. She pulled Jamie tight to her with her right arm and reached back for the rock bluff with her left. They teetered there, out over the edge.

Alesha screamed, then covered her mouth and turned away.

Amy reached behind her and grabbed onto a protruding rock, pulling herself backward with all her strength. Slowly her body responded. Still holding Jamie tight, she closed her eyes. Tears of relief streamed down her face. Then she put her son down. "Stand very still, Sweetheart. Don't move, okay?"

Jamie nodded.

Amy looked at her sister. "Your turn."

Eickher pushed past Alesha. "I'm next," he announced and stood poised on the edge of the gap. "Get back out of my way." With incredible agility he leapt into the air, landing softly on the other side, with room to spare. He picked up Jamie and dangled him off one hip. Eickher yelled at Alesha, "Get on with it!"

Alesha looked down, her body swaying precariously. "I can't," she said.

Eickher nodded knowingly. "So, now we know that you are Alesha," he said. "Stop this silliness and jump!"

Again, Alesha reacted to him. She pushed off the ledge. But she didn't have enough height.

Amy stifled a scream. Alesha wasn't going to make it.

CHAPTER 52

Larson joined Dallas on the ledge and handed him the coil of rope. "Here's your cowboy lasso, Sheriff."

Dallas slung it over his shoulder. "Don't knock it, Larson, this is the only rope you can throw over a rock, or a person, for that matter. There's just no substitute for what this rope can do."

Larson grinned. "All of us know that, but you're the only one who can make that damn thing work." He looked along the steep bluff, saw the situation, and raised his rifle. "You want to take the shot, Sheriff, or you want me to?"

"You're better at long shots. You see an opportunity, take it. That bastard's going to get them killed. Trouble is, with the angle we're on, it's all but impossible to get a shot off without risk to one of the others."

Larson put his sights on Eickher. "Yeah, you're right." He tried different positions. "There just isn't a clear shot. Not from here." He watched Eickher leap with ease across the gap. "The man's part elk."

"Yeah, and the rest is complete psycho," Dallas said with distain. He'd seen what happened with Jamie. One twin froze, leaving the boy dangling precariously over the brink. To his relief, she had recovered enough to send the child across. The other sister had to lean out so far to grab Jamie that it threw her off balance.

She and the boy almost fell into the void. It was clear that one twin had a debilitating fear of heights. Remembering how Amy was with heights, he knew it wasn't her.

Suddenly Alesha jumped.

"Shit! She's not going to make it!" Dallas yelled to Larson, "Give me the rope." Dallas raced for the gap.

CHAPTER 53

Alesha's death flashed across Amy's mind. She pictured her twin falling onto the rocks, her body gored by the pointed pinnacles. "NO!" Amy screamed.

Alesha was falling a foot short of the landing ledge, her arms out, her feet sending her end of the blanket into the void. Amy reached out, grabbed Alesha's arm, and holding tight, Amy dropped flat onto the ledge. Grasping onto Alesha's other arm, Amy pulled hard, swinging her sister into the rock wall below. Amy braced for Alesha's full body weight to hit her. Suddenly, Alesha's weight yanked Amy's upper body out over the precipice. Amy's arms and shoulders felt like they were being ripped from their sockets. Her muscles burned.

Alesha hung momentarily from Amy's hands before her arms started sliding from Amy's grip. Amy squeezed hard but couldn't stop the slippage. Then she felt Alesha hands in hers and they locked onto each other. Amy could barely breathe. The weight was too much. Suddenly, Alesha was slipping away again.

Alesha searched in desperation for a foothold on the rock face. She found a protrusion. Quickly, she transferred her weight from Amy.

"There's another ledge about a foot up," Amy called out. Alesha found it. Now, Amy could wiggle backward to safety. Their hands were still locked.

"Leave her!" Eickher yelled. "The stupid woman can get up herself. If she can't, she deserves to drown. You hear me Wench, I said, get up!"

CHAPTER 54

Dallas moved quickly, darting in and around rock outcroppings. Eickher spotted him, leveled his revolver in Dallas's direction, and waited for the sheriff to come into view.

A few feet from the gap, Dallas stopped to assess the situation. The second he stuck his head out, Eickher fired. Dallas ducked back. The scientist had the gun raised in one hand and Jamie tucked under his other arm, dangling over the edge. If anything happened to Eickher, the boy would be gone. Neither Dallas, nor Larson could shoot. Meanwhile, one of the sisters, likely Alesha, clung precariously to the rock wall below the gap and there wasn't a damn thing Dallas could do to help her.

He pulled out the radio and spoke to Larson. "You got him in your sights?"

"Yeah, but the prick's still got the boy hanging over the edge."

Dallas told him, "They're moving out. Son-of-a-bitch is leaving one of the women hanging off the wall."

"I'm almost there, Sheriff."

CHAPTER 55

The gunshot sent a bolt of terror through Amy. She glimpsed Dallas on the other side of the gap, about thirty feet down the trail, and hoped Eickher had missed.

Amy waited for Alesha to grab onto a ledge before reluctantly letting go of her sister's hands. "Dallas is close behind us," she told her, "Hang on tight. He'll be here soon."

Amy stood and took one last look at Alesha before turning around. When she turned, what she saw stopped her dead. Eickher was holding Jamie over the edge of the precipice. "Put him down!" Amy screamed at him, reaching for Jamie.

Eickher knocked her back. "One wrong move and I'll drop him," he said. His voice was like ice. His eyes bored through her. "I've had enough of your games. Now, get in front of me where I can see you, and move your ass!" He stepped tight to the edge, forcing Amy to squeeze by on the inside.

"Get moving!" Eickher commanded.

Amy led off, fighting panic. Inside, she was a caldron of churning fear and horror. She was terrified for Jamie, but if she let those fears get a grip on her, they'd paralyze her. She had to focus on finding a way to get Jamie from Eickher, and then get safely away.

265

Beneath her fear, a different emotion began to surface: a deep, burning anger at the psychotic who played them for personal gain. Human life had no value to Eickher. He would toss her beautiful son to his death at the first sign of insubordination or risk. She had to do something fast.

A premonition flashed across her mind and she knew without a doubt that to save her son, she would need to kill Eickher. A dozen scenarios crossed her mind. Never had she ever imagined that some day she would have to kill a man. The thought was revolting, horrifying, and gruesome. Life wasn't supposed to throw a woman into harrowing situations. Life was supposed to be a picket fence and the American dream. Where had it all gone?

CHAPTER 56

Both Larson and Dallas had their weapons trained on Eickher. The man kept Jamie positioned over the ledge. The scientist mocked them, knowing he was safe. Leaving one sister down on the wall, he pushed the other in front of him and followed her out of sight. Just before he disappeared, he turned and tipped his hat to Dallas.

"Bastard!" Dallas cursed, his eyes boring into Eickher's back.

"Egocentric prick," Larson spit out.

"His time is short," Dallas promised, grabbing the coil of rope and dashing for the gap. He called to Alesha, "Put your head down, I'm coming over," and using the forward momentum, he leapt off the ledge, landing heavily on the other side. He knelt down and reached for her, "Alesha?"

"Yes," was the shaky response.

"Okay. Take my hands; I'm going to pull you up. Use your toes to push," Dallas instructed. He pulled with steady strength until he could help her up onto the ledge. It had taken longer than he liked. He had to get to Amy and Jamie.

Alesha stood, relieved. "Thank you, Sheriff," she pushed Dallas down the trail, "I'll be fine. Please continue on. The second Helmut sees an opportunity

267

to flee he'll kill Amy and Jamie. They're only alive because he needs them.

CHAPTER 57

The trail sloped downhill toward The Caves. They were now only about twenty feet above the swirling sea. The ocean surged through a narrow opening in the rock and was trapped by a huge horseshoe of low rocks. The inbound ocean formed a massive whirlpool. One slip and she'd be sucked into the swirling vortex.

Eickher slid over the wet rocks and moss, descending behind her, still holding Jamie near the drop-off.

Amy estimated they were only about thirty feet from the nearest cave, but between them and the entrance a cascade of water rushed down the bluff face. On the other side was a thin, perilous overhang. The water had eroded and undermined the trail, leaving only a small protrusion sticking out. There wasn't much support. Would it hold them?

Amy stopped beside the waterfall. It cascaded straight down. The only thing she could do was jump onto the ledge on the other side and pray it would hold her weight.

"Get going, Wench." Eickher snapped.

Amy reached back and touched Jamie's soft, damp cheek. The child was so weary his eyes were half-closed. "You're a brave boy, Jamie," she told him. "Mommy loves you very much."

Jamie's small hand reached up and caught hers. "Love you, Mommy," he said sleepily.

Amy scanned the ledge for signs of instability. There was a deep fissure about two feet ahead of her landing position. A bad sign. It was crazy to put weight anywhere near there. The entire outcropping could break off the minute they stepped on it. She knew Eickher would never turn around with Dallas behind them. Even if she pointed out this new danger ahead of them, Eickher would tell her to keep going. His escape depended on that.

Suddenly, she was thrown against the rock wall. His right hand flew against her chin, driving her head into the rock. "You whore." He put his face into hers, his breath hot and rancid against her cheek. His jaw snapped uncontrollably. His black eyes were pinholes. "You're only alive because of Alesha's stupidity. You'll take her place. But when I'm done with you," he slid his hand down over her neck, "I'll take the greatest pleasure in breaking your neck!" He yanked her off the wall and flipped her around. "Now, get the fuck over to the other side before I drop this kid in the drink."

Amy tried to catch her breath and stop shaking. She was ill with fear of what was going to become of her and Jamie. *Keep going. Don't do anything to maker him angrier.* She stepped back, took a few steps, and jumped. Mid-air she reached for the rock wall trying to defer some of her body weight and landed as lightly as possible on her toes.

Immediately, she felt the ledge shift. She froze, waiting. It stabilized. Slowly, she turned around. With Jamie on his hip, Eickher weighed almost double what she did. She was certain the outcropping would never sustain his weight. She reached for her son, calling out to be heard over the rushing water. "Pass Jamie to me." She could see the scientist's mind ticking, wondering if he could risk it.

"Get back." Was the chilly response.

Amy stepped gingerly back, looking at the deep crack by her feet. If the ledge started to give away, she needed to move with lightning speed.

Eickher checked behind him. Amy hadn't seen Dallas since the gap and assumed he had stopped to help Alesha. Satisfied the sheriff wasn't in sight, the scientist stepped back, and with Jamie on his outside hip, he leapt over the waterfall and landed heavily on the other side.

The ledge moved. Suddenly, the area beneath them slipped. Instinctively, Eickher let go of Jamie and grabbed for the rock wall.

Amy had anticipated that. A split second before the scientist let go of Jamie, she had her hands around her son. In the next second, she was flying toward the cave, the ledge crumbling and falling behind her. The entire ridge would go at any second.

Eickher screamed, but she didn't dare look back. Her eyes were pinned on the cave opening. Her feet seemed to have lost the ledge. The trail gave way with her every footfall and dropped into the sea.

The cave entrance was only four feet. Three. Two. Then, the ledge went out from under her.

CHAPTER 58

Eickher's hands flailed along the buff wall, looking for something to grab onto. He slipped down about ten feet before his fingers found a hold. Then, the entire ledge slid out from under him. His legs flew free. Desperate, he searched for a place to put his feet, his knees scrapping the rough area left behind. He found a rock for his feet and put his toes on it.

Sweat mixed with mist from the waterfall. He saw Amy race for the mouth of the first cave, the ledge going out from under her. She dove for the entrance, barely making it. Conniving bitch had saved the boy. She must have figured this would happen.

Eickher checked the trail. No sign of the sheriff. Yet. Eickher knew he was an open target where he was; he had to get into the cave. The ledge between him and the cave entrance had vanished into the swirling sea below him. Adeptly, he found new places to put his hands and feet, moving slowly and steadily sideways toward the cave. He grew impatient. If the sheriff came around the corner, that would be it. Move faster. No time for caution. Almost there. I'll get that bitch.

CHAPTER 59

With Jamie in her arms, Amy dove through the small rocky opening to the cave. She landed on her right side, trying not to injure Jamie, and wiggled her legs in behind her.

It was dark and damp inside. The rock curvature dripped water, chilling her to the bone, but she was glad to be alive and to have her son away from Eickher. They were in the smallest of the three caves, with no room to stand, but it was quite deep inside. Amy pushed into a corner beside the entrance and pulled Jamie tight to her. Already she felt claustrophobic.

She savored the reprieve from Eickher. With every step down the trail Eickher sunk deeper into madness. The scientist had become an evil, terrifying force. But where was he now? Had he fallen into the sea when the ledge collapsed?

"Where's that man, Mommy?"

Amy peered out. To her horror, she saw him a few feet below her. Cold black eyes bored into her. "You're dead, bitch." he screamed. "You set me up for this. You're going to pay!"

Amy jumped back, her heart pounding. The moment had come. If Eickher made it into the cave, he'd kill them. He had to be stopped. Amy looked around. No loose rocks, nothing to use as a weapon. The thought of touching him with her bare hands was deplorable. There had to be another way.

CHAPTER 60

A sinister rage burned in Eickher. He recognized it and tried to curb it. He knew from experience that when these black episodes occurred, he lost rationality and did things that subverted his best interests. He tried to calm down, but the ravaging fire that burned inside him was flaring out of control. He could barely think now. The heat was searing his brain, like it always did. He panted, spittle running from his mouth.

He would kill that bitch. And the kid. He could barely wait. He could feel her neck in his bare hands already! Yes! The excitement of the kill coursed through his veins, energizing him. His muscles pumped, his heart raced.

The wall he was climbing crumbled as he inched his way up. With a burst of energy, he scaled the rock face, his bitd-like eyes on the entrance above him.

She was in there. Suddenly, she appeared above him. "You're dead, bitch." he screamed. "You set me up for this. You're going to pay!"

CHAPTER 61

Amy moved Jamie deep inside the cave. "Stay right here, Jamie. Don't move, okay?"

The boy nodded.

Amy scrambled back to the entrance. Eickher was coming for them. His madness had overtaken him. Amy knew he was going to kill both of them. There wasn't much time. He'd reach the cave entrance any second.

She reached back into her pocket and pulled out the insulin syringe that Alesha had given her back at The Cliff House. Holding it up, she pulled back on the plunger sucking air into the syringe, the way Alesha had instructed. Air bubbles mixed with Humalog and injected directly into the carotid artery would finish him instantly. Amy prepared herself, and then peeked out of the cave to see where he was. It was a huge mistake.

He was hanging off the vertical wall right under the entrance, his head almost level with the floor. With reptilian speed, his arm slithered up. His icy hand grabbed her neck in a death grip. "Ha! I've got you now, Bitch. Say goodbye to your boy." Still outside the cave, he leapt upward, yanking her down to the rocky floor of the entrance, his grip on her enabling him to scramble up a little higher. He squeezed her windpipe with his skeletal fingers.

Amy's entire body flew into overdrive. Using her left hand, she pried at his fingers, trying to free them. They were like steel around her neck. She couldn't breathe! Her windpipe was collapsing. Her vision grew blurry. He was clinging to her, his face contorted, ugly, his black eyes bloodshot and evil, his breath vile.

Her hand tightened on the syringe and with one last effort, she focused on his pulsing carotid artery. *Do it!*

CHAPTER 62

Eickher squeezed hard, her windpipe fragile in his grasp. "You fucking, whore! You've destroyed everything!" he screamed. "Everything! My life's work is incomplete because of you!" He wanted her to suffer, to gasp, to beg, and to writhe in pain. He wanted her to pay for desecrating his plan, for obliterating everything he'd worked a lifetime for. He wanted to watch her grovel in agony, convulse, and then die with the knowledge that her life was ending very slowly. Very slowly.

Eickher felt himself slipping down the rock bluff and grabbed onto the lip at the cave entrance with his other hand. He tried to pull himself back up. His shoes kicked and scratched at the rocks, looking for a purchase, but pieces of the wall crumbled with each impact. A huge section gave way beneath him and he slid down, dragging Amy halfway out of the entrance.

Suddenly, a hypodermic needle flashed by him. He jerked backward to avoid it. At the same instant, the ledge gave out. He was falling!

"No-o-o-o-!" His scream pierced the air. Then—an abrupt silence.

CHAPTER 63

The earsplitting scream echoed through the cave, bouncing off the rock.

As if in slow motion, Eickher fell, his arms reaching out to Amy, his eyes riveted on hers, his scream piercing in her eardrums. His feet cut right through the outside of the massive whirlpool and he disappeared into the swirling sea.

A moment later, he burst back up through the surface. Fighting to stay afloat, his willowy arms pumping, he was washed around the circumference of the giant whirlpool, his arms flailing now as he fought the deadly suction. It caught his legs and sucked him into the dark green vortex.

He was gone.

A moment later, as a final coup de grace, an enormous wave broke over the protective horseshoe of rocks, obliterating the whirlpool, and smashing into the rock bluff, sending spray right up into the cave.

Amy rolled back inside, her eyes squeezed shut, unaware of the tears streaming down her face. Her world went dark, her heart cried out, and her soul ached. The cave echoed only the sounds of the sea and water dripping all around her. His was the face of a madman, contorted and ugly, and it was overpowering in her mind.

"Mommy, are you asleep?"

The clear, sweet voice penetrated her pain. She was on her back at the cave entrance. Her throat and neck ached. She couldn't swallow and it hurt to breathe. It took her a few minutes to sit upright. "Mommy's awake," Amy croaked.

With trepidation, she leaned over glanced out of the entrance.

Eickher was gone.

From the cave, there was no way back to the trail. The outcropping she had traversed had fallen into the sea. The wall that Eickher scaled was still crumbling. In fact, a huge section was missing beneath her, leaving a large hollow below the cave entrance. From where they were, even Dallas wouldn't be able to help them.

The tide was rising quickly. Without the protective horseshoe of rocks, one powerful wave after another rolled in and crashed against the bluff. Soon the ocean would come roaring into the cave.

Amy turned away. Jamie was exactly where she left him. She went to him, pulling him from the recess where she had placed him, and hugged him tight. Never, had it felt so good to hold her child. That wonderful, special warmth flooded through her. She felt a kiss land on her cheek.

"Love you, Jamie. I love you so much," she whispered hoarsely.

They huddled together for a few minutes while Amy collected herself. She had to find a way out of the cave. Jamie was shivering with cold. She opened his wet jacket and her own, and pulled him tight to her chest, warming him.

Looking around, she saw a pinnacle of light near the very back recess of the cave. Maybe there was another way out. When Jamie stopped shivering, she zipped him up, took his hand, and half crawled toward the back wall. With each step, the ceiling grew lower, forcing her down. Her pulse quickened. Sweat broke out on her forehead. Small spaces. She hated them and glanced back at the opening, trying to calm herself.

Jamie shivered next to her. His clothing was soaked. Being so little, his body heat dispersed quickly and he'd been wet too long. They had to find a way out. Amy crawled forward until her head hit something hard. She was at the end of the cave, but light was filtering from a tunnel that curved off to her right.

A tunnel? Narrow, constricted, dark—

She'd never be able to go in a *tunnel*.

CHAPTER 64

Dallas wrapped the rope around Alesha and tossed the end to Larson, who stood waiting on the other side of the gap. "Okay," he instructed her, "take a run at it and head on over to Deputy Larson. He'll catch you on the other side."

This time Alesha made the jump with no problem. When she landed, she turned around and gave Dallas a small proud smile. "Go now, Sheriff," she called to him, "and thank you."

Larson undid the line, coiled it, and tossed it back to Dallas. "How do you want to handle this, Sheriff?"

Dallas told him, "Winds down. Chopper's on its way. SAR is on the north trail. I'm going to keep going." Dallas looped the rope over his shoulder. "Take Alesha back."

Alesha called back, "Please hurry, Sheriff. Amy needs you. She's in desperate trouble."

CHAPTER 65

The narrow tunnel was barely big enough for both of them. Amy couldn't get enough air. They were in a dark, damp, constricted space. Her penlight battery had died long ago. Icy sweat trickled into her eyes and down her back. Her heart raced. She felt trapped. Panic descended on her. The ceiling was too low… the space too small. She wanted out so badly, it was all she could do not to slide back out of the tunnel.

"Mommy? I'm cold."

His small shivering body snapped her away from the terror. She had to get Jamie out of there. She had to keep going. She forced herself to concentrate on the light ahead and inched along.

Then, she inhaled fresh air and wiggled forward. The tunnel grew brighter. She moved forward another foot. And another. She bumped into a wall and found herself looking straight up into a tube. The gray overcast sky was visible high above her. She squeezed upright into the pipe and wiggled to a standing position, pulling Jamie up with her. The tube, about twice her height, was sheer and damp with no handholds.

How would they ever get to the top?

CHAPTER 66

Dallas stood by the waterfall, a sense of devastation overtaking him. The trail had collapsed into the sea. Obviously, it had just happened. Had Amy and Jamie tried to make it to the cave? Had the trail fallen out from under them? Did they fall to their deaths? Or did they make it to the entrance? Where the hell were they?

"Amy! Amy, are you in the cave? Amy…" Dallas called out over and over, but no answer.

With the tide rising and the giant waves pounding against the bluff, there was no way of reaching the entrance. He examined the rocks that followed the waterfall up the bluff. If he was careful, he could climb up the side. He checked the knot at the end of the rope and adjusted the loop, and then using it like a lasso, he tossed it up high, over a boulder, but the loop slipped off. Dallas tried again. This time the rope landed behind a crack in the boulder. When Dallas pulled the rope taut, it slipped into the crack and caught. He started up.

The climb was slippery, slimy, wet, and steep. On the positive side, the rain had stopped. As he worked his way to the top, he thought about Amy. It was hard to think of anyone or anything else these days. She had captured his heart. The past few hours had been hell. He was afraid for her and Jamie's lives. Somehow, no matter what it took, he had to find them.

When he reached the top of the waterfall, he re-coiled the rope and headed north through the woods. A while later, he found himself onto the north trail. The largest cave was ahead of him, but where was the small one? He climbed to the top of the big cave and stood, looking back toward the waterfall. From up top it was difficult to determine where one cave began and another ended.

Suddenly, a huge plume of spray blew from a nearby hole.

CHAPTER 67

The tide rose steadily. Coupled with powerful ocean surges, waves reached far beyond their high tide lines in storm season. Amy knew this. Suddenly, it happened. With a roar, the next wave surged into the cave, through the tunnel, right past them, and up the tube.

Oh no! It's a blowhole! We're in a blowhole. The Devil's Pipe!

They had to get out, and fast. Amy had no idea how much higher the tide would rise. She did know that with every inch of rise, the force would increase, making it difficult to keep hold of Jamie. In the end, the extreme force would either blow them out of the pipe or kill them. *Dallas, where are you? Help us. Please, please help us.*

Then it came again! The roar. White water rushed toward them sending icy seawater swirling around them. It struck with tremendous force. She held Jamie with every ounce of strength she possessed, but she underestimated the sheer power of the surging ocean combined with the trapped air.

The water tore past her, nearly tearing her clothes off her body. Then the back suction pulled at her as the water receded.

Amy knew what she had to do. *The only way out of the pipe is to go with the flow,* she thought. *We can't stay here any longer.* It had been years since Amy had been to The

Devil's Pipe, but she did recall sloping, mossy ground surrounding it.

She lifted Jamie up and explained what she was about to do. "Okay, Jamie, we're going to use the water to get out of this pipe. I'm going to lift you up as high as I can. Are you ready?"

He nodded, "I'm ready, Mommy. But I'm so cold."

"I know, but when we get out of here, I'll warm you up," she promised. She heard the roar and hoisted him high over her head. "The water's going to lift you out of the tunnel. When you get out, find a safe place nearby, and wait for Mommy. Okay?"

"Yes…"

She never heard the rest. The roar filled the pipe and a split second later the ocean blew past her. It tore at her skin, pushed water up her nose and into her ears, mouth, and eyes. Suddenly, Jamie was ripped from her grasp. With a gigantic whoosh, he was sent skyrocketing up the pipe!

Moments later, the surge stopped, leaving Amy choking on seawater. Then came the suction. It pulled at her feet, her legs, and her body. "Jamie!" she called out, wondering if he was okay. No response. She had to go next and find him.

CHAPTER 68

Dallas stared at the geyser of water spewing from the pipe. A *blowhole.* The Devil's Pipe. Seawater spewed from the hole, high into the air. When it subsided Dallas climbed toward it. There would be another plume of seawater soon, and it would continue to grow higher as the tide came in.

Suddenly, he heard a small voice cry out. A geyser of water surged from the pipe, and to his shock, a small boy flew into the air. "Jamie!" Dallas rushed to catch the child before he hit the ground. With his feet sliding out from under him on the slippery moss, he dove for the boy and landed on his good knee, the wet child dangling from his arm.

Jamie spit and coughed water, then choked, "Mommy's down there," and pointed to the hole.

Dallas sat Jamie on a knoll. "I'll get Mommy," he told the boy. "Stay right here. Understand?"

Jamie nodded and sneezed and then stuffed his little hands into his wet pockets.

CHAPTER 69

A gigantic roar and a huge torrent of water ripped through the tunnel toward Amy. The wait was terrifying. The seconds ticked by. *Will it take me all the way out of the pipe? What happens if it doesn't lift me high enough? Would I fall back down? How will I stop that from happening?* She raised her arms over her head and held her breath. The roar of water was deafening. The air pressure changed. It was almost there!

It hit hard and fast. The huge geyser of saltwater and trapped air roared into the pipe. Amy was propelled upward. Her outstretched arms collided with the walls. Her cheekbone struck hard against the rock, but she continued flying toward the open vent.

Suddenly, the lift diminished, leaving her about three feet from the top. She wedged her feet and legs hard against the walls of the pipe and pushed against each side of the pipe to keep herself from sliding back down. The next surge should lift her out. She didn't have long to wait. There was another roar of water surging toward her. The seawater and trapped air joined forces once more and she literally flew out of the pipe. Her eyes, ears, and nose were full of saltwater. She could see nothing. But suddenly, just before she hit the ground, someone grabbed her. Then she heard his voice. "It's okay, I've got you!"

They slid down onto the mossy knoll and Dallas pulled her into his arms. "Are you all right, Amy? Are you hurt?"

Coughing and sneezing, she looked up at Dallas. There were huge dark shadows under her eyes and her skin had a bluish tinge. She was soaking wet, her hand and face were badly scraped, but she had a huge smile. Dallas lifted her up and carried her over to where Jamie sat.

Amy slid her arms around Dallas's neck and rested her head on his shoulder. Gently, he put her down beside her son. She kissed Jamie, and then reached up and put both hands on Dallas's cheeks, her eyes steady on his. "Dallas," she whispered, kissing him, "I'm so glad you're here."

He pushed a strand of wet hair from her eyes. "I was so worried," he said. "It took a day from hell for me to figure out just how much you mean to me."

Then, the deep thump of rotors caught his attention. The chopper. At last.

CHAPTER 70

Dallas stood on the balcony of The Cliff House, hands on his hips, deep in thought, looking at the trail below. He was steaming mad. The search team had gone back and forth along the trail and had scoured the surrounding property looking for clues to Alesha's disappearance. No one in the house had seen her. The Marine Patrol was checking the coastline. He unclipped his radio. "Any sign of her?"

"Nothing yet, Sheriff."

"I can't understand how you could have let her go! Who dropped the ball? What the hell happened?"

"Larson handed her off to Matson. That's all I know, Sheriff. We haven't got a thing to go on."

Dallas clicked off as Larson joined him on the balcony. "I can't figure it, Sheriff. She was fine when I handed her off to Matson."

Dallas tried to curb his anger. "Tell me again what happened."

Larson scratched his head. "Alesha did okay coming back along the trail. She told me that likely the exposure to heights had actually cured her phobia. She was quite happy about that. At the same time, she told me repeatedly that she was terrified of what Eickher could do to Amy and Jamie. When we got to the house, we entered through the side door here," he said pointing to the door behind Dallas. "Matson met us at the landing

291

and I handed her off to him and went inside to catch the elevator up to the parking lot. I got into the cruiser and headed up to the north access trail. So, that was the last I saw of Alesha, Sheriff." Larson shrugged. "It beats the hell out of me."

Dallas agreed. "Yeah. Me too. And according to Doris, she and Alesha are very close. It doesn't make sense for Alesha not to see her mother considering everything that's happened."

Dallas turned and went back inside, with Larson. Neither man wanted to say what they were really thinking.

The living room was taped off. Matson ducked under it and approached Dallas. "Crime Scene Unit says it's pretty clear cut. Eickher pulled the trigger killing Johnstone, then fled the scene."

The detectives had already apprised Dallas of that. He tried to contain his anger. "Larson passed Alesha Eickher off to you. No bullshit this time. Tell me exactly what happened next."

Matson looked at Larson, then back at his sheriff. He hesitated too long.

Dallas stared him down. "We have a missing person. Not only were you the last one to see her, that woman was in your charge. Your responsibility, Matson. Now, let's hear what really happened."

Matson cleared his throat. "Larson brought her in through that door up there and passed her over to me. As soon as she got inside, she told me she needed to use the washroom and off she went. Meanwhile, one of the detectives had some questions for me, so I came back down here and talked to him."

Dallas grew impatient. "And then what?"

Matson studied the floor. "That's it."

"Don't give me that!"

"I got involved with things down here and—'"

Dallas finished the sentence. "You forgot about her!

Matson twisted uncomfortably.

"You stupid son-of-a-bitch! You're the most incompetent, irresponsible, useless, sorry excuse for a deputy. If I didn't respect your old man so much, I'd throw you out on your ear. In fact, I might just do that anyway." Dallas put his hands on his hips and turned away in sheer frustration. Without looking at Matson, Dallas asked, "How much time went by before you remembered your charge?"

Matson scuffed the floor with the sole of his boot. "I'd guess about thirty minutes."

"Jeez." Dallas looked at his watch and ran his hand through his hair. "She's been missing over an hour."

Larson asked, "You think she went back down the trail to look for Amy, Sheriff?"

"Anything's possible. I'll be in with Doris Eickher, if you need me."

Dallas found Doris down the hall in the den. She was sitting in a chair, staring at the bookcase. When Dallas walked in, she jumped up. "Did you find her, Sheriff?" she asked, hopefully.

Dallas shook his head. "Not yet." Dallas took her elbow. "Why don't you sit down, Mrs. Eickher. I have a few questions."

"Please call me Doris. I'll be legally changing my name back to Sanford."

Dallas nodded. "Doris, tell me about Helmut Eickher and his project."

"Well, we met at university in the late sixties. We were young. We studied together, graduated together, got our doctorates together, and did our post-grad research together. Then we married. Helmut was always intrigued with the human brain, IQ in particular. In fact, it was an obsession with him. It formed the basis of most of his research. He had no patience for stupidity. He saw it everywhere, but what infuriated him most was the fact that he thought the nations of the world were most often held back by what he called *thick-headed, undereducated, inexperienced, power hungry, low-level thinkers*. He was going to change that. He had this idea to create new generations of highly educated, super brains who he could strategically position globally. His vision was to see the nations of the world influenced by a unified, high-thinking race with common goals." Doris explained the rest to Dallas, then went to the window and looked out. She continued, "We couldn't have children of our own. Lord knows, we tried. So, when the first tiny baby arrived at the facility, I fell in love with her. That was Alesha. I raised her as my own, educated her, and taught her everything I know. She has a doctorate in biochemistry, you know. There's so much good she can do—" Doris's voice broke, "I couldn't bear to lose her. She's all I have, Sheriff. I love her so much."

Dallas put his hand on her shoulder. The woman had succumbed to tears. There was no point in continuing. His questions could wait while he checked in with the search team. "We're doing all we can to find her. The minute we hear anything, we'll let you know.

Leaving the room, he said, "The FBI will be here soon. You realize that there'll be a federal investigation into the abduction of the infants from the US?"

"Yes, I know."

"Your involvement will be scrutinized."

Doris sat down heavily, her head downcast. "I understand."

Dallas was about to leave when she looked up and asked, "How is Amy?"

Surprised, Dallas told her, "She's recovering in hospital, but I don't think she'll be in there for long."

Walking out of the study, Dallas wondered how he was going to tell Amy that her sister had disappeared.

CHAPTER 71

Amy was sitting up in bed when Dallas walked into the hospital room. Jamie slept soundly in the next bed. Happy to see Dallas, she swung her legs off the bed and stood up, throwing her arms around his neck. "My dear Dallas," she whispered.

He kissed her tenderly and pulled back to look at her. "How are you?"

She sat back down on the bed and pulled Dallas down beside her. "I'm okay. Took hours to warm up. Lots of bruises. Lots of terrible memories..."

Dallas put his arm around her and pulled her close. "I know. How's Jamie?" he asked, looking over his shoulder at the boy.

"Poor little guy was exhausted. They immersed both of us in the warming tub. Afterward, I helped him put on hospital pajamas and held him for a while. He fell asleep right away." Amy snuggled into Dallas and closed her eyes. "I'm glad it's over. Finally." She felt him stiffen. She looked up at him. His pale blue eyes searched her face and she got that feeling again. "What?" she asked. When he didn't reply, she repeated, "What is it, Dallas?"

He turned to her and put both hands on her shoulders. "It's not good news," he said gently. "It may not be bad news either," he said, "but right now we just don't know."

295

Alarmed, Amy stared at him. Her mind raced across the possibilities. Jamie was right beside her, so it wasn't him. Gramps was up to see her a few hours ago, so it wasn't him. He'd told her Grams had improved significantly, so it wasn't her. Even better, the doctors had nullified the Alzheimer's diagnosis. That left one person.

"Alesha," she whispered, dreading what Dallas was going to say.

"Yes, it's Alesha."

She saw the pained look on his face and turned away. Fear and dread filled her heart. "No, please, no. Not Alesha." Her twin's beautiful face flashed before her, choking Amy with tears. She could still feel the warmth of her sister's hug. There was so much for them to learn about one another, so much to share. "Oh, no, Dallas."

Dallas reached across and rubbed the tears from her cheeks. "We're not sure what happened. The teams are still out there looking."

Amy put her hands over her face. A sick feeling flooded her chest. *Alesha, Alesha. No!*

Then Amy sat bolt upright. Her hands dropped to her lap. Her eyes grew wide and she was still. She reached across for Dallas's hand and sat for a few minutes struggling to understand what had just happened to her. "Dallas," she said softly, "you know they say that monozygotic, or identical twins, intrinsically know things about each other, even when they're miles apart?" Amy's voice was hushed. "Well, I know this is going to sound very odd," Amy hesitated, trying to understand the sudden knowledge and awareness that overwhelmed her. "But Alesha's okay. I know that for certain."

CHAPTER 72

Paraguay
Friday, November 20 3:12 PM
From: AleshaE@tmail.net
To: AmyJ@gennison.com
Hi Amy,

I arrived back in Paraguay this afternoon. With connections, it took two long days of flying. I stepped off the plane into our hot, stifling, humid air and immediately decided that when I'm finished here, I'm going to return to Oregon to live.

I want to tell you why I left so quickly. Deputy Larson brought me back to The Cliff House and told me you and Jamie were okay, and that Helmut had drowned.

I knew that with his and Johnstone's deaths, the FBI would likely raid the facility, here in Paraguay. I had to get back here right away. The research done here is invaluable and could do a lot of good, so I'm currently having the computer hard drives and documents removed.

As this facility is close to the capital city of Asuncion, I'm giving the building over to be used as a hospital and research center to benefit the Paraguayans. I'm trying to get everything done before the investigators arrive.

I'll be back very soon. Please apologize to Dallas for me.

My love to you, Amy,
Alesha

CHAPTER 73

Four Weeks Later...

Slashes of yellow and lavender streaked across the evening sky, reflecting off the glassy surface of the Pacific. Dallas walked with Jamie down the old boardwalk bordering the beach, the little boy holding tight to Dallas's hand. In his other hand, Jamie hugged the Frisbee. As they approached the pathway to the beach, Jamie tugged Dallas's hand. "Come on, Dallas, this is the best spot."

Amy watched them run down to the packed sand and hooked her arm around Alesha's. "Jamie idolizes Dallas."

Alesha nodded in agreement. "I sense he's not the only one."

A smile played on Amy's lips. "What do they say? Smitten, enamored, head over heels? I qualify on all counts. And speaking of which, I noticed Deputy Larson came by the other night."

Alesha flashed her gray eyes at Amy. "Kev. He's a really nice guy. He's asked me to the office party this weekend." She heard Jamie calling her and looked up the beach. "Oops, looks like it's my turn on the Frisbee. Here comes Dallas." She gave Amy a squeeze. "You two can have a romantic moment and enjoy the sunset while I wear Jamie out. Then, it's over to the restaurant with us. I'm famished."

"Your turn," Dallas told Alesha, passing her on the boardwalk. He put his arm around Amy and led her to a sun-bleached log, where they sat, their eyes following Alesha and Jamie, on the beach.

Amy dropped her head on Dallas's shoulder, "Jamie finally asked me what happened to his dad."

"What did you tell him?" Dallas asked, concerned.

"I told him that Daddy loved him very much, but he got hurt badly, and we couldn't make him better." Amy looked up at Dallas. "That's enough for now. He's only five. One day he'll ask more questions and then I'll have to answer them best I can."

Dallas looked down at Amy. "What about you?"

Amy slid her coat sleeves over her hands. "I'm relieved it's over, for all our sakes, but especially for Jamie's. You know, Dallas, life is strange. Everything is completely different from what it was six weeks ago. I don't even feel like the same person. Yet, in spite of everything I went through, I came out the other side with so much to be thankful for. I have you, and Jamie, and Alesha. Gramps and Grams. Amy put her hand on Dallas's cheek and looked into his pale blue eyes. "How about you?"

He hesitated. "I never realized how alone I was. Always coming home to an empty apartment. No one to share a meal with or a conversation. Only company I had was my memories." Dallas reached for her hand. "Truth is, Amy, I can't wait until we move into our new place."

Amy looked at him skeptically. "You sure it's not too much—too fast?"

"No, I'm happy, Babe. What more could a man want?"

Amy smiled up at him. "Well...I was thinking of a little girl."

Note To My Readers

The Oregon coast is unique and spectacularly beautiful. It was during one of our camping trips on this pristine shoreline that my husband and I experienced the sudden onslaught of a fall storm so fierce that it not only gave us pause, it became the inspiration for this novel.

I enjoyed writing WINTER'S DESTINY and would love to hear from you. To send me your thoughts, please feel free to visit my website http://nancyallan.net/Contact.php

Made in the USA
Lexington, KY
12 April 2012